MERCENARY INSTINCT

MERCENARY INSTINCT

Mandrake Company, Book 1

RUBY LIONSDRAKE

ISBN: 1517451221
ISBN-13: 9781517451226

ACKNOWLEDGMENTS

Thank you for trying out a new adventure by a new author. Before you jump in, please let me thank my editor, Shelley Holloway, as well as Sarah Engelke, Cindy Wilkinson, and Samantha Nolan for offering feedback on an early version of this novel.

CHAPTER ONE

Ankari Markovich dangled from a rope, making faces as she chiseled fossilized gunk from the walls of a twenty-thousand-year-old latrine shaft. It wasn't as if the bumps and nodules she was scraping into sample containers smelled after all this time. It was just that she hadn't imagined herself with such a hands-on role when she had incorporated her latest business. She was the marketing specialist *and* the majority stakeholder, not the—she scraped a particularly large piece off and into a bag—ancient alien feces collector. At least her mother wasn't here to sigh with disappointment at yet another "foolish scheme," as she called Ankari's dreams.

The rope shivered. A nervous jolt ran through her, and Ankari forgot her indignation.

"Someone coming?" she whispered toward the hole at the top of the crumbling shaft.

"No," Lauren Keys, microbiologist and business partner, whispered back. "I mean, I don't think so. Two more ships have landed while you've been down there, but nobody's come this way yet. I was just shifting my weight."

Two more ships. What was that now? Six total in the area? Six ships full of treasure hunters who had come to scavenge the ruins, but who would gladly scavenge the contents of the *Marie Curie* for the valuable scientific equipment inside. Not to mention scavenging her and the other two women in her crew, as well.

"Warn me next time, will you?" Ankari tapped a button on her mechanical rappelling harness. It whirred softly and lowered her a few more inches, so she could scrape at a new spot.

"I'm sorry. I didn't know I had to update you when I was scratching my backside."

"Just…if you're doing it vigorously."

Ankari shined her flashlight on the stone now visible underneath the patch she had scraped free, then rubbed it with her sleeve. It gleamed dully, interesting threads of green and silver shooting through the dark black. Andorkan Marble, or this world's equivalent. A half ton slab of low- to middle-grade quality sold for two thousand aurums on the stone and metals market. With the gold and artifacts largely stripped from the ruins, someone would doubtlessly be down here with excavation equipment, going after the marble before long.

"Ankari?" Lauren whispered. "I heard something—a shifting of rocks over the hill."

"I'm almost done." Ankari lowered herself further, until she reached the uneven earth at the bottom. "You said to get some samples from down here, right?"

"Yes, and I also said we should do this at night."

"We barely found this hole by day." They had spent two hours dodging treasure hunting teams, hiding in the ruins, and following a map neither was certain was accurate to find the midden heap. Ankari scraped as she spoke, rushing to fill her collection bag. She was as worried as Lauren. This was some corporation's protected planet, and there weren't any settlements—or any police—on it. Anyone they encountered would be, at the very least, a trespasser and likely much worse. "I'm done. I'm coming up."

Lauren didn't answer. She must have ducked behind that wall off to the side to hide. Ankari debated whether to go up or to wait until she got the all-clear from her partner. Seconds ticked by.

"Lauren?" she whispered. "You better not have wandered off. You're the one who knows what to do with this fossilized poop."

When she still didn't get an answer, Ankari touched the comm-pin stuck to her vest and thought about contacting her that way, but there might be unscrupulous people out there, listening in on the various frequencies. She didn't hear any voices or scuffs drifting down from above, so she tapped her harness, this time having it reel her up. Slowly. She kept her ear trained toward the hole's entrance as she approached. Nothing.

At the top, she poked only her eyes out of the shaft.

The wind scraped across the remains of towers, buildings, and walls, most crumbled into barely recognizable shapes. Thorny vines meandered here and there, one of the few plants that grew in this dry desert zone, but there wasn't much foliage to hide behind, only the ruins themselves. Ankari looked upward. Days were short on Libra, and the sun had moved across the hazy blue sky in the short time she had been down in the hole. Before long, it would be dark, and their third crew member, Jamie, who was back on the *Marie Curie*, would be wondering about them.

She risked tapping her comm. "Lauren, are you all right?"

The sound of someone speaking came from a pile of rocks a few feet away. Ankari flinched, her hand whipping to the Tiger 420 pistol strapped at her waist, before she realized what she was hearing. Her own voice being echoed back to her. A comm-pin identical to the one on her chest lay in the dust beside a rock. Lauren's medical records and identification were encoded in that pin, and Jamie could have tracked her with the ship's sensors…if she were wearing it. The sturdy fastener wouldn't have fallen off on its own.

"Not good," Ankari mumbled.

She didn't take her eyes from her surroundings as she picked up the pin and stuffed it in her pack. She unbuckled the rappelling harness and thrust it and the rope into the pack too. She wasn't sure whether to search for Lauren here or run back to the ship, where they could search from the air. Unfortunately, the *Marie Curie* had the same problem down here that she did: as soon as it left its hiding spot, it would become a target. The bulky modified freighter wasn't exactly a warship. It was possible would-be captors would be too busy laughing at its rainbows-and-flowers paint job to attack, but Ankari would prefer not to test that hypothesis.

She tapped her comm again. "Jamie? Are you listening? Have you heard from Lauren?"

A splatter of static answered her.

"Wonderful."

Ankari slung her pack over her shoulder and turned around. She halted before taking a single step along the path that led back to the ship.

Six well-armed people stood on the ridge, all with cold, hard faces, most displaying a fearsome collection of tattoos, piercings, and scars. One was a woman, dark-skinned and broad-shouldered, with a build just as muscular as that of the men. They all had the miens of soldiers—or ex-soldiers—even if they weren't clad in anything resembling uniforms now.

Ankari's shoulders slumped. The man on the far side held Lauren, his meaty hand wrapped around her arm, as yielding as a shackle. His laser pistol was pressed into her temple.

Ankari was a decent shot, but didn't doubt that these people could blast her before she got her own weapon out. And, depending on what they wanted, they might kill Lauren if Ankari ran or dove for cover. Or twitched in a way they didn't like.

"If you're looking for aliuolite, I can direct you to a good source." Ankari pointed toward the midden hole rather than mentioning the samples stashed in her pack. Fossilized alien feces were only worth a few aurums an ounce, but there were a lot of ounces down there.

The burly thugs looked to the person at the center of the group, a broad-shouldered man in a leather duster and boots that seemed antiquated next to his intricate mesh vest armor and a digital scanner he wore over one eye. The armor, which could deflect bullets and lasers, was standard issue for police and Galactic Conglomeration Fleet soldiers. Ankari doubted the man was either. He was handsome, in a cold and aloof way, with green eyes that stood out from his olive skin and short black hair, but there was nothing friendly about his face as he considered her words. Or perhaps he was considering what fancy dinner he might treat himself to with the money he got from selling her into slavery.

"What's aliuolite?" the man holding Lauren whispered. He was a squat tank with bronze skin and almond-shaped eyes.

The woman squinted thoughtfully, like the term might be familiar, but ultimately she shrugged and didn't answer.

Without taking his eyes from Ankari, the leader said, "Old alien shit."

"That's what aliuolite is?" Lauren's captor asked. "Or that's what we're standing in?"

"Probably both."

"If you were known for your sense of humor, Captain, I'd assume you were joking with us."

Captain? Maybe this was some kind of military outfit after all. Either that, or treasure hunters these days had delusions of grandeur. But nothing about the man's grim face, scarred hands, or hard eyes said he was a poser. He looked like a veteran who had survived a lot of battles, including some that hadn't gone his way.

"It's used in the jewelry business," the captain said, surprising Ankari with his knowledge—it wasn't a widely known piece of trivia. "For those who can't afford real gems. Or just like quirk." His eyebrow twitched. He was still staring at Ankari, and she wondered if that was a dig. Did he think her a freak because she was collecting the stuff? He couldn't possibly know what her team really wanted it for, so he must. She scowled at him. As if collecting fossilized poop was any less noble than kidnapping people.

"It worth anything, Captain?" Lauren's captor asked, speculation narrowing his eyes.

Another man snorted. "How much can shit earrings be worth? I think you're right, Corporal. The captain *is* joking."

Most of the men smirked, their faces losing some of their hardness, though it was difficult to find them anything but menacing when the corporal still held a gun to Lauren's head.

"Enough," the captain said. No smirk had ever softened his face. "Striker, get the girl before those vines start growing up our legs."

Ankari took a step back, lifting a hand toward the spiky-haired man who approached her. He wore no less than four guns, numerous daggers, and what looked to be a chain of grenades on a bandolier across his chest.

"You're right," Ankari rushed to say—her hand wasn't doing anything to stay the brute. "Aliuolite is used for jewelry, and it's actually trading for more on the market this year than it has in the past twenty." A true statement. "There's a fascination with all things related to the ancient aliens, you know." Also true. "And there's enough aliuolite down there that you could make a small fortune." That was less true, but wouldn't it be brilliant if they all dove down that shaft in their eagerness to get at the stuff? "Far more than you'd ever get for us."

The captain snorted. "If you think that, you don't know how much you're worth, girl."

The comment surprised Ankari. He couldn't be talking about anything other than the slave trade, but she couldn't imagine she would command any great price on the auction block. She was attractive enough, she supposed, but certainly wasn't some stunning virgin beauty that could be served up on a platter to some self-proclaimed backwater prince or horny old finance lord.

Though she was confused by the comment, Ankari reacted before the walking knife collection could grab her. She leaped backward, landing in a fighting stance. It was more by habit than rational thought—her father had insisted on training her as a mashatui practitioner all through her childhood—because what could she possibly do against so many armed men? But a clatter arose from behind a wall of ruins on a nearby ridge, and all except one of the brutes turned toward it, their weapons shifting from her to the noise.

The man who had been tasked with grabbing her—Striker—didn't falter. He lunged for her hand, pulling out a gun as he did so. With the others distracted, Ankari felt more brazen—less like she would get herself and Lauren in trouble for defiance—and jumped back. He was as fast as she and might have caught her wrist, but his toe smacked against a rock. She snatched up a handful of sand and threw it at his face, then scrambled up the side of what had once been a small tower.

She glanced back as she went over the top and into the broken structure. His gun was pointed at her, and he could have fired, but he grumbled and didn't. Ankari didn't question her luck. She jumped down and squeezed out through a dog-sized opening on the back side of the tower, trying for silence in the hope that he would think she was staying inside to hide.

A low wall ran off to either side of the tower, and she scrambled along the back of it on hands and knees, trying to avoid his view. If he thought she was running, he should expect her to go the other way, but she angled back toward the group. If some trouble came from up on that ridge, and there was a chance she could use it to her advantage and get Lauren, Ankari had to try. Not only would she feel horrible about getting Lauren captured by slavers, especially after talking her into coming out to help collect samples, but unemployed microbiologists didn't wander into her orbit every day, and the business was useless without one.

A laser gun fired, the whine abrupt and over quickly. Ankari's stomach sank. Lauren? Had Ankari's choice to run cost her partner her life?

But more shots fired, not only from nearby but from that ridge, as well.

"Take cover, Striker." That was the captain's voice. "We'll get her later. Deal with these idiots first."

Ankari risked poking her head over the wall. Red and orange bursts of laser fire were streaking across the ruins, bright against the fading light of the afternoon sky. She picked out the backs of the woman and two of the other men, including the brute holding Lauren. They had taken cover behind crumbling walls and were all facing the ridge, where two figures hid behind ruins of their own, leaning in and out of sight to shoot. Lauren was the only one looking in Ankari's direction, and her face lit with hope when they made eye contact.

Ankari aimed at the back of the head of Lauren's captor. She had never killed someone before, and she had no way to know for certain that these were criminals with bounties on their heads. Hoping she wouldn't regret it, she shifted her aim to the man's shoulder. That ought to get him to release Lauren.

"Ready?" Ankari mouthed.

Lauren nodded vigorously, her tangled, shoulder-length black hair flopping in her dark eyes. Her alarmed gaze darted from Ankari to the laser blasts streaking through the ruins and back again.

A scream came from the ridge.

"Nice, shooting, Captain," someone said. "Didn't think any of us were going to get past that full body armor. Best armed scavengers I've ever seen."

"Stolen gear," the captain said. "It doesn't fit properly."

The men kept ducking, dodging, and shooting as they traded this casual exchange. Another scream came from the ridge, a shot fired from the female warrior this time.

"You're right, sir," she said. "Armpit was open."

The kidnappers were making quick work of their opponents. Ankari didn't have time to waste, but she made herself wait until Lauren's captor finished shooting a spray of red beams and paused to reload his gun. He wasn't holding Lauren at the moment. She probably could have lunged free and run, if she wasn't afraid of being hit by the stray beams herself, but she merely crouched there, her round eyes riveted on Ankari. Well, nothing on her résumé had said she was good in a fight. So long as she ran when she had the chance.

Ankari fired.

The beam lanced into the back of the man's shoulder, charring through his shirt and into his skin. He didn't cry out. He only grunted and spun toward her.

Lauren leaped to her feet without looking and sprinted toward the half wall Ankari hid behind. She didn't so much as glance at the beams lancing through the air all around, but luck favored her mad dash, and she flung herself over the stones and to the ground. The brute who had lost her jumped to his feet, as if to charge after them, but Ankari pointed her pistol at his eyes. He considered her for a long second, but the burning hole in the back of his shoulder must have convinced him that her aim was decent. He gave her a wry smirk and even a salute, then went back to shooting at the people on the hill.

"Suppose I shouldn't feel indignant that he sees me as so little of a threat that he's turning his back on me," Ankari said and dropped below the wall again. "That way," she added when Lauren gave her a questioning look. Ankari jerked her head in a direction that would take them away from the conflict but that should let them circle back to their ship. She hoped the *Marie Curie* was still hidden beneath that overhang and that nobody had noticed it. She didn't want to return to a league of bounty hunters—or slavers or whatever these people were—lined up in front of the craft.

Shots continued to fire, but they grew less loud as Ankari and Lauren scurried through the ruins. If other treasure hunters lurked in the area, Ankari and Lauren didn't run into them on their way back to the ship. Scavengers or not, they were probably smart enough to stay away from a firefight—at least until the carrion birds were circling and the bodies could be looted. As she weaved around and over the dusty ruins, Ankari acknowledged that she

and her team were technically scavengers down here too. And they, too, ultimately wanted to make money from what they were pulling off the planet,
if in a roundabout way.

"Judge not lest ye be judged…" Wasn't that some saying from one of
the old Earth religions?

When the *Marie Curie* came into view, sans a brute squad, Ankari gasped
a relieved, "Yes!"

The rainbow-striped freighter with its flower highlights wasn't exactly
designed to blend in here—or anywhere—but with night's approach, the
deep shadows beneath the overhang should be hiding it, at least from the
air.

"Jamie, you there?" Ankari asked into the comm. "If you could open
the door, we'd appreciate it." No need to mention the squad of men she
feared would be tracking them to this spot within minutes.

"Mission accomplished, boss?" Jamie asked as the big cargo bay door
on the back lowered, providing a ramp for Ankari and Lauren to run up.

"Yes, but we may have company soon. Get us out of here."

"Will do."

The deck shivered beneath its shaggy blue carpeting as Ankari and
Lauren ran past the science stations that dominated the old cargo hold.
Ankari charged into the compact navigation cabin first, breathing hard.

Jamie, hands on the controls, glanced back, her blue eyes widening.
"You weren't kidding. Someone really is after you."

Twenty years old with blonde pigtails, Jamie didn't look old enough to
be a pilot, much less the ship's engineer, but, like Lauren, she was willing to
work for a share of the business. Few people with more experience—and
without criminal records—were so inclined.

"Yes. Are we in the air yet?" The view on the screen was depressingly
similar to the view Ankari had left behind.

"We're almost out from under the ledge," Jamie said dryly.

"This ship's a real cheetah, isn't she?"

"She's not that bad." Jamie gave the console a friendly pat.

Lauren stepped into the hatchway. "If you'll give me that pack, I can get
to work." Her face was red, her clothes were torn, and she was smeared with
dirt, and she wanted to get right to her research?

Ankari could have hugged her, though she wasn't ready to drag her eyes from the viewer to remove her pack, not with the dusty ground inching along at a snail's pace. Once they were in the air…Better yet, once they were completely off the planet, it would be a different story.

"Let's see if we make it out from under this ledge first," Ankari said.

"Almost there." Jamie tapped a display flashing a clearance warning.

The burly captain stepped out from behind a boulder, and Ankari almost peed down her leg. He had removed the scanner on his head, and his two hard green eyes were staring straight at the view screen. She expected him to raise his pistol and point it at them, but even if the freighter wasn't a sleek warship, its hull would easily withstand the firepower of a hand weapon. Those grenades that other brute had been carrying might do some damage, but Ankari didn't see him. The captain was alone. But his lips were moving. Issuing some command to the rest of his team? Letting them know he had found Ankari's ship and that he needed help bringing it down? Well, the *Marie Curie* wasn't waiting around for that.

"Who's *he*?" Jamie asked. "He's handsome. Pissed looking, but handsome."

"Calm your teenage hormones down and get us some altitude," Ankari said.

"I haven't been a teenager for weeks now, you know."

"He wants to kidnap us, not get in bed with us. Now, go."

"Really? Kidnap all of us?" Fortunately, Jamie's fingers danced across the controls as she spoke, and the captain disappeared from view as the ship rose from the ground. Soon, he and his men would be powerless to stop them.

That didn't keep Ankari's fingers from digging into the back of Jamie's chair. "Lauren and me for sure. I don't know if they're aware of your existence."

"Typical." Jamie sniffed. "Let me get us turned away from that mountain, and it'll be a clear shot into space."

"Good." As the view rotated, Ankari was on the verge of loosening her fingers when a sleek black shuttlecraft glided out of the twilight sky. Before she could do more than wonder if it had weapons, a torpedo launched from its bow.

"No, no, no," Jamie said over and over, trying to navigate out of the way.

But even the most agile GalCon fighter couldn't have dodged at that close range. Ankari didn't have time to brace herself before the world exploded in her face.

Her last thought, as she was hurled backward, was that she should have known the captain was calling to a ship, not talking to his crew. Then her head struck the bulkhead, and darkness swallowed the world.

———

Captain Viktor Mandrake led his team toward the smoking wreckage, grimacing at the damage Frog's torpedo had done. The ugly little freighter would never fly again, and—worse—its passengers might not have survived. He flipped open his pocket tablet and skimmed the wanted hologram that formed in the air above it. Yes, alive. The prisoners were supposed to be delivered alive.

"Problem, sir?" Sergeant Hazel asked, falling into step beside him.

Corporal Jiang had also caught up with them, clutching at a shoulder smoldering from a laser blast, and wearing a chagrined expression. He probably felt abashed after letting the girl out of his grasp. He should.

Striker, Dunhill, and Chen were making sure all of the thugs who had ambushed the team were either dead or knew better than to bother Mandrake Company again. Viktor also wanted to know if there had been a reason behind the ambush, or if the riffraff had simply been trying to take advantage of distracted people. Maybe they had overheard that woman's lie about the fortune to be made in fossilized crap.

"They're wanted alive," Viktor said.

"They weren't very high up when Frog hit them, sir. The crash shouldn't have killed them."

"The torpedo hit right below their nav cabin."

"Oh. That might have cut them up."

The torpedo, or the crash, or both, had left a jagged hole in the side of the freighter. That was fortuitous, because the cargo door looked too smashed to ever open again.

Viktor ducked circuitry and jagged pieces of hull, but paused before charging inside, inhaling, listening, and looking in all directions. He wouldn't expect a handful of civilians to lay a crafty trap or have the wherewithal to mount a defense, but one never knew. The woman who had seemed to be in charge—Ankari Markovich, the wanted poster said—had been agile. She might have some combat experience. If she was still alive. According to the write-up, they were criminals, so their deaths shouldn't bother him, but he hated bungling a job. Even if Mandrake Company was more known for killing people than kidnapping them, his crew ought to be able to manage either in a competent, professional manner. Otherwise what was to separate them from all the ill-trained mediocre mercenary outfits in the galaxy?

Aware of Sergeant Hazel shadowing him, Viktor stepped inside before she could offer to go first and remind him, as she so often did, that it was foolish for the captain to come on these missions personally and risk his life. No matter how many times he pointed out that he was a combat specialist and would be bored into insanity if he never left the ship and saw action, she never failed to point out that captains weren't supposed to be expendable. Few others would presume to lecture him, but she was from Grenavine, the same as he and a handful of others in the company, and she had known him for years. They were part of the original crew. The survivors.

Ceiling panels dangled everywhere in the warped corridor, and Viktor had to walk in a hunch to reach the nav cabin. A woman's unmoving form lay crumpled on the shaggy floor covering—a carpet, he supposed it would be called, though it looked more like the fur off an animal that seldom bathed. As he knelt to check the woman's pulse, he spotted the other two crew members slumped against the base of a nav console so devastated it was barely recognizable. Blood smeared one of the women's faces, and neither person was moving. At least this one—Lauren Keys, according to the poster—had a pulse.

Viktor winced when another panel fell from the ceiling, banging down between the two other women.

"I'll get that one, sir," Hazel said, "if you want to grab the others."

Viktor stepped past the Keys woman, letting Hazel pull her out, and gathered the other two, draping one over each shoulder. Dr. Zimonjic wouldn't approve of using anything other than a stretcher, but she wasn't here, nor did Viktor want to wait for someone to grab first-aid equipment out of the shuttle.

Ducking panels and buzzing circuits, he toted the women back to the hole in the hull. Maneuvering out of the smashed corridor with two people balanced over his shoulders was awkward, but he had carried heavier loads.

One of his passengers stirred and moaned as he stepped out into the night. The temperature was plummeting now that the sun had set, and it had already dropped below freezing. The shuttle should land on the flat hilltop a quarter of a mile away. After eyeing the winding, rocky path leading up to it, Viktor handed one of the women to Jiang to carry.

"Don't let that one go, eh?" he said.

Jiang wasn't one of the original crew, and he gulped noticeably at Viktor's slight censure. He was cocksure with his comrades and most people he met, but he gave a mild, "I won't, sir," here.

"Someone get that shuttle down here," Viktor ordered.

He wondered if Frog was taking his time because he was afraid of being chastised. At least their quarry hadn't escaped. That would have been annoying. This was nothing more than a side trip to earn extra cash for repairs and new equipment. He had never had any intention of chasing these women across the system.

Viktor's remaining captive, Markovich, groaned again and tried to push her way off his shoulder. He put her down, getting a face full of dark wavy brown hair in the process. It had been tied back in a more practical ponytail earlier, but it must have fallen out in the crash.

He fished out flex-cuffs and secured her wrists behind her back before she had stopped blinking her eyes in confusion—or perhaps that was less confusion and more an attempt to focus them. He patted her down, checking her dusty khaki jumpsuit for weapons. Full of pockets, the baggy outfit did little to accentuate her figure, but his search revealed some nice curves. He made himself keep the pat down quick and professional—he shouldn't be noticing a criminal's curves anyway.

"Sir, she needs the doctor, not a prison cell," Sergeant Hazel said, waving to the flex-cuffs.

Probably so, but the old habits, those that had been drilled into him in a previous life, had served him well as a mercenary and kept him alive. Never underestimating enemies and never leaving prisoners unsecured were two of those habits.

Viktor tensed when the woman stumbled against his chest, though it was doubtlessly due to her barely being able to stand rather than an attempt to get close to attack him. Though his better judgment argued for it, he didn't push her away. They had been on the defense of Maritoba without relief for more than six months. It had been a long time since the crew's last shore leave, and he hadn't had anything softer than a gun pressed against his chest for far too long. She smelled nicely feminine, too, despite the dust and grime she had acquired mucking around in those ruins, and he let his chin droop a bit, ostensibly to look her in the eyes, but also because he was trying to identify the scent of her shampoo. Lavender and...lilac? The scent surprised him with a pang of nostalgia, as his brain stirred up memories of his homeland, of walking through the gardens on the edge of the forest, where such flowers had grown along the winding dirt pathways.

"What do you people want?" Markovich mumbled, wincing as she looked up at him. A headache from hell, no doubt. He'd been knocked out enough times to know how wonderful it felt when you woke up.

Realizing he was staring at her, Viktor quashed his memories of home, a home long gone now, and he also quashed any sympathy that he might have otherwise felt toward a woman in pain. She wasn't someone to be empathized with; she must have done something particularly vile to warrant a bounty so high. Besides, "Captain Mandrake" was hardly known for showing sympathy. His crew would think him under a witch's spell if he treated this woman differently than he would any other prisoner.

"We want you," he said.

"Me? Why?"

"To collect your bounty."

The look of utter confusion that crossed her face was...a fine bit of acting.

"What bounty?" she asked.

He doubted very much that she didn't know. Still, he pushed her away from his chest, keeping a hand on her shoulder so she wouldn't pitch to the ground, and showed her the holographic poster. Her mouth opened and closed a few times. Nothing came out. She leaned toward it, squinting, but looked like she was still struggling to focus her vision. She had caught the gist though. That much was clear.

The shuttle finally reappeared, descending from the stars to land on the hilltop. Its lights brightened the path leading up to it.

Viktor folded the tablet and stuck it in his cargo pocket. "Get moving."

He turned his prisoner to face the shuttle, its rear hatch already opening. She balked, or maybe she was stunned, because in looking in that direction, she saw her ship—what remained of it. Tension bunched her shoulders, and he expected the outburst before it came. How could Frog be so good at destroying enemy craft and so pitiful at disabling them?

"You destroyed our *ship*?" Markovich spun back toward him. The shuttle's landing lights offered enough illumination that he had no trouble seeing the rage in her eyes. "Do you know how long I saved, how much I gave up to come up with the down payment, and how much I still *owe*? No, you wouldn't care, would you? You think I'm some criminal, and it would never occur to you to double-check to make sure this wasn't a mistake or vicious prank or…" Her eyes drifted toward his cargo pocket, and she wound down, finishing with, "Who the hell would put a bounty on me? On all of us? We've only known each other for a few of months. How could we have possibly committed a crime that quickly?" Then her head jerked up, and she spun around again. "My partners. Are they all right?" She spotted Sergeant Hazel and the woman she was carrying over her shoulder and onto the shuttle. Jiang was walking up the hill after her, his prisoner draped in his arms. "Lauren? Jamie?"

"They're alive." Viktor didn't think either of them had regained consciousness. "When we dock, I'll send the doctor to the brig to check on all of you."

"Well, aren't you a thoughtful bounty hunter?" Markovich grumbled.

"We're mercenaries," Viktor said stiffly. As if it mattered to her. He wasn't even sure why the distinction mattered to him. Catching criminals, fighting wars. Was one activity more virtuous than the other? They were both jobs, neither the kind that was idolized by the entertainment industry and their mindless dramas. Sometimes, very seldom, his company got hired to help the side they truly wanted to help, the outnumbered and beleaguered, but in the end, it rarely mattered. Those in bed with the Galactic

Conglomeration always won. He hadn't even been able to help his own people, and now only graves remained on Grenavine. "Walk," he said, not caring that his tone was cold, not caring that it made her flinch. "Walk, or I will carry you."

She threw back her shoulders, lifted her chin, took a step...and her legs gave out. With her hands locked behind her back, she would have fallen on her face, but he caught her. Viktor might not be as young as he once was, but his reflexes were still decent. He picked her up and carried her to the shuttle. It had been a while since he swept a woman up to carry her somewhere, but he was fairly certain that irked expression on her face wasn't a good sign. As if this was his fault. She shouldn't have annoyed Lord Felgard to the extent of a hundred thousand aurums. The owner of Trak Teck Enterprises had deep pockets, but that was a hefty bounty, even from him.

As he watched his crew strap in the prisoners for the ride up to the *Albatross*, he wondered what they had done to earn the powerful entrepreneur's wrath.

CHAPTER TWO

"I don't understand," Jamie said, sitting hard on the bench built into the back of the cell and crossing her legs with a huff. "We haven't *done* anything. You two have been back in the lab with your noses stuck to your microscopes. How could we possibly have done anything?"

Technically, Ankari had been reading books on what her microbiologist was doing with her nose stuck to a microscope, but all she said now was, "I don't know." She stood near the front of the cell, gazing down the corridor to a security desk at the end. All she could see was a pair of boots propped up on it.

Ankari paced back to the bench and patted Lauren on the back. "You doing all right?"

Blood stained the back of Lauren's hand, and the side of her face had been burned. She needed a doctor more than any of them. Ankari hoped the captain hadn't been lying, that he would send someone with medical expertise to tend to them. If he truly believed they were criminals, he had no reason to treat them decently.

"My ribs hurt," Lauren whispered. "And my head. Is the ship really... gone? All of our equipment? Our samples? My research?"

"The ship won't fly again," Ankari said. Nor had she heard anyone give an order to bring it along, even if it was only for scrap. The scavengers would be delighted to pick over the remains—some of that equipment had to have survived the crash and doubtlessly still had value. Her soul ached, knowing it would all be gone by the time she and her partners escaped and made their way back there. *If* they escaped. "I did see someone carrying our packs to the shuttle. Probably because they want to cash in on the aliuolite I gathered." She snorted. "In case our bounty isn't enough."

"Did you see who issued our bounty?" Jamie asked.

"Lord Someone. Felgard, I think. I was seeing about three blurry copies of the captain standing in front of me. I could barely read what he showed me."

"And to think I thought he was handsome."

"The handsome ones always break your heart," Lauren said.

"And blow up your ship," Ankari growled. "Sometimes your head too."

She probed the swollen knot at the back of her skull. She still felt woozy and nauseated from smacking that wall and wouldn't mind some attention from the doctor herself. Even more, she wanted access to the tablet the captain had shown her. If she could get on the net, she could learn everything about the bounty poster, and she could mail her friend, Fumio, programmer and hacker extraordinaire, to find out who had created it. Was it truly one of the self-proclaimed lords of finance, or had some enemy of hers simply wanted to get her in trouble, making it *seem* like someone who had a lot of money wanted her? She allowed herself a moment of smug pleasure at the idea of Captain What's-his-name showing up on the steps of some mansion's front door, trying to collect a bounty that had never been issued. But she couldn't imagine who would have gone through the trouble to arrange such a farce. She was only twenty-six. How many enemies could she have? She couldn't even think of any, beyond old rivals on the streets where she had grown up, but those people shouldn't have the resources to do this. And she couldn't imagine many of them had even thought of her once she had left.

"Wish I'd thought to steal his tablet," Ankari muttered. She had been a fair pickpocket once, much to her father's chagrin, but it wasn't a craft easily undertaken when one's wrists were handcuffed. At least the thugs who had stuffed them into this cell had removed their bindings before activating the force field.

A door swooshed open, and the boots disappeared from the desk. "They're all there, sir." Striker's voice floated down the corridor. "I haven't been bugging them."

"Good." That was the captain's voice, but the first person to walk into view was an attractive woman with black hair, one temple shot through with gray. She wore the same civilian-style clothes that everyone on the crew favored, at least everyone Ankari had seen so far, but her leather instrument bag and a thin gray cardigan with bulging pockets gave her a doctorly look.

The captain came into view next, though all he did was put his palm on the wall lock outside of the cell to drop the force field. Ankari took note of a small electric sensor under the handprint pad. Was it possible to lower the barrier with some kind of key as well?

The doctor walked in while the captain leaned against the wall, watching everything. He wore the same clothes as he had on the planet, though he had taken off the vest and eye apparatus. His guns still hung in a holster at his waist. Ankari had to try extremely hard not to let her loathing show on her face. She still couldn't believe he had ordered her ship blown up. Even if money were no object, it would take forever to reacquire all the specialized lab equipment they'd had inside, and money *was* an object. When wasn't it?

She fantasized about blowing up *his* ship. He would be left with nothing except scrap metal. Maybe ten thousand aurums worth, she calculated, judging how much the recyclers might offer for the raw materials from this size craft. That wouldn't pay his crew's wages for long. Of course, she would need to find a way *off* his ship before blowing it up...

For now, she painted a bland expression on her face. She might not have read any books on war and combat when she was growing up, but she had a feeling one wasn't supposed to telegraph one's hatred to one's enemy. Better to take him by surprise later on.

"I'm Dr. Zimonjic. Who's first?" The woman's voice was pleasant. She smiled too.

"Lauren, please." Ankari gestured to her injured partner and turned her back on the captain. It would be easier to keep that loathing off her face if she wasn't looking at what she loathed. "Where are your muscles, doctor?"

The woman's brows rose. "Pardon me?"

"Everyone else we've seen here...bulges. Even the women." Speaking of bulges, Ankari wondered if any of those lumps in the doctor's pockets would be worth checking out. Might there be something that could facilitate an escape? Though she trusted the skills she had acquired in her sketchy youth, the thought of trying to steal something with the captain watching made her nervous. Her wanted poster might have said she was to be delivered alive, but there were a lot of levels of aliveness one could exist on. It *was* promising that he had brought the doctor, but he had also had her ship destroyed with the wave of a hand. She couldn't assume that he would treat her well, no matter what.

"It sounds like you've met Sergeant Hazel," the doctor said dryly, taking out a scanner. She waved the handheld device over Lauren. "It's true the women here all train as hard as the men, the combat specialists anyway. And the pilots and engineers, too, come to think of it. The captain seems to think everyone should be fit enough to repel a boarding party with one hand tied behind his or her back." She smiled over her shoulder as she said this, a playful quirk to her lips.

The expression, directed at the humorless captain, surprised Ankari. Maybe they were lovers or had been once.

The captain's eyebrow ascended a millimeter, but that was the extent of his acknowledgment of the doctor's teasing. A hint of wistfulness entered Zimonjic's expression as she turned back to her patient. Ah, not lovers, but she might wish they were. Hard to imagine. The captain looked like he'd be about as cozy in bed as a Deruvian fang lizard.

"How did you come to be here?" Ankari asked the doctor.

"The army decided I was no longer trustworthy, and, thanks to the notes they wrote on my discharge, I had trouble finding work as a civilian." The doctor took out a repair kit and punched in a few codes, then lifted Lauren's shirt and affixed it to her ribs. While that was doing its work, she turned her attention to Jamie.

"Why weren't you trustworthy?" Not a failing in her doctoring skills, Ankari hoped.

Zimonjic's lips flattened. "Because of where I'm from." Her expression didn't invite further inquiries.

A man ambled into the corridor to join the captain. Ankari recognized him as one of the brutes who had been along on the mission, the spiky-haired thug with all the knives and guns, the one who had tried to capture her. Striker. That had been his name. She wondered how big the crew was. From the back of the shuttle, she had glimpsed the gray outline of a winged ship before they had docked. It hadn't been a small craft, but she had no idea whether it held fifty people or two hundred and fifty. She had seen a half dozen new faces on her way to the brig. The idea of escaping past all of them was daunting, and she didn't even know what they would escape in, with the *Marie Curie* left on the planet. One of those shuttles? What was their range? Could Jamie fly one?

"They going to live, sir?" Striker asked, taking up a position that mirrored the captain's on the opposite wall.

"Looks like."

"That's good money being offered for them. I'd hate to lose my percentage."

The captain grunted. A real chatterbox, that one.

If they were mercenaries and money was their prime draw, maybe they could be tempted by the allure of more. The promise of fossilized poop might not have tickled their greedy spots, but could something else work? Ankari didn't have a lot of free cash after buying all of that equipment, but maybe the mercenaries could be enticed by a share in the company. Those shares weren't worth much now, but if Lauren's second round of tests went as promisingly as the first, they could have a high value someday. That knowledge made Ankari reluctant to give them away, but this situation called for desperate moves.

"How much *is* the bounty?" she asked.

"I showed you the poster," the captain said.

"My eyes were busy crossing at the time."

"A hundred thousand aurums," Striker said cheerfully.

Ankari stared at him. A *hundred thousand*? Who would pay that much for her team? And why?

"And as Chief of Boom, I get two percent of that," Striker added. Chief of Boom? Was that some way of saying he was an artillery specialist without using so many pesky syllables? "Once we finally get our shore leave, that'll buy a lot of drinks. And women." Striker gazed thoughtfully at Jamie and smiled. Aside from the doctor and Sergeant Hazel, Ankari hadn't seen any women on board. That must not leave the men with many mating options during the long months in space. Striker turned his thoughtful gaze on the captain, as if he meant to ask if these particular women might be available.

It was a silent question, but the captain's lack of a response wasn't reassuring. He was simply staring into the cell. Actually, he was staring at *Ankari*. Something else that made her nervous. It wasn't a lascivious stare, the way Striker's was; it was more like he was scrutinizing her. Why? What exactly was on that wanted poster anyway? For the fiftieth time, she wished she had gotten a better look. If she could find a way to a computer, she needed to do some research.

"You have teams picked out for Sturm?" the captain asked, finally looking away from Ankari to meet his soldier's eyes.

"Yes, sir. Alpha and Charlie for sure, but maybe Delta too. Waiting for intel to get me a report on our thief's most recent hideout, but it sounds like he's got a big bunch of uglies working with him. You coming down with us on this one?"

"I might."

Ankari had to take advantage of the captain's attention shift. The doctor was bent over Lauren, checking the repair device, and her pockets were accessible. Ankari touched the knot on her head with one hand, drawing Zimonjic's eye, and said, "I could use some attention from your devices, too, Doctor. Got a lump bigger than most of the ruins on that planet."

In the seconds that Zimonjic was looking at her face, Ankari's other hand went shopping in her pocket.

"What were you looking for in the ruins?"

"Fossils." Ankari met the doctor's eyes and didn't look at what she had fished out of the pocket, but it felt like one of those syringes that stored a number of medications in the handle. Either that or it was a sonic toothbrush. Ankari doubted the latter would get them out of the cell, so she decided to hope for the former.

"Poop fossils." Striker snickered. Amazing that the captain would consider putting someone with the maturity of a toddler in charge of a combat mission.

Both of the men were staring through the force field again. Ankari slipped her stolen medical tool—or tooth tool—into her pocket to examine later. They had been searched before being shoved into the cell, so another search shouldn't be forthcoming. But there were doubtlessly video monitors; since Striker had left the desk, she hoped that meant nobody was watching the feed.

"We were collecting samples for the R&D department of our company," Ankari said, extending a hand toward Lauren, who managed a wan smirk despite her weary visage. "If you get excited by two percent of some grubby mercenary earnings, you should see what a percentage of our company would be worth, if you were to partner with us, Mr. Striker." She might not be able to promise anyone a hundred thousand aurums, but she could promise more than two percent of a hundred thousand. She smiled at Striker, though she glanced at the captain, as well, wondering if he might be intrigued. His flat stare didn't suggest it.

Striker, however, did perk up, his gaze shifting from Jamie to Ankari. "Yeah?"

"We could use a weapons expert for our business, as is doubtlessly apparent." Ankari made a gesture to encompass her team and their forlorn position inside the cell.

"That much is obvious," Striker said. "What kind of money are you making now?"

The captain's eyes narrowed, but he watched the exchange in silence. He either had to think Ankari was brazen for trying to steal one of his soldiers away in front of him or…stupid. And maybe she was. She didn't truly expect anything to come of her offer, but one never knew. There were two sets of ears in the area besides the captain's—all it would take was for one to find the offer intriguing to make something happen.

"We're a pre-revenue startup at this point," Ankari said, "but we've talked to a number of biotech firms, and they'll either pay us enormously when we deliver or they'll buy us out." Granted, only two of the twenty firms had actually listened to the idea, while the others had laughed Ankari out of their fancy gold-gilded reception halls and slammed the doors behind her.

"Pre-what?" Striker asked.

"They haven't made any money yet," the captain said.

"Oh. Well, honey, I ain't real interested in a percentage of nothing." Thus Striker proved he had a better understanding of math than Ankari would have guessed.

"What's your company do?" Dr. Zimonjic asked, removing the repair kit from Lauren's ribs and giving Striker a little frown. That frown didn't extend to the captain, even though his flat statement had been nearly as sarcastic.

Lauren, who must be feeling better now, straightened on the bench. "You're interested? It's fascinating, really. As a doctor, you're of course aware of the importance of human intestinal microbiota in determining a person's overall health, including his ability to combat aggressive micro-organisms, and properly digest foods and produce certain key vitamins, yes?"

Striker's lip curled in confusion, or maybe that was a sign of incredulity at how disinteresting he found the subject. They would probably have to look elsewhere for a burly security guard to cut in.

"Yes…" Zimonjic said.

"Depending on your specialty, you may also be aware that there's been research done, tying epigenetic changes—such as those that might cause a person to merely be a carrier for a certain autoimmune disease versus actually expressing it—to a person's overall gut health. The human micro-biota—the tens of trillions of microorganisms that live in our intestines—" that aside seemed to be for the soldiers, "—can be drastically different from person to person, with an individual's particular makeup being determined by a great many things, with diet and environment lying at the top of the list. We've been debating for centuries what the optimal mixture and popu-lation of intestinal flora is for a human being—did you know that there are scientists that argue that we're not even human anymore, not in the sense that the original colonists from Old Earth were, because our microbiota has changed so much as a result of the existing microbes in the system we now call home? Up until two years ago, the focus of my work was in heal-ing people with gut dysbiosis issues that were affecting their health. I would transplant the microbiota from an individual with a healthy gut into that of the ill person, often to fantastic results. Then, after meeting Ankari through my clinic—"

When Lauren gave her a cheerful wave, Ankari forced herself not to grimace. She didn't particularly want to talk about all the pathogens she had picked up as a result of growing up on the streets and being so often forced to eat and drink from less than optimal sources. Fortunately, Lauren didn't go into that.

"—we got to talking about the microbiota of the aliens who lived in this system thousands of years ago."

"Is that so?" The doctor's eyes dulled at the mention of aliens; yes, she would sympathize with those eighteen companies who had shown Ankari the door when she had brought up their company's latest research. At least Zimonjic was still working. She had scanned Ankari's bump and laid a repair kit against the side of her head, before shifting her attention again to Jamie. The device hummed softly, reverberating in Ankari's skull as it amplified her body's own ability to heal the injury.

"*Yes*," Lauren said, not noticing the doctor's tone, thanks to her own enthusiasm—or just because she never could understand that people wouldn't be as fascinated by her work as she was. "As you've doubtlessly heard, the archaeologists who've been studying the remains of the original inhabitants of this system have declared that they were remarkably similar to us in body and brain makeup, and even in culture and thought, except that fossils and other evidence suggest that they were faster, stronger, and physically superior to us in most aspects and that they lived two hundred years or more. They rarely fell to disease, instead dying of old age or because of intra-system wars. *Our* studies have been fascinating." Lauren pointed to Ankari as well as herself, even if Ankari was more the marketing and business side of the enterprise and, after throwing out the initial idea, had done precious little actual studying. "They suggest that the secret to the aliens' long and healthy lives was their intestinal microbiota, rather than any superior genetics they might have possessed. Think about it: if genetics alone held the key to health and longevity, as people thought for so long, we'd have already *made* the superior human being. Our company is working on isolating—"

Ankari stopped her partner with a hand on the shoulder. Striker looked like he was about to fall asleep; Zimonjic had long since decided Lauren was a quack; and the captain was checking something on his tablet. Probably something really important. Like what the ship's cook was making for dinner.

"They haven't signed a non-disclosure agreement," Ankari said. "Let's not give away too many of our secrets, eh?"

Lauren's eyes widened. "Oh. Of course."

Zimonjic plucked the repair device from Ankari's head and stepped back, tucking her tools away. "You three will live. Until you get to your destination, anyway." She stepped out of the cell, nodding toward the captain.

He folded his tablet and palmed the force field on again. The screen stretched across the cell with a flash of blue and a hint of ozone before becoming a clear barrier that one wouldn't notice until one touched it.

"That was boring as hell," Striker muttered, his voice not quite low enough to be indistinguishable. "But that one's tits bounced nicely when she was waving her arms about with all that crazy enthusiasm."

Ankari couldn't make out the captain's response. She supposed it was too much to hope that it was along the lines of, "Get your mind out of the brothel, and try reading a book and learning to think about more than sex some time."

"Captain," Ankari called before he disappeared around the corner. She smoothed her face and smiled—no loathing here, no, sir. "If you're not committed to whoever made that bounty offer, I'd like to discuss with you the potential of us buying out the contract."

The captain looked back at her. "With the earnings from your pre-revenue startup? I'll pass."

Ankari flushed. "I *might* be willing to negotiate in shares, but I was thinking in terms of straight cash. I can muster up ten percent now and pay the rest back as a loan with a fair amount of interest based on the current prime rate." Never mind the loan she was already going to have to pay back for her ship…There was no way her insurance was going to cover her, not when she'd taken the *Marie Curie* to that dangerous, parasite-laden planet.

The captain grunted. Not exactly a sign of interest, but he wasn't walking away.

"We have tremendous potential," Ankari tried. "After we do the clinical trials, we'll have customers lined up for our services, whether we get GalCon approval right away or not. We've already had amazing results on mice. You could be one of the first to receive a transplant. What do you think? Would you like to gain greater strength and stamina than you've ever had? Live an extra hundred years?"

The captain hadn't been receptive to start with, but at this question, his face shut down like a reactor gone critical. "That sounds like a punishment rather than a reward," he muttered. He didn't explain why. He simply turned his back and headed for the exit.

"Would you at least consider returning our packs to us so we can continue our research?" Lauren called after him.

He disappeared without responding.

"I'm eager to examine the specimens you gathered," Lauren explained when Ankari looked at her.

"We're trapped in the brig of a mercenary ship, being delivered to what could be our deaths, and that's your primary concern right now?"

"Well, I thought you were working on that part of the problem." Lauren waved to Ankari's pocket.

Ankari snorted. Lauren was either more observant than she would have guessed, or her sleight-of-hand skills weren't as good as they had once been.

"We'll see." Ankari walked to the corner of the cell, turning her back on the force field. Hoping to avoid the security camera, even if she had no idea where it was located, she slipped her stolen find out of her pocket. It wasn't a toothbrush. She had been right; it was a combo syringe. Now she just had to figure out what was housed in it…and how she could get close enough to someone to use it.

———

Viktor's tablet bleeped, letting him know he had a request for voice communications. Lord Felgard. It looked like it came from the man's personal account too. Not that of some secretary. Huh.

It had been less than an hour since Viktor had transmitted the fact that he had acquired the three women, and it was the night cycle on Felgard's private island, wasn't it? The stamp on the message said three a.m.

"You want to beat on each other in the gym for a while, sir?" Striker asked. They were walking the corridors from the brig to the mess hall, neither on duty now. It was the night cycle here too.

"Later, yes. I've got to answer this first." Viktor waved the tablet, then veered into an alcove to take the ladder up to his deck.

Striker surprised him by following, his boots clanging on the rungs. "Sure thing, sir. But I've got a question first, if you don't mind."

"*I* don't mind. *Felgard* might wonder why I'm being delayed."

"Aw, that rich old crotch sock, I'm not worried about him."

"I'll let him know that."

"Go ahead. Just, uh, don't use my name when you tell him. Or my description. Or anything about me."

"What about your comics?" Viktor asked, referring to Striker's legendary—at least among the crew—drawings that depicted everyone and their adventures. Striker was still waiting to acquire galaxy-wide recognition.

"Oh, you could tell him about those. Maybe he'd find me a publishing deal with one of the media empires, eh?"

"What's your question, Striker?" They had reached the door to Viktor's quarters. It recognized him and slid open.

"It's about those girls. Can I foist them off on Tems, or am I still responsible for them?"

Viktor had assigned Sergeant Striker to watch them on the shuttle, more as a punishment for losing one of them on the planet than out of a fear that they would escape in front of so many soldiers. He hadn't specified that this watching should continue once they were in the brig. If he had, he'd be annoyed that Striker had left his post to rush after him with questions. He might be annoyed anyway. He hadn't decided yet.

"Tems is security chief. I've notified him of their presence. He'll make sure someone keeps an eye on the brig."

"Oh, good," Striker said. "I don't think they like me. 'Course I like them fine." His eyebrows waggled.

"I'm sure you do." Viktor stepped inside, expecting the door to shut and for Striker to leave.

Striker slapped his hand against the jamb to keep it open. "They're real cute. Especially the young one."

Jamie Flipkens, Viktor's mind supplied. He had memorized every detail of the women's poster before going down to retrieve them. Flipkens was twenty and had been some whiz mechanic in her little farming community. How that translated to becoming a ship's pilot and engineer, he could only imagine, but her record hadn't contained much more information than that.

There hadn't been much on Ankari Markovich, either, though the microbiologist had a long list of publishing credits, and it wasn't clear why she'd left academia to join the other two nuts. The Ankari nut, specifically, since she was clearly in charge. She must have been smoother when recruiting the others than she had been when trying to inveigle someone over to her side down in the brig. Viktor wasn't sure why he had listened as long as he had. Probably because she was attractive and her inveigling attempts had been moderately entertaining. But only an idiot would allow himself to think of a prisoner as anything other than a prisoner. An idiot...or a horny combat sergeant.

Striker was still standing in his doorway, waiting for an answer.

"Sergeant," Viktor said, putting an edge in his voice. "You have a mission to plan."

An edge that Striker was, as usual, oblivious to. "Yes, sir. But can I have the young one to, uhm, I mean I can watch her real good when I'm off shift, and put her back in the brig when I'm on."

Viktor faced the man, letting Striker see the hardness in his eyes. "You know we don't rape or otherwise molest prisoners." He had seen enough of that bullshit when he was in the GalCon army, especially on those outer core duty stations where soldiers thought nobody was watching, that nobody cared. "We may be mercenaries, but we can choose to act with honor, and that means with prisoners, not just on the battlefield."

"Oh, sure, sir." Striker lifted his hands, an expression of purest innocence widening his eyes. "I wasn't thinking rape...exactly, but I'm a handsome fellow; you can't deny that."

Viktor said nothing.

"What if she *willingly* wants to come with me? She's got to be bored down there, and maybe tortured in her head listening to that science woman prattle on. Might be I'm an appealing alternative."

Viktor doubted it.

"Come on, sir. I haven't been any trouble of late. I've worked real hard for the crew, for you. I took that bullet on Vasquelin, remember?" He tapped his side. "And we haven't had leave in months and months. I'm tired of nothing but my hand for company. I was so desperate last week, I tried to get Sergeant Hazel to come see my gun collection, and you know how she responds to that kind of thing." Striker's hand twitched protectively toward his groin. "Can I at least *ask* that girl? If she says no, I won't be any trouble to them. I swear."

Another bleep came from Viktor's tablet. Damn, Felgard was in an insistent mood. Viktor wasn't one to jump at anyone's summons, but if there was more information to be had or a change to the deal, he needed to know about it promptly.

"They're prisoners, and they'll be looking for ways to escape," Viktor said. "I don't want them taken out of the brig. You can go down there if you want, and if you can get her to jump your gun in there with both of her friends watching, I don't care. But no force."

Striker grinned, as if this posed no problem. "Thank you, sir."

Viktor snorted as the door shut. He shouldn't have agreed to even that, but none of those girls was going to willingly do anything with him. Striker could get himself a little excited then go off and have another date with his hand.

Viktor tossed his tablet onto his standing desk, and the three-dimensional video display came to life. "Felgard," he said, letting the computer handle the connections.

While he waited, he added water to the reservoir for the system that fed the dwarf apple trees potted in a grow station along one wall of his cabin. Two were flowering and needed pollinating, but his comm pinged first. In less time than he had expected, especially given the lag as the request for communications was relayed across six planets and a whole lot of empty space, Felgard came into view.

A reed-thin man with a protruding jaw and wispy gray hair sticking out from beneath a top hat, the legendary entrepreneur had keen gray eyes framed by old-fashioned spectacles that doubtlessly camouflaged some state-of-the-art technology. An expensive and much more sophisticated version of Viktor's Eytect scanner, maybe.

Viktor folded his arms across his chest and waited for the other man to initiate the conversation, so he could get a feel for his thoughts and attitude. He had never spoken to the lord of finance before, nor had any direct dealings with any of his employees, but he *had* once blown up a munitions platform that belonged to Trak Teck Enterprises as part of a raid by a competitor. That had been more than five years ago. He would find out how fine Felgard's memory was, and if he was the type to hold a grudge.

"Captain Mandrake," Felgard said. "I wasn't expecting you to be the one to capture those criminals. You don't usually deal in the bounty collection business." Felgard smiled and waited for his words to transmit.

The words came across as polite, almost friendly, but Viktor knew Felgard was letting him know how much he knew about the business of Mandrake Company. Given that there were hundreds, if not thousands, of mercenary outfits spread across the system, many much larger than Viktor's, this meant Felgard had done some research. Five years ago likely. At the time, he must have decided retaliation wasn't worth it—especially when he had been busy dealing with an upstart competitor—but now? Who knew?

"Lord Felgard," Viktor said, managing not to show how much it grated on his nerves to call someone a lord, as if he were some Old Earth descendant with noble blood rather than someone who had simply earned enough money to be listed as a lord of finance in the *Rothmore Journal*. "You're correct. Collecting bounties wouldn't keep a crew of one hundred plus in armor and rations, but your offering was particularly lucrative, and we were quite literally on the way past the planet where your villains were hiding." He raised his eyebrows slightly as he said villains, to let Felgard know he was wondering what those three women had done. He wasn't going to ask. Bounty hunters who wanted to live long enough to spend their earnings didn't pry into their patrons' business. Still, he found himself hoping for an answer as he waited for his words to transmit and for Felgard's response.

"That is fortunate for me. I trust you're en route with them now?"

"We have business on Sturm and a few repairs to make, then we'll head straight to your planet."

For the first time, Felgard's polite smile faded, and his eyes hardened. A blue light blipped on the frame of his spectacles. Accessing some report, was he? Probably finding out what was happening on the mining and lumber moon of Sturm.

"You plan to engage in a manhunt for that self-proclaimed Robin Hood who's supposed to be hiding out there?" Felgard asked.

"Sisson Hood is the name he's taken. He's stealing from the rich, pocketing ninety percent, and spreading the other ten amongst the poor, trying to gain their support. But he's also kidnapping young women when he's dropping off the money and returning them somewhat used to their families. The local government isn't pleased, nor is the Buddhist temple there. They've each offered to pay us for getting rid of the problem." Viktor wouldn't normally explain so much of a coming mission to someone who had nothing to do with it, but he suspected Felgard already knew all the details.

"Noble work, I'm sure," Felgard said. It actually *was* nobler than many of the assignments Mandrake Company was offered, and Viktor was looking forward to it, especially after seeing the images the temple had sent, the battered faces of some of the ravaged women. If it had only been the government sending these images, he might have expected a hoax, that the Robin Hood angle was truer than they were admitting, but he respected the monks more than the representatives of most of the religions in the system. They were always so adamant about not taking money from corporations, and he had rarely been led astray by anything they said. "But," Felgard went on, after a delay that might have been his own or might have been a lag in the connection, "that could keep you for weeks. I must have my prisoners."

"It won't take weeks, my lord. My people are good."

"Any delay is unacceptable. You must bring them immediately to me if you wish your payment, and then you may go on your other mission. Sisson Hood isn't going anywhere, I'm sure."

Actually, it was possible a bounty hunter would come in and take him down if Viktor's people didn't get there first. Sturm was also on the way into the core worlds, where the *Albatross* was scheduled for repairs—their last assignment had been long and bloody and run the ship down as much as the crew. It would add two weeks to their travel to detour to Felgard's and then come back to the moon and the mission. Viktor had promised his people they would be on leave by then. As he was so often reminded, these weren't soldiers in the army, men who had sworn oaths to serve, protect, and kill in the name of GalCon. They were mercenaries, and they expected to be paid and allowed to take regular vacations, as promised in their contract. If the entire crew was as restless and horny as Striker, he could have people abandoning the company before long.

"I have other obligations, my lord. And with all due respect, you won't receive your prisoners if you're not prepared to relinquish payment,

whenever I arrive." Anticipating Felgard's irritation, Viktor added a concilia-
tory, "I'll see that my arrival is prompt, however. If it does look like we're to
be delayed on Sturm, I'll arrange to have them sent ahead."

Felgard's face had grown harder, all trace of the earlier politeness gone.
Viktor expected the lord to come back with more arguments, but after a
pause during which the light blinked on his spectacles again, Felgard said,
"See that your delay is short, Captain." Then he cut the communication.

That last blink stayed with Viktor after the hologram faded from his desk.
Maybe it was nothing. But maybe he needed to make very certain he wasn't
delayed on Sturm. It was true that Viktor could withhold the prisoners if
Felgard tried to withhold the payment, but the wealthy old entrepreneur had
the power to make life unpleasant for him and his company. He hated the
tap-dancing he had to do when dealing with these lords, but he ought to be
used to it. After all, hadn't he tap-danced for the senior officers in the fleet?
He might have started his own company, thinking it would be different if he
was calling the shots, but nothing had really changed. He could plot his own
course now, but the stars were always the same.

Feeling the familiar mix of longing, frustration, and rage, emotions that
often boiled near the surface, Viktor hit a button. A ceiling panel opened,
and a heavy punching bag dropped down with a clank-thud. He spent the
next fifteen minutes pounding it. It was exercise, but it was a venting of
frustrations too. Better to take his feelings out on an inanimate object than
on his men.

When he was out of breath and bathed with sweat, he hit the button,
storing the bag again. He walked the five steps to the other side of the
sparsely furnished cabin. The lack of chairs made it seem larger than it
was—there were a few katas he could do on the padded matting when he
preferred calmer exercises than what the bag offered—and didn't encourage
people to stay long when they visited. He never sat himself, not having the
personality for such inaction, and only laid down for sleep and for time in
sickbay. The clock said it was time for one of those things now. He couldn't
remember when he had last eaten, so he grabbed a meatloaf log from the
tiny kitchenette built into the wall and pulled out the blender to make one of
his "horrible green drinks," as the crew called them. A doctor and old friend
had recommended the crushed ice and vegetable concoctions to him long

ago, since he had a habit of avoiding leafy things at his meals. He always threw in an apple from his trees, and that made the drink sweet enough to be palatable.

As he stood at his desk with his meal, smelling the blossoms on the flowering trees, the memory of the gardens back home came to mind. Strange. It had been almost ten years since his world had been destroyed and twenty since he had walked those flower-, leaf-, and fruit-laden paths. Why think of them now? Because of the trees? No, they were always in his cabin and had been for years.

No, he knew the reason. That Markovich woman, with her lilac and lavender-scented hair, had brought the gardens to his mind earlier in the night. Viktor wished Felgard had let something slip about his prisoners, about why he *wanted* them.

On the one hand, he could believe they were criminals, even if they didn't seem that polished, because he had seen all kinds of people break the law, and it wasn't uncommon for those who sought to climb into the business world to be the first to cheat and steal and do whatever they could to reach those lofty heights. For those who made it all the way, being dubbed lords of finance, the rewards and privileges were endless. Even those who simply created a decently profitable business could live a much nicer life than galactic standards.

On the other hand, that microbiologist was passionate about her studies—Viktor had skimmed the abstracts of a few articles related to what she had been blathering about, enough to know that they were researching in a legitimate field and it wasn't all quackery designed to flummox dumb soldiers. Nothing about her came across as duplicitous. Further, the young mechanic-turned-engineer had struck him as innocent rather than conniving. And the leader, Ankari Markovich…she seemed a schemer, and he could see her as the brains behind a fraudulent operation, but she had put on a good show when he had shown her the tablet. If she knew she was a wanted criminal, she had feigned otherwise convincingly. She had been a lot less convincing when she had been feigning that she didn't hate Viktor's microbe-filled guts. She might have smiled and been trying to interest him in her ludicrous upstart—startup, whatever—company, but he'd read the fury simmering in her eyes. She'd had that look for him since she realized he was responsible for destroying her ship. He recalled her eyes *before* she had realized that, when she had been waking from her concussion and blinking up at him without artifice or anger. Bedroom eyes. That was what they called it. She had those. And she also had those nice curves that had been pressed against him.

Viktor snorted at himself. Striker wasn't the only horny one around; that was a certainty.

Even allowing that he was attracted to the woman, he couldn't quite pin down why he found himself wanting to go down to the brig to talk to her. He wasn't intrigued by her business, but he wanted to know more about her and what she had done to irk Felgard. He had a fondness for people with the balls to stick it to those megalomaniacal finance coots. Which probably meant he *shouldn't* go down to talk to her, or have anything to do with her. The last thing he needed was to develop an attachment for someone he was going to hand over to a man who might shoot her once he got her.

Besides, Striker was already down there, talking to the women. Viktor snorted again and took his dishes to the cleaner. He ought to get the security feed later to watch that. In part to make sure Striker didn't violate his orders, and in part to see how entertaining his rejection was.

In the meantime, he lay down on his bed, thinking thoughts of lavender and lilac…and a home that was no more.

CHAPTER THREE

Ankari woke up when the lights, which had been dimmed for the night cycle, powered up to full strength. Striker was back, standing on the other side of the force field and staring at her. At Jamie, actually. It was creepy. How long had he been there?

A pair of boots was visible on the desk at the other end of the hall. Ankari found that reassuring, though she didn't know if she should. The crew might look the other way as this Striker dragged a prisoner off to his cave for unspeakable torments.

"You rethink my offer?" Ankari sat up. She and Jamie had been sleeping on the floor, while Lauren took the bench. Every surface in the cell was equally hard.

"Nah," Striker said, "but the captain said we could have sex."

"Uh, what?"

Jamie was awake now, too, and hadn't missed the fact that the big brute was looking at her as he spoke. She pulled her knees up to her chest and wrapped her arms around her legs. With her eyes wide, glancing back and forth between Striker and Ankari, Jamie appeared young and vulnerable. Ankari had been anything but young at twenty, but when Jamie had spoken of the small rural community she had grown up in and the strict father who had shooed away boys, Ankari had gotten the impression that she might still be a virgin without a birth-control implant or anything. Not that anyone of any sexual experience couldn't be alarmed by Striker's words.

"He said we could get horizontal if you agreed to it." Striker grinned. "Or vertical. I'm easy."

That much was obvious. That the captain had deemed it appropriate to let this thug wander down here and proposition them gave Ankari one more reason to want to clobber him. Still, this could turn out to be an opportunity.

"Who exactly are you propositioning?" she asked.

"That one." Striker pointed at Jamie, who squeezed herself into a tighter ball. "But I'd poke any of you." He looked at Ankari's chest, making her glad she wasn't wearing anything revealing. His pleased smile had all the charm of an auto-tram barreling down the mountain at a woman tied to the tracks.

"How magnanimous." Ankari touched the cylindrical lump inside her jumpsuit pocket. She hadn't decoded all of the options inside the syringe tool—the display showed the full medical names rather than ones a layman might know—but she had recognized a sedative. She had risked showing Lauren, for verification, though she had been worried about the camera picking up the tool.

"Who's interested?" Striker puffed out his chest. "I'm good at my job, *all* of my jobs, if you catch my meaning."

"Shocking," Lauren muttered, her eye lingering on Ankari's pocket.

The real shock would be if this idiot had ever convinced a woman to sleep with him without paying her. A lot.

"No, thank you," Jamie said politely. The wariness hadn't faded from her eyes. She must wonder, as Ankari did, if the thug would take no for an answer.

Striker's face remained unperturbed, or maybe optimistic was the word, for he merely turned toward Ankari. "What about you?"

"Where would we do it?" Ankari asked. "Do you have a private cabin?" She gave the boots on the desk a significant look. She couldn't see around the corner to see the rest of the security man's face, but he had to be entertained by this conversation.

"I *do* have a private cabin. I'm a senior sergeant, been here since the beginning, you know. Got all kinds of perks. But the captain said we'd have to do it in here." Striker tapped his fingers on the wall beside the door pad. "Shall I come in?"

If he'd still been wearing the bandolier of grenades, Ankari might have been tempted—surely the three of them could have overpowered him, grabbed a few, and made a stand—but blowing up the brig wasn't what she wanted. She needed a chance to roam free for an hour or two and find the ship's library—if a mercenary ship had such a thing—or someplace quiet to access the net. She needed to get Fumio researching for her and to learn more about Lord Felgard. She'd heard the name before, but had no idea why he might be after her team. All she could think was that this might somehow be related to their company, but they hadn't set up a clinic yet or taken on any clients. How could he have even heard of their business? Aside from that handful of meetings Ankari had arranged, they hadn't told anyone what they were doing.

"Look, I might be interested," Ankari said, "especially if you might be willing to put in a word to the captain on our behalf and perhaps get our samples and equipment returned to us…" That ought to add a little verisimilitude. As dumb as Striker seemed to be, he would probably be suspicious if one of them jumped at a chance to ride his…poker. "But, I'm afraid I prefer privacy for sensuous matters."

"I can make it dark." Striker thumbed a panel, and the lights dimmed, then went up again. "And your friends can turn their backs."

Gee, how private. "Sorry, big fellow. I need to be in the mood too. Privacy, romantic music, and a strapping gentleman with a nice muscular chest."

Striker's brow had been furrowed, but it smoothed at this. "I have a nice muscular chest."

"I'm sure you do. And if we go up to your cabin, you can show it off to me."

"And you'll show off your chest to me."

"That's generally how these things work." Ankari did her best to give him a flirtatious smile. No one had ever accused her of being a great actress, but he wasn't the most perceptive audience, either.

"But the captain said…" Striker chewed on the side of his lip. "Maybe we could…" He glanced back at the boots. "I mean, of course we could. I'm a trusted part of this crew. I can take a prisoner out if I want. Not like you're going to get away from me and run off." He gave her a dismissive sniff.

Whatever got him to let her out of the cell.

"Ankari," Jamie whispered, "you shouldn't…I mean, you can't really be thinking…?"

Either Jamie hadn't seen Ankari pickpocket the tool, or she had little faith in her ability to use it on Muscles over there. Or maybe she was playing along, making this all seem more realistic to Striker.

"Aw, there's nothing wrong with me. I'll be nice. Unless you don't like nice." Striker grinned. "I'll even show you my comics."

"Er, how can a girl say no to that?" Ankari asked.

"You can't. You already agreed." His triumphant smile made her nervous. If this didn't work and she wasn't able to sedate him, she had a feeling he wasn't going to let her change her mind later. Not easily anyway. She tried to draw some strength from the fact that she'd had years of her father's training and had used it on the streets a few times. But this wasn't some brute from one of the roving gangs; he was a trained soldier. He would have seen unarmed combat in all its variants at some point in his career, and he would have an answer for her attack unless she caught him off guard.

The force field dropped, and she was out of time to second-guess herself.

Striker extended his arm, as if he were inviting her to stroll out to a ballroom floor with him. Right.

Ankari licked her lips and stepped out. She resisted the urge to look back at her partners with a what-have-I-done expression on her face. Instead, she laid her hand on Strider's arm and smiled up at him. He reactivated the force field and led her past empty cells and to the door at the end of the corridor.

"Gotta sign her out," said the soldier at the desk. He was watching a movie on his tablet—maybe he hadn't been all that entertained by Striker's attempts to woo a prisoner after all.

"The captain said—" Striker started, but the soldier interrupted him.

"I don't care what the captain said. I'm not getting busted on account of your oversexed tent pole. Gotta sign her out." He flipped from his movie to a signature form and held it up for Striker.

Ankari was beginning to wonder what the captain *had* said. It seemed to have changed from the time Striker had first entered to now. Rewriting the conversation in his head as he went along, was he?

Striker shrugged and scribbled his name with his finger, then led Ankari out the door. He slung an arm around her and started groping her as they walked. She hoped it wasn't far to his quarters, but if it was...she let her hand dangle close to her pocket.

"This is going to be fun," he promised.

"Can't wait," she mumbled.

"Really?" He stopped in front of an alcove with a ladder going up, his eyes burning like he might strip her down right there.

"No, I can wait." The man was literal, wasn't he? "I want the romance. The music, remember? And your comics."

"Oh." He brightened, then stepped onto the bottom rung. "Yes, I just drew a new panel. You'll like it."

He was an artist? She couldn't even imagine what he might draw. Something lurid, probably.

"Follow me," he said.

Between one eye blink and the next, she realized he was giving her the opportunity she had been hoping for. While he was climbing, he wasn't holding her and couldn't see what she was doing. She lunged up the rungs behind him to catch him before he clambered out on the next level. Fortunately, he was going up two levels. They were halfway to the top deck when she got close enough to stab him in the butt with the needle. She jammed it in without mercy, knowing it had to go through a couple of layers of clothes and also knowing that he would jerk away as soon as he felt it. She pressed the button that released the drug.

"What was that?" he roared, spinning on the ladder and staring down at her.

"My fingernails," Ankari said, trying to hide the syringe from view and hoping the sedative kicked in quickly. "I saw your hard butt and couldn't resist—"

He dropped down, smacking her arm away. "That wasn't any fingernail."

Her knuckles banged against the side of the ladder well, and the syringe flew from her hand. It bounced off a rung, dropped a floor and a half to the deck below, and rolled into the light spilling in from the corridor.

"You drugged me?" Striker demanded, taking another step down and reaching for her hair.

And that was her cue to run.

Ankari let go a hair's breadth before he could grab her hair, skimming down the ladder and dropping to the deck. She lunged out into the corridor. Fortunately, it was late enough that nobody else was around. She thought of sprinting in a random direction, but plastered herself against the wall instead. If she fled, she risked running into someone.

Striker barreled out of the ladder well. He must have expected her to run—he started to sprint, then stopped himself with a jerk, his arms thrown out for balance, and she got her split-second of surprise. She launched a foot at his exposed torso. The side kick slipped under his arm, hammering him in the ribs. She'd thrown all of her weight behind it, but he was so big that he didn't even stagger to the side. He might have a bruise in the morning, but that didn't keep him from lunging at her.

She evaded his long arms by dropping to the floor and launching a second kick as she fell, this one taking him in the side of the knee. It affected him more than the blow to the ribs had. There was less muscle to protect the joint, and his leg crumpled. He didn't lose his balance and go down, but he did pitch forward for a moment, having to grab the wall to support himself.

Ankari rolled backward in a somersault and came up on her feet, facing him. He glowered at her, rage blazing from his eyes.

Anytime, that sedative could start working anytime...

Striker lunged at her. Were his movements the tiniest bit slower than before? She didn't know his norm and couldn't be sure, but she had time to leap back, throwing up a block to deflect his grasping fingers.

"Stop moving, you tricky bitch," Striker snarled. "I'll—" He lunged again, punching toward her face.

Expecting it, Ankari leaped back again. This time, he had been feinting, and he followed his jab with a rush and a fist toward her stomach. Under normal circumstances, his speed and strength might have gotten through her defenses, but he was definitely moving more slowly. He almost stumbled over his own feet too. She blocked both attacks and threw a heel strike at his groin. Her first thought had been to go for the ribs, but she had already felt how much muscle plated them. The groin was a different story.

He yowled, and she winced at the noise. She needed to shut him up somehow, or she would never get her chance in the library. Soldiers would be streaming out into the corridor any moment.

But the sedative finally kicked in, and he didn't get another yowl out. He was clutching his groin with one hand and reaching uselessly toward her with the other when his eyes rolled back in his head. He crumpled to the floor.

Though Ankari's instincts were to run, to get space between her and the commotion and who cared about the direction, she took fifteen seconds to pat him down first. If he had a tablet on him, she wouldn't need to find a library. But he didn't have anything in his pockets besides folding knives.

Ankari thought about pulling him into the ladder well or maybe even a cabin, if she could get a door to open, so she would have more time before he was found, but he was well over two hundred pounds and too heavy for her to drag far. She dared not waste any more time, so she left him as he was and ran down the corridor, glancing at doors. Some had labels, some didn't. This level had shuttle bays, weapons and sensor stations, and cargo bays, rather than cabins—that might explain why nobody had burst out to check on the noise yet. More out of curiosity than anything else, she tried to open the shuttle bay door. She couldn't leave without her comrades, nor did she have any idea how to fly some random mercenary craft, but it would be good to know if she *could* get into that room. Alas, the doors were keyed to people's palms, and it didn't budge. Would *any* of the doors open for her? What if she found her library and couldn't get in? Like the security pad in the brig, this one had that little sensor below the palm pad. Maybe she could find the key that activated it.

She reached the end of the corridor and was on the verge of running back to the brig and trying to sedate that guard who'd had a tablet when she spotted a door labeled "recreation." That was probably for drinking and gambling and watching movies, but it might also have the computer she longed to hijack.

She reached for the palm pad next to the door, dreading a rejection, but the entrance opened before she touched the panel. "I guess anyone is allowed to recreate," she mumbled, slipping inside.

The room inside stood empty. Ankari had to weave around pool tables, floor dart lanes, and through an aerial star-fighting game flashing its lights in the air, but she spotted what she sought. A bank of computer stations waited on the far wall, and she jogged over, sitting down at one. A hologram flared to life in the air above the desk and waited for a voice prompt or physical commands. Glad for a familiar operating system, she swiped at the air, bringing up the mail program, and she logged into GalNet. She tapped her fingers on the desk, and a keyboard flared to life. She sent a hasty plea to her hacker friend, Fumio, explaining her situation in as few sentences as possible, then pulled up information on Felgard at the same time as she located a copy of her wanted poster. They were a ways out from the core planets, so the net wasn't very fast, and she drummed her fingers with impatience as she waited for her search requests to be answered. She was all too aware of her limited time. More than once, she second-guessed herself, wondering if she should be doing something better with these minutes of freedom, something that might lead her to an escape. But where could she go? Even if she *could* acquire and fly a shuttle, her options would be limited if they weren't close to a planet.

The information on Felgard came up, and she skimmed through it, trying to commit as much to memory as she could.

Far too soon, the hiss of a door sliding open sounded behind her. Ankari kept reading, kept devouring information, until a hand landed on her shoulder. She held her open hands out and turned, expecting a security guard. But it was the captain. His hair was tousled, and he was wearing a rumpled short-sleeve sleep shirt. She stared down at the corded muscles of his forearm beneath black tattoos of leaves and thorns stretching from his wrists to his elbows, and belatedly realized she should have hunted around and found the syringe before leaving Striker. She could have jabbed him with a dose of sedative, or something more toxic if she could have found it. The bastard deserved it.

Someone shifted in the doorway. Ah, there were the security guards. The syringe probably wouldn't have mattered when there was backup so close.

Ankari lifted her gaze to the captain's eyes, wondering what she would see there. Irritation, most likely. Especially if he had been woken from sleep.

"You seem to have left your date," he said blandly.

For reasons she could only guess at, he seemed more…amused than irritated. It flustered her. Perhaps because he wasn't wearing all of his weapons—or his habitual glower—she had a hard time remembering that this was the man who had destroyed her ship. Or maybe it had something to do with the way that shirt so nicely hugged his form. Who had dreamily pointed out he was handsome? Jamie? It was true, especially without the glower.

Ankari lifted her chin, determined not to acknowledge any attraction—and determined to stop looking at his nicely outlined pectoral muscles. "He had roaming hands. I find that unacceptable on a first date."

The captain snorted. "All right, woman. Back to your cell." He took her elbow and pointed her toward the door. His grip wasn't harsh, but it *was* firm. She would have to be content with the information she had gathered, because she wasn't getting any more tonight.

———

Viktor yawned but kept his eyes focused on the video feedback from the brig. He wasn't going back to bed until he figured out how his prisoner had acquired Dr. Zimonjic's syringe. Viktor had been standing there, watching the women the whole time that medical treatment had been going on. He'd already scoured the footage from the corridor and, even though there weren't recording devices in the ladders, had gotten the gist of what had happened in there from Strider's outcries of rage, which a nearby camera had picked up. What had happened after, out in the corridor, had surprised him. Not the fact that Striker had been bested by a woman—Hazel often took him down on the wrestling mat, because he had a tendency to underestimate the fairer sex—but the fact that this scheming little entrepreneur knew mashatui, a martial art that had developed on the world of Spero. Spero had been destroyed—wiped clean of life and left a radioactive mess—twenty years ago, much as his own Grenavine had been annihilated. Both planets had been used as examples for the rest of the system, a blunt, terrifying, and devastating way to end rebellions that had been centuries in the making. Now everyone knew, those who defied GalCon suffered total eradication.

Questioning his assessment, Viktor had played that short fight in the corridor countless times, watching the flowing style of her kicks and blocks. It was that flow that made the martial art unique and memorable. For centuries before the rebellion, Spero had been ruled by a pair of finance lords who had treated the populace like indentured servants, allowing little to no freedom. Among other things, they hadn't been permitted to carry weapons, nor had they been allowed to study unarmed combat. The oppressed citizens, always planning for a day when they might overthrow their unwanted rulers, had practiced an ancient martial art on the sly, adapting it so it looked more like a dance than a style of combat, turning it into something their rulers wouldn't recognize as a means of attack and defense, even if they were watching the katas being performed. There were precedents, some that dated back to Old Earth, but mashatui was the only living style of this type, as Viktor well knew; every unarmed combat system had been drilled into him during his military training. And even mashatui was barely considered "living." Not when so few of Spero's inhabitants remained.

Markovich couldn't have been more than a few years old when the planet was destroyed. Did this mean her family had left before the devastation? That a father or mother had trained her? Viktor hadn't heard of the art being taught in schools.

He rubbed his eyes and yawned again, not sure why he was expending so much mental effort on musing about her. She knew mashatui, and she might have been born on Spero. So, what? It didn't change anything. She was still a criminal and still had to be delivered to Felgard, especially since Viktor had told Felgard he had her. If he hadn't sent word so early, he might have...

"Might have what?" he grumbled to himself. Let her go? Why? Because she might be from a world that had been destroyed? Because he was from a world that had been destroyed? It wasn't as if they were even the same worlds. "Nothing in common; nothing that matters."

He waved at the holographic display above the desk to restart it. He hadn't been paying attention, and Zimonjic was already walking out of the cell. This time, he watched more carefully, but it wasn't until the third iteration that he spotted Markovich's quick move, her lower hand subtly delving into the doctor's pocket. On the video, he couldn't even see what she had pulled out or where she had hidden it, but he had seen enough. She had deft fingers.

A thief, a martial artist, and an entrepreneur. And a criminal. "Busy girl."

A chime sounded. His sleepy mind thought it was the door—he was expecting Striker, as soon as a nurse cleared him as fit for duty and he couldn't hide out in sickbay any longer—but he realized it was just his comm. "What?"

"It's Thomlin, sir. I got into Markovich's account and have the message you asked for."

"Good. Send it to me." Viktor felt a little sheepish at prying into her personal mail, but he had to know whom she had contacted and why. For all he knew, she might be arranging some ambush for the *Albatross*, so she and her friends could slip away. *He* would certainly be trying something of that ilk.

"Yes, sir." Thomlin, his chief intel officer, didn't sound that excited about the message, so it probably didn't promise a nefarious threat to the ship.

Viktor read it right away, anyway. Whether he wanted to admit it or not, this woman had piqued his curiosity. When he finished, he wondered if he should have read it after all. It could have been part of her on-going act—she must have suspected that someone on the ship would be talented enough to hack into her account and read her outgoing messages—but her plea for her friend to figure out why there was a bounty on her head made him shift his weight uncomfortably. He had already seen the research she had been doing in the rec room, first reading over her wanted poster, and then finding everything she could on Felgard. He was getting the unpleasant feeling that maybe, just maybe, she had been telling the truth, that the poster was a mistake or a fraud and that she wasn't a criminal.

"Just because she isn't aware of her crime doesn't mean she hasn't committed one," he told himself sturdily. Because to believe otherwise would mean he had captured her and destroyed her ship for no good reason at all.

The door chimed. This time it was Striker.

"Get in here," Viktor said.

Striker slouched inside, halting half a step inside the threshold, clearly not wanting to come farther. "Sir?" he asked warily.

"You disobeyed my orders," Viktor said softly, in what the crew recognized as his dangerous voice. Sometimes, at times like this, it was an affectation, but there were other times when he barely knew he was using it. That was when he was truly irritated. This was a mild inconvenience, an example needing to be set.

"I know, sir. I thought...I mean, I didn't think—"

"No. No, you didn't."

Striker hung his head.

"You'll take an extra shift for the next two weeks, during which you'll run a diagnostic on every piece of battle armor for every crew member. I want each suit cleaned and polished, as well. You'll be up at five a.m. every day, too, to teach the morning unarmed combat class. It seems you need a brush-up."

Striker winced. "I was drugged, sir. I couldn't move as fast as usual."

The captain wasn't all that sure that would have mattered, but he wouldn't argue and humiliate the man further than he already was. "Yes, sir, is the expected response, nothing more," he said, his tone cold and clipped.

"Yes, sir."

All in all, it wasn't much of a punishment, so Striker shouldn't have reason for resentment. It was more of a warning. Viktor preferred not to dock men their pay or reduce their rank, since things like that *were* cause for resentment, but he couldn't have prisoners roaming free about the ship.

"One more thing before you start your extra duties," Viktor said.

"Yes?" A wary glance.

"Find the women's gear, check it for anything that might be used to facilitate an escape or overpower someone—" Viktor raised his brows with significance, "—and remove it. But give them the rest of their stuff. Their fecal samples and equipment for examining them, or whatever they have in there."

"All right...but why, sir?"

Why, indeed? "Because I said so."

"Yes, sir."

CHAPTER FOUR

The morning brought two gifts: the team's bags of equipment and three egg logs, the latter being the mercenary equivalent of breakfast. Nobody had offered them dinner the night before, so Ankari was hungry enough to rip open the wrapper of her "log" without scrutinizing the ingredients list. Some things were probably better left a mystery, anyway.

"I don't understand this," Lauren said, standing over her open pack, "but I'm tickled to see my collapsible BioEye 973." She pulled out a compact field unit that was a combination microscope and sensor unit. "My field generator is even in here."

Ankari opened her own pack and immediately noticed that the rope and rappelling kit had been removed, along with a multi-purpose knife and a laser cutting tool. All of the samples she had gathered were there. "Guess they assumed we couldn't use fossilized remains to formulate an escape."

"I'll take those," Lauren said brightly, holding out her hand. She had already settled cross-legged on the floor and didn't seem daunted by the notion of setting up a field lab in a tiny room with no tables, sinks, or power outlets.

"It takes so little to make you happy." Ankari laid the samples out beside her. "You were a good investment."

Lauren smiled. "Of course I was."

"Let me know if I can help with anything."

Lauren didn't respond. She had already bored into one of the samples and scraped out fine particles to make her first slide, and she was busy with the microscope. The humming sensors doubtlessly told her more than eyes alone could.

Ankari settled on the floor against the bench, sitting next to Jamie, who was inspecting the wrapper before opening her egg log.

"Eat it," Ankari suggested. "You're already on the lanky side. You shouldn't be missing meals. Not if you want to keep attracting the eye of sexy mercenaries."

"Uh. Which one was the sexy one, because I know you're not talking about that thug from last night?"

"You liked the captain, didn't you? Though he is a little old for you."

Jamie snorted. "*I'm* not the one he watches when he comes down here."

"No, because you're not the one who talks a lot and pickpockets his people." Ankari bit into her breakfast and eyed the corner of the desk at the end of the corridor. The day guard didn't throw his boots on it—maybe he considered himself more professional than the movie-watching night-shift man—but he was up there. He'd brought them the gear and food, then disappeared into the alcove. What could she try next to escape? At the least, she wanted a chance to read whatever message Fumio might have sent back. But preferably, she'd find a way for them to get off the ship altogether.

"No doubt, that's why you left with the thug last night and came back with *him*. You must have done something he appreciated." Jamie waved to the packs.

"I don't know what, since I was knocking out his men and breaking into his computer system." Ankari supposed logging onto the rec room computer wasn't technically "breaking into" anything. And she'd only knocked out the one man...But her words earned her an admiring smile from Jamie.

"You're so brave. I would have been terrified of going off with that Striker. I *was* terrified."

"An understandable reaction. He was dangerous. I'm just too busy scheming to realize I'm in danger sometimes."

"Are you scheming now?" Jamie asked.

"I'm—"

The guard chose that moment to walk back to their cell. He didn't say anything, but he watched Lauren for a moment. He was probably making sure they couldn't blow anything up with the gear they had.

"Morgen," a voice said over his comm.

He tapped the patch. "Here."

"Striker assigned you to his team for the scouting mission. When you get off shift, report to the staging room. You'll be going down tonight."

"Good. Thanks."

"Going down where?" Ankari asked casually. Just out of curiosity, of course, not because she wanted to know if they were approaching a planet or station where three women might find a way to disappear if they were crafty enough to escape their captors...

"Nowhere that has anything to do with you," the guard said and walked back to his station.

"Wanna bet?" Ankari muttered.

"You *are* scheming," Jamie whispered.

"Always. Listen...do you think you could fly one of these mercenary shuttles if we managed to get aboard one?"

Jamie's face crinkled dubiously. "Maybe eventually, but probably not right away. I'd have to familiarize myself with everything first and find the technical manuals."

Something that she wouldn't have time to do if they knocked out guards and blew their way into the shuttle bay. Not that Ankari could imagine a scenario in which that happened anyway.

"I'm sorry." Jamie poked at her knee. "If you had a real pilot, she would have gone through military or civilian flight school and would be familiar with a lot of the models out there."

A *real* pilot would have commanded a hefty salary and a big share of the company too. Jamie had been so eager to escape her home world that she probably would have worked for free. As it was, the five percent share she had accepted had thus far amounted to nothing, and she *was* working for free. Though she didn't seem to mind, Ankari vowed to see her vision completed and her company worth something before the year was out. She eyed the confines of the brig. They just had to get past one small obstacle first...

"You're doing fine," Ankari said. "And maybe I can get you a technical manual that you could study beforehand."

"Beforehand? What's happening...after hand?"

"We're going wherever he's going," Ankari murmured, nodding toward the guard desk. She had no idea what this new mercenary mission might entail, but if there was going to be a preliminary scouting mission, there should be a full-fledged assault at some point after that. If most of the crew went along on that, that could be the perfect time to escape.

"Tonight?"

"Tonight or more likely tomorrow. We'll get off the ship, disappear on the world or station or whatever we're approaching, and leave our mercenary friends forever. And find somewhere safe to hide until we can get this bounty problem solved." Ankari scooted up to Lauren, tapping her on the shoulder. "You know that generator you mentioned? Didn't you once say that it could make electromagnetic pulses?"

"That's one of the energy forms it can generate, yes."

"And you said they left it in there?"

"Yes." Lauren tapped the pack—hers had always been the heaviest. "They took my nail file, but not an energy generator."

"Because it looks like scientific equipment, not a weapon."

"It *is* scientific equipment."

"I know, but is there any chance it could disrupt the force field?"

"Uhhh." Lauren gave the invisible shield a skeptical look. "Maybe with Jamie's help, I could try to come up with…something. But I couldn't make any promises."

"Do your best." Even if the generator could free them from the brig, Ankari would still have to figure out a way to get into the shuttle bay, not to mention finding a manual for Jamie. Still, if the ship would soon be light on crew members, that would be the time to try an escape.

"This is another instance when a technical manual would be useful," Jamie said, waving toward the force field. "One of *this* ship, this time."

"The manuals for the ship and the shuttles are probably on the tablets the crew all have. I'll see if I can get you one." Ankari stood up, hoping the guard would respond if she called him back here.

"How are you going to do that?" Jamie asked.

"Chat with the captain." Ankari wriggled her fingers to imply she might do a little more than *chat*.

"Without the force field being involved?"

Yes, picking pockets through that would be challenging.

"Well, I'd like to thank him for his generosity." Ankari waved at the packs. "Maybe he'd let me do that over lunch or dinner."

Jamie's face grew skeptical. "If you can make that happen, I'll be impressed. I'll be even more impressed if you can get something better than an egg log out of him." She lifted her unopened breakfast package.

"I will."

"Better stop glaring so hard at him then," Lauren added without looking up from her work. "I'm pretty sure he knows you want to fry his balls off for blowing up your ship."

"Er, was I that obvious about that?" She had been trying hard to be civil the day before...

"I don't know. Maybe only to people who know you."

"We'll see."

———

Viktor was changing into his exercise togs when his comm chimed. Just when he thought he was off duty for the day...

He didn't recognize the face that popped into the air above his desk, along with the request to speak. The unshaven man had a nose as pointy as a spearhead, wore a bandana over greasy dark hair, and his eyebrows had been pierced twenty or thirty times, each little ring sporting a small colorful gem. Wryly, Viktor wondered if any of them were made from aliuolite. The man's scruffiness—and jewelry choices—meant he wasn't fleet, but didn't proclaim much else. Viktor called up the communications and intelligence station before answering.

"Yes, sir?" Lieutenant Thomlin asked.

"Someone's calling my private line. Any idea who?"

"No, sir, but I can find out."

Viktor could find that out for himself in about two seconds, but he said, "Do that and trace where he's calling from too."

"Yes, sir."

Viktor answered the request—the caller had waited rather than leaving a message. "Captain Mandrake here."

"This is Captain Goshawk."

The name was vaguely familiar. A bounty hunter? That sounded right.

"I reckon you're a busy feller, so I won't take much of your time, Mandrake. You've got some prisoners that Lord Felgard wants right now. Actually he wanted them last week."

Viktor folded his arms over his chest. He hadn't told anyone outside of the ship about the prisoners except for Lord Felgard himself. It was possible he had a spy on board—it wouldn't be the first time—but it seemed even more possible that Felgard had put the word out in an attempt to hasten Viktor along his course.

"So?" Viktor said.

"You're a man of many words, aren't ya, Mandrake? The *so* is that I'm willing to offer you eighty percent of what's on their heads, take them off your hands right now, and deliver them straightaway to Felgard while you finish your business on Sturm. You'll get paid right away, and I'll take over the risk in delivering them, for a fair percentage of the bounty of course."

Interesting. Had Felgard suggested this to Goshawk personally? Or had he merely made Mandrake Company's cargo and coordinates known to those who might be able to get him his prisoners more quickly? Either way, it pissed Viktor off.

"Risk in delivering them?" Viktor asked. "They're three academic women. They're not much of a risk." No need to mention that one of them had already escaped a couple of times.

"Even if they're not a threat, there are always external risks, Mandrake. You know this. Space is dangerous. You never know what obstacles might fall out of the stars and into your path." A smile spread across Goshawk's face. It was as greasy as his hair.

Viktor knew a threat when he got one.

Lieutenant Thomlin's face popped up in the air beside Goshawk's, and he made a keep-him-talking hand motion. He must be close to pinpointing the location of the bounty hunter's ship. Good.

"Do you even *have* eighty percent, Goshawk?" Viktor asked. "That's a lot of money, and you look like you can't even afford razor blades." Or soap.

"Not everyone likes that military look, Mandrake. I'm surprised you, of all people, keep it up."

"What does that mean?" Viktor asked, though he already knew. Anger welled in his chest in anticipation of an insult.

"It means I know you're a deserter, Mandrake. Everyone does. And nobody would miss you if you were to disappear. I also know your people are trying to trace me, but you know what? I don't care to have you showing up on my doorstep uninvited. Think about my offer. I'll be in touch again."

His face winked out, leaving only Thomlin staring back at Viktor. Actually Thomlin was frowning down at his control panel. "He's got a scrambler, sir. A good one."

Viktor grunted, never enthused with excuses.

Thomlin rushed to add, "I can tell he was calling from a ship, though, and that it's in orbit around Sturm, not on the planet or any of the other moons."

That was more information than Viktor had expected. Did Thomlin think he'd wanted to know the pub Goshawk would be drinking at that night? When he'd been in the fleet, his unit had possessed equipment that would have allowed that sort of precision, but Mandrake Company couldn't afford anything that sophisticated, so Viktor kept his expectations realistic.

"So he's waiting for us," Viktor said.

"Maybe so, sir," Thomlin said.

Goshawk might have been in the area for other business when Felgard had contacted him, but for the promise of a hundred thousand aurums, he would have made this his only business. For twenty thousand, he might not have, but Goshawk probably hadn't been sincere when he'd made that offer.

"Get me everything you can on Captain Goshawk, and pass the word to keep an eye out for him, but we'll continue with our mission on Sturm." Viktor stopped himself from saying "as planned," because he decided, in the middle of that sentence, to change one thing.

"Yes, sir."

As soon as Thomlin's face disappeared, Viktor called up his second-in-command, who was on shift at the moment.

"Yes, sir?" Commander Garland asked from the bridge, his short gray hair and leathery face coming into view.

"Our shuttles are scheduled to dock at Morgan's Rest tonight. Cancel that. We're going to go down unannounced. Pick a spot in the jungle, somewhere close to Sisson's camp. Don't tell anyone except the pilots."

Garland's brows rose. He clearly wanted an explanation—Viktor would apprise him later—but all he said was, "Yes, sir."

In case there *was* a spy, Viktor wouldn't make these updates widely known. He would also make sure they left some good men behind on the ship, in case Goshawk decided to come knocking on the door while most of the crew was gone. The *Albatross* had weapons and shielding enough to defend itself, even with a minimal crew, but bounty hunters tended to be crafty. The ones who survived in the business, anyway.

Another chime came in as soon as Garland disappeared from view, and Viktor grumbled to himself. He was supposed to join some of his men for a workout, and the need to pummel people was building in him like water set to boil.

"Sir? It's Cutty from the brig. One of the prisoners has been bugging me all day, saying she needs to talk to you. I didn't want to bother you when you were on shift, but she harassed me until I promised I'd at least ask you. Says she wants to thank you."

To thank him? For the return of their equipment? That was all Viktor could think of, and he promptly assumed it was part of some ruse. She probably wanted to steal his tablet so she could check to see if that acquaintance of hers had replied. Viktor found himself curious about what that acquaintance might have come up with too. And he wouldn't mind talking to her, to get answers to some of the questions he had, of course.

"Sir?" Cutty asked. "Should I tell her you're busy?"

"Is it Ank—Markovich?" Viktor wasn't sure why his brain wanted to insert her first name. It wasn't as if she had invited him to use it. He was probably the last person she would invite to use it.

"Uh. I don't know. It's the one with brown hair, dimples, and a mouth you wish she'd use for something other than talking."

Viktor snorted. So, he wasn't the only one who had noticed Markovich's attributes, the ones the jumpsuit didn't hide anyway.

"All right." Viktor checked the time again. He needed his exercise session, and people were waiting for him, but after that, he was off duty and free of expectations until they reached Sturm. "Take her to the mess hall in an hour. I'll meet her there."

"You *will*?"

Viktor didn't know how to respond to the shocked tone, but felt he had to say something, lest rumors get started about how the captain was rolling one of the prisoners. He supposed it didn't really matter, but some might question his professionalism. He had flaws enough for an entire army, but he wasn't one to take advantage of his position when it came to personal desires. He had already seen Markovich more often than he had seen any other criminal they'd turned over to the law—or the highest bidder—and the crew might be wondering about it.

"I have questions for her," Viktor finally said.

"Oh, about the business? Striker said we might be able to make some piles if we got in on that. Too bad she's going to Felgard, eh? Or *is* she still going to Felgard?"

Striker had a big mouth. And a poor understanding of what pre-revenue meant. But if he had started rumors about that instead of about the captain asking a prisoner to dinner, then that suited Viktor well enough, at least for the moment.

"She's going to Felgard," Viktor said, "but her research may have some interesting applications that might serve *us*. It's worth learning more about." In truth, he was skeptical about her business, but he doubted anyone would question his desire to improve the health and stamina of his crew, if something like that was truly possible.

Cutty chuckled. "So she goes and her research stays, and we either use it or sell it to someone else? Crafty, sir."

Crafty, right. That was him. "Mess hall in an hour, Cutty."

"Yes, sir. She'll be there."

CHAPTER FIVE

The captain wasn't in the mess hall. A handful of crew members were sitting in pairs, eating from plates of food that looked somewhat more promising than breakfast logs, but not much more. If anyone who served in the capacity of chef or cook worked on the ship, it wasn't apparent.

Ankari quickly moved on from inspecting the food to inspecting the people. She spotted a bulge in a mechanic's pocket that might have been a tablet. Maybe she could accomplish this part of her mission before she met with the captain. Pickpocketing a random mechanic ought to be easier than pickpocketing him.

Unfortunately, her guard, the all-too-alert Corporal Cutty whom she had been wrangling with all day, had her handcuffed. Her wrists were in front of her instead of behind, so she might still be able to pick a pocket, but it wouldn't be easy. The flexible material that comprised the cuffs might be pliant enough to conform to a prisoner's wrists, but it was still stronger than steel.

"The captain is coming here?" Ankari asked, even though Cutty had already explained that to her.

"To question you, yes."

Not for coffee, eh? "So, I should sit and wait?" Ankari lifted her hands toward a table on the other side of the one where the mechanic and another man in coveralls were dining.

Cutty shrugged. "Can if you want."

All day, he had vacillated between being laconic and being exasperated with her, sometimes both. It had made her long for the witless lust-infused conversational style of Striker.

Ankari strolled toward the table she had indicated, pausing at the side of the mechanic. She bent to peer at the men's plates—and to place her hands close to his cargo pocket. She would be disappointed if that bulge was nothing more than some rolled-up gloves stuffed in there. But it had more of a rectangular form. She kept her back to Cutty, hoping to hide the movements of her hands.

"What are you two eating?" Ankari asked when the men gave her inquiring frowns. "It smells—" good wasn't quite the right word, "—better than the wrapped bars they've been giving us." A truth, though that might simply be because this food had been heated up. The plates had the lumpy, even portions of a meal that had come out of a box or a bag.

"This is supposed to be a quiche," the mechanic said, "and that's a dogeater."

As he pointed at his comrade's plate, Ankari checked his pocket. Buttoned, naturally. She tilted her chin toward the second plate as she worked to thwart those buttons without touching the man's leg and alerting him. "A *dogeater*? I haven't heard of that, er, dish. What is it?"

"Your guess is as good as mine," the man eating it said. "A meat patty of some kind. It might have been something big enough to eat a dog. It might have been a dog once."

Ankari finished with the buttons and slipped her hand into the mechanic's pocket. Yes, those were the hard corners of a tablet. She leaned closer, touching her chest to his shoulder. She would have made a poor professional thief, because she always felt sleazy using her body for misdirection, but in her experience, men were less likely to notice their pockets being picked if there was a boob pressed against some part of their anatomy. "Wouldn't the people who supply all of your fine and hearty fare have called it a dog log, if that were the case?"

"Uh," the mechanic said, glancing at her chest—and not, fortunately, his pocket—"I think a dog log is something else."

"Who *are* you?" the second man asked and glanced past her to Cutty. Uh oh, if the direction of his glance was correct, Cutty wasn't in the position she had left him in.

Ankari smiled and slid the tablet toward her own pocket as she straightened. "I'm—"

"A prisoner," Cutty said from behind her ear.

His hand clasped about her triceps, and Ankari almost dropped her prize. She fumbled it, caught it, and stuffed it in her pocket, all the while keeping her face bland and friendly and giving no indication that her heartbeat had just tripled.

"One who's waiting to see the captain," Cutty said.

"Should she be roaming around the mess hall while she waits, Corporal?" the mechanic said, an edge in his tone, along with that subtle snottiness that implied that he outranked a corporal.

"Probably not," the second diner said, scooting his chair back. "Here, let her sit in my lap until the captain comes. She's cute."

Cutty sighed, turning Ankari around. "Why do I have a feeling you get in trouble everywhere you go?"

Ankari did her best to hide the new bulge in her own pocket. "That's not...strictly true."

"Come on." Cutty pushed her toward the door. "I'll take you to wherever the captain is. I'm *supposed* to be off shift now."

Ankari looked for an unsuspicious way to tell the man she would be happy going back to her cell. The longer she wandered around with a tablet in her pocket, the more likely someone would notice it. Or the mechanic would notice it missing and realize what had happened during the dogeater discussion. But, after trying all day to arrange a meeting, Cutty would know she was up to something if she suddenly lost interest in it. He was already talking to someone over his comm and getting information on the captain's whereabouts.

"He's in the cargo bay. This way."

Hm, what of interest had happened in the cargo bay to make him forget a date with his favorite prisoner? Ankari trailed her guard down to the bottom deck, the ladders awkward to navigate with the handcuffs, not that

Cutty cared. He huffed and grumbled as he waited for her, then led her to one of the doors she had passed by the day before.

The grunts and smacks coming from the chamber inside surprised her. A hoot and some jeers followed. It sounded more like a boxing arena than a cargo bay.

Cutty led her out onto a grate platform with stairs leading up to a catwalk and down to a floor covered with friction matting. A woman was already on the platform, leaning against the railing and looking down. The noises were coming from the floor. A couple of crew members were using weight-lifting equipment set up in one corner, but a dozen others were gathered around a knot of barefoot men alternating between throwing punches and trying to ensnare each other's limbs for take-downs. Two were topless and two others wore short-sleeve black T-shirts. At first, Ankari thought the wardrobe choices might represent who was on whose team, but it soon grew apparent that three of the men were ganging up on one. Granted that *one* could take care of himself; his hands and feet were a blur of motion as he avoided being trapped between the others and dealt damage of his own at the same time. Even if most of Ankari's own training had been with her father and her siblings, and she'd only had to defend herself on the streets a few times, she recognized a skilled practitioner when she saw one. *All* of the men were fast and agile, but the solo figure did an amazing job of anticipating attacks and responding, almost before they were launched.

"He can't keep that up forever." Cutty sighed and leaned against the wall beside the door.

Only then did Ankari realize they were watching the captain. From up here, the gray sprinkled in his dark hair wasn't noticeable, nor was there any sign of what had to be forty years in his movements as he fought off all those attackers. More than that, he was getting in numerous good blows of his own. One man tried to jump him from behind, only to take an elbow in the solar plexus with enough force to go flying backward. He rolled to his feet quickly, so he wouldn't be vulnerable to further attack, but it was clear from the way he grasped his chest that he'd had the wind knocked out of him.

"I'm sure he'll have time to interrogate you soon," Cutty added.

Interrogate? Disgruntlement replaced her admiration for the captain's speed and strength. Was an interrogation what Mandrake had planned for her? Not the acceptance of an apology? Even if she had lobbied for this meeting all day with the sole intent of stealing his tablet, she found herself disappointed that he'd had military matters in mind when he had agreed to see her. The emotion confused her—what else could she have expected? She ought to be more worried about what this interrogation might involve. Last night, he had seemed amused by her escape, almost amiable in his rumpled nightclothes, but maybe that had been an act. Maybe he had secretly been furious that she had fooled his people, and he now intended to extract every iota of information from her in whatever manner possible.

The woman at the railing turned at the sound of voices behind her. It was Dr. Zimonjic. Her expression grew wry when she saw them. She must have been informed about the syringe. Maybe she'd been disciplined for her carelessness. Ankari didn't know whether she should approach or not.

Zimonjic touched the front of her black-and-silver wrap. "No pockets."

No, Ankari had already noticed that. The doctor wasn't carrying any of her equipment, so she must not have been called down to attend to an injury. Although, with the way the men were going at each other, it was surprising nobody had cried out for first aid. Or grunted out. She supposed such fierce fighters wouldn't cry, scream, or whine about injuries.

Ankari lifted her wrists, drawing attention to her handcuffs, and approached the railing. With the tablet stuffed in her pocket, standing with things in front of her body was a good idea. "I had to try whatever I could to escape," she said apologetically.

"Is that what you're doing right now? Escaping?" Zimonjic raised her eyebrows at the handcuffs.

"Apparently, I'm being interrogated now. Or I will be soon." Ankari looked toward the captain. He only had two opponents now. The other one was sitting on the matting beside the rest of the onlookers, nursing fresh bruises.

The doctor followed her gaze and smiled. There was that wistful look on her face again. "He looks like a brute, I know, but he'd have Striker or Liang question you if violence was going to be involved. They like that sort of work. Viktor doesn't."

"Viktor? That's his first name?"

"One of them." Zimonjic's smile changed again, from wistful to mischievous. "You'd have to ask him to tell you the other."

At that moment, "Viktor" smashed one of those men in the chest with a kick that launched him into the spectators, who jeered and whooped.

"He doesn't like violence, you say?" Ankari asked.

Zimonjic chuckled. "Oh, he'll knock you into the next galaxy if you pick a fight with him, but standing in front of a defenseless prisoner and inflicting pain on him—or her—he doesn't care for. From what I've gathered, he used to do that, and all manner of other unpleasant things, in the fleet. One of the reasons he left…Well, I don't really know. He's never told me these things, and I romanticize him, I suppose. But I've seen his military record, what unit he was in, the training he received." Her humor disappeared, and she shook her head. "I doubt he knew what he was signing up for when he was a kid—he was probably drawn by the fact that Crimson Ops soldiers get trained to parachute out of shuttles, hijack ships, and travel all over the system. That's what the recruiting posters say, anyway, but…" She shrugged. "You're aware of the reputation of the units, I'm sure."

A cold hand seemed to wrap itself around Ankari's heart. GalCon's Crimson Ops were trained to be the most versatile—and deadly—warriors in the galaxy. They were feared as much as they were admired. The press made sure their deeds were known and that their reputations for delivering death never faded from the populace's mind. If something awful happened in the system, whispers of Crimson Ops were always made. Some people said it was just propaganda and fear-mongering by the corporations, and there had to be some of that, but Ankari had always believed…There had been those who said the Crimson Ops laid the explosives that had destroyed her home world. Her family had moved right before that happened, and she hadn't been there in the end, but she had been old enough to remember the images on the news: cities being blown up, people dying horribly…

"I'm sorry," Zimonjic said, watching Ankari's face. "I meant to ease your concerns, not make them worse."

Ankari didn't know what expression had been on her face, but she tried for a nonchalant visage. It was a struggle, though. Her body had broken out in a cold sweat. She remembered the calm way the captain had ordered her ship destroyed. Could such a man have calmly ordered a planet destroyed twenty years ago? No…He wasn't old enough for that. Even if he had been there, he would have been someone following orders, not giving them. That thought didn't reassure her as much as she would have liked, and the smile she tried on the doctor had to be anemic.

"He won't hurt you," Zimonjic added.

Ankari glanced at her guard, wondering what he thought about the doctor sharing all this information on the captain, but he was listening, his expression intent, as if he was hearing it all for the first time. Maybe he was.

"I'm taking heart in the fact that I'm wanted alive by this Felgard," Ankari said. "I figure I don't *really* have to worry until I'm tied up like a parcel and deposited on his doorstep."

"Probably true. I wonder what Viktor wants to talk to you about." The doctor went back to watching him, or perhaps admiring the way his sweaty shirt stuck to his back. She had the look of a woman memorizing the body of the man who was going to star in her dreams that night, something she probably couldn't do that easily most of the time, at least not without the captain noticing. He was down to one opponent now, and their attacks were less frenzied. It had wound down to more of a coaching session than an all-out battle.

"Are you two…?" Ankari prompted, even if she was fairly certain of her guess. There was no reason for her to ask—this information surely couldn't be useful in her escape planning—other than curiosity. Earlier, she had been toying with the idea of expressing her gratitude toward the captain in the way of a kiss, thus to get close and pick his pocket, but with a tablet already in her possession, there was no need for her to lower herself to such chicanery. It had been bad enough, rubbing up against the mechanic. Three days ago, she would have told anyone that she had long since found enough success that she'd never have to pick another pocket again. What a debacle this week had become.

"No," Zimonjic said, lowering her voice so the corporal wouldn't hear. "In the three years I've been here, I've never known him to be in a relationship with anyone. He seeks out companionship when he's on leave, the same as the other men, but if he ever keeps in touch with any of those brief lovers, I've not heard about it."

"Sounds lonely."

"I think he prefers it that way." Zimonjic hitched a shoulder. "I asked him once if he wanted to be more than colleagues. I don't know if it was just an excuse, but he said I reminded him of some counselor he had to go to when he was in the fleet."

"Counselor?"

"Well, he called her a mind-fucker, but the GalCon term is counselor. These are the people who do whatever they have to do to make sure their soldiers are the perfect killers without a thought toward questioning orders."

"Oh."

"I will give you one warning," Zimonjic said, her voice returning to a normal tone, "because you seem the type of woman who could inadvertently—or perhaps *advertently*—irk a man."

That prompted a noisy snort from Cutty.

Zimonjic's smile was a little too knowing. She waved at the captain. "He's pretty good at controlling it these days, much better than when I first crossed his path years ago, but there's a lot of rage in there. I've seen him kill a man in anger, one of his own crew. The man had betrayed the ship and deserved some kind of punishment, but…" She spread her hand. "It's why people tiptoe around him."

Yet more information that Ankari didn't find comforting. Had Zimonjic truly meant to assuage Ankari's concerns about the "interrogation"? Or had this all been designed as some mind-game, some revenge for stealing her equipment and using it to knock out Striker? Because Ankari *hadn't* been worried about dinner with the captain *before* this chat. Now, there were Mercrusean tangleworms wrestling in her stomach. The tablet felt like an anchor in her pocket. If the captain found it on her, would he be amused? Or would some of this rage appear?

"They're done," Zimonjic said. "I'd better go. Good luck."

She *sounded* sincere, friendly even, but Ankari's voice was raspy with concern when she uttered a quick, "Bye."

"Cutty," came a cool call from below. "This isn't the mess hall."

"No, sir." The guard rushed forward, hands clasping at the rail. The stern, exasperated authority he had been exuding all day had evaporated. Maybe listening to Zimonjic had put wrestling worms in his stomach too.

"You didn't show up, and she was getting into trouble. And I'm supposed to be..." He must have decided he didn't want to whine that his shift had ended over an hour ago, because he switched to, "I just wasn't sure if you'd forgotten and wanted me to put her back."

When the captain's gaze landed on her, Ankari kept herself from quailing, though she feared he would immediately see through the railing to the bump in her pocket. She raised her chin. "I was *not* getting into trouble. I was merely walking to a table and stopped to ask a man what a dogeater was."

The captain's eyebrows didn't so much as twitch, but her comment drew a few snickers from the onlookers. A couple of men had grabbed towels and were heading for the door, but one stopped to ask. "Did you get an answer? Because I've been wondering that for years."

"Apparently it's a mystery, even to the mechanics."

"There's a lot that's a mystery to the mechanics," someone else snickered.

"Oh, please, Frog. Don't act like you're a brain because you know how to fly a ship. Nine out of ten people here beat you at space rocks."

"That's a game of chance."

"Only for you, my friend."

"The mess hall, Corporal," the captain said. "I'll be there in ten." Throughout his men's banter, his eyes had never left Ankari's, and she was doing her best not to look guilty, but she continued to feel that he already knew she was up to something. She was relieved when Cutty led her out of the cargo bay but knew the feeling would be short-lived unless she could figure out somewhere to hide the tablet on the way back to the mess hall. But if she did that, how could she be sure to find it again?

———

The lush green landscape of Sturm was visible through the portholes by the time Viktor walked into the mess hall. It had taken him twenty minutes instead of ten, because he had first showered, changed, and checked to make sure the scouting team had made it to the moon without trouble. When he saw Ankari—Markovich—sitting at a table near the view, he almost apologized to her, but her hands were folded in front of her, the flex-cuffs clearly in view, and he kept the words to himself. By now, the hour had grown late, but there was still a table occupied by a group of fighters from Delta Squadron, and they had grown silent when he walked in. They must be insufferably curious about this meeting between captain and prisoner.

Viktor had initially planned to meet with Markovich in plain sight of everyone, to keep rumors from spreading and any resentment from starting up in the ranks—we haven't had leave for months, but the captain gets to shag prisoners? What the hell? But when he saw the nervous way Markovich watched him enter, he found himself wanting to set her mind at ease, not turn her into a spectacle. He had seen Zimonjic up there talking to her and wondered what the doctor had said. She was a talented medical officer, but she'd come from GalCon, too, and knew more of his secrets than he was comfortable with. While he couldn't imagine why she would share any of those secrets with a random prisoner, he had caught her pointing to him a couple of times while she had been talking, and he wondered.

Corporal Cutty was standing at parade rest behind Markovich, clearly ready to go, but clearly doing his best to appear a model soldier until he was dismissed. He was trying harder than usual. What *had* Zimonjic been talking about?

Viktor grabbed a couple of plates of food, avoiding the "dogeaters" in favor of meatloaf and a mashed side dish that could have been potatoes, parsnips, or a pale squash. The smell didn't give any clues. "Give me the key, and hit your rack, Cutty."

"Yes, sir." The corporal should have been off duty a couple of hours ago, but he would survive a late night here and there. He gave a quick salute, tossed Viktor the electronic key that opened the cuffs, and trotted out of the mess hall.

Plates in hand, Viktor tilted his head toward a door at the back of the room. "Officers' mess," he said and headed that way. Markovich hesitated, maybe not quite catching his invitation, but pushed back her chair and followed when he walked past her. A few soft groans of disappointment came from the Delta table as the entertainment disappeared. Too bad.

"Sit." Viktor set the plates down at the single oval table inside, then jerked a thumb toward the outer room. "I'm getting a drink. Want something?"

"Whatever you're having is fine." Markovich sat at one of the seats with a plate.

"Probably not." Viktor waved the key over the cuffs, and they popped open. He tossed them to the center of the table.

"Pardon?"

"It's green." At her blank stare, he added, "My drink. We've got whiskey if you want some. It's not good, but it has a high alcohol content."

"Your drink is green?"

"Green as grass. It's vegetables mostly, some fruit, some seeds. Mashed up in a glass." He stuck the electronic key in his pocket, noticing that Markovich tracked the motion with her eyes. He would have to make sure it was still in his pocket at the end of the night, since it could open a lot of doors on the ship as well as all of the flex-cuffs.

"Is that the secret to your speed on the wrestling mat?" Markovich asked.

It was silly, but he found himself pleased that she had noticed. "My last doctor would have said so. Mostly, I've only found it the secret to keeping regular."

She blinked a few times. Viktor kept himself from wincing. Barely. It had been years since he tried to woo a woman, and he'd been horrible at it even then. Not that he was trying to woo this one, but he vaguely remembered that there were some topics that were perfectly appropriate to talk about with one's soldiers and that were completely inappropriate to discuss with women. Women who weren't soldiers anyway. Sergeant Hazel never seemed to care.

"Well," Markovich said when she recovered from her surprise. "Then I'll have one of those."

Viktor arched his brows. He had offered the concoction to people before, but never had a taker. He wasn't even sure why he still drank them. Doc Aglianico, the one who had insisted soldiers consume greens now and then, was long gone, dead in the line of duty, like so many others before him. Maybe that was why Viktor still drank them. Aglianico had been Grenavinian, one of the original crew and one of his few confidants.

"My routine has been disrupted of late, and those meal logs you give to prisoners…" Markovich shuddered. "Something with a vegetable in it sounds lovely."

"Everybody gets the logs when they're on assignment. There actually might be some pulverized vegetables in them somewhere. But no promises."

Viktor's step was light as he returned to the kitchen area. The Deltas had cleared out, and for whatever reason, Markovich wasn't glaring daggers at him tonight. He didn't believe for a second that she had forgotten her anger over her ship, but maybe having the prisoners' gear sent to the cell had quenched some of that rage.

When he set the tall glass of green juice in front of her, she took a sip without hesitation. While she didn't smack her lips in delight, she gave it a considering head tilt, then a nod of approval, as if she were judging some much-lauded vintage of wine.

He drank half of his glass before setting it down. That was probably one of those things that wasn't proper in front of a lady, either, but he was thirsty after the gym workout. He would switch to water shortly. He had to be hydrated and ready if the scouts found the camp quickly and called for the rest of the fighters.

He took a bite of the meatloaf, noticed Markovich hadn't started eating, and asked, "What did you want to see me about?"

She looked up at him. "Oh, I forgot. This is to be an interrogation." A flash of nervousness crossed her face.

Viktor tried to figure out what he had said to bring that on. "What do you mean?"

"Well, you're standing. I thought dinner…I mean, I don't know. I wasn't expecting a casual chat, but I guess I'd thought…" She bit her lip. It was an alluring gesture, though he didn't think she meant it to be. No, she looked uncomfortable and confused.

Great. He had flustered her, and he didn't even know how or why. "I always stand. And who said this was going to be an interrogation? I told Cutty I'd see you—you asked to see me, remember?—and that I might ask some questions. That was it."

She searched his face, as if he were the puzzle here. Hardly that. "You always stand when you eat dinner?"

"I always stand for everything. Except sleep. I've done that a few times, but you inevitably pitch over at some point." Viktor tried a smile. He wasn't very good at them—he had been told they looked more like bear snarls than signs of friendliness or pleasure. But despite her nerves tonight, she seemed like someone who wasn't easily daunted.

"You never sit? At all? Why?"

"I'm not good at relaxing. And it's easier for people to get the jump on you when you're sitting." Maybe he shouldn't be explaining this. She would think him paranoid. Which he was, but that wasn't the sort of thing that impressed women. Not that he was trying to impress her. He took a long drink.

"What if a woman wants to make out with you on the sofa?" Markovich asked.

Viktor almost choked on his juice. Not so much because of the question—he had been asked it before—but over the fact that, for whatever reason, she had been thinking of him in such a scenario. He had made exceptions to his rule for situations such as that, but he decided not to confess to it. "I don't have a sofa. We'd have to use the bed." He hadn't ever brought a woman aboard the ship, so his lack of furnishings hadn't come up much. The men on the crew thought it was practical that he had room for the punching bag.

"Er, we?"

Was she alarmed or intrigued by the notion? He couldn't tell.

"Whoever wanted to kiss me on a sofa." Viktor took another bite of meatloaf. This wasn't how he had imagined this meeting going. "I do have a couple of questions for you, Ms. Markovich, if you'd be inclined to answer."

"Go ahead. I have nothing to hide." She nodded, looking relieved at the change to a more formal tone. She even took a bite of her dinner.

"Where did you learn mashatui?"

She sputtered, flecks of meatloaf flying out of her mouth. Apparently that had been too blunt a question to start with. He handed her a napkin.

"Thank you," she murmured, wiping her mouth, and then the spattered table. Thoroughly. Buying time before answering, was she? Because she did, indeed, have something to hide? Or because it was an uncomfortable subject?

"My father," she finally said.

"He was from Spero?"

"We all were."

Ah. One question answered. "You escaped the destruction."

Had she been nearby when it happened? Perhaps been in orbit and seen it with her own eyes? The way he had for his world's destruction?

"We'd left a week earlier. My father had a job offer on Novus Earth, one that evaporated after…Let's just say GalCon didn't trust Speronians for a while." Markovich gave him a puzzled expression. "Why do you…? I mean, these aren't the kinds of questions I expected you to ask." Or care about, her tone said.

Yes, and why *did* he care? Why *was* he asking? "You're something of an enigma. I'm trying to figure you out." That sounded plausible. Maybe.

"I'm not that complicated. Really. My father didn't get the job, and there was no home to go back to—" her mouth twisted, "—so my brothers and sisters and I grew up in the slums of Calimar on Novus Earth. Sometimes we had a place to stay; sometimes we were on the street. My father always kept us together though, made sure we didn't starve. Financially, he had nothing, and he had to do jobs well beneath his education level, but he loved us, and he gave us…his culture, his sense of honor. I don't know what you'd call it. He taught us a lot, and he always made me want to be a better person than our situation and my own tendencies might have otherwise warranted." She smiled faintly for the first time. She was still wiping the table, though she didn't seem aware of it. "He hated it when we stole. Better to starve than to act without honor, he'd say. Though…" She squinted up at Viktor and pointed a finger at his nose. "I'm positive he'd have no qualms about stealing if it was to escape an enemy."

"Hm," Viktor said, not ready to give more, not ready to admit that his mind was working over her words, what it would mean to be raised by a Speronian practitioner. "This business of yours, it's not the first?" He didn't want to mention her ship and bring the loathing back to her eyes, but he was trying to work out how someone who had grown up in poverty could have acquired a craft. Even if it had clearly been a clunker, spaceships weren't cheap under any circumstances, and it had apparently been full of expensive scientific equipment.

"Oh, it's at least the tenth." Markovich tapped her fingers on the table, counting. "The eleventh. Twelfth if you count the recycling craze. To this day, I can give you the spot price of more than two hundred metals that trade on the market. Well, I haven't had a chance to check the market for a couple of days, but…" She spread her hand.

Viktor grunted. Then, feeling he should say more, thus to encourage her to continue speaking, he added, "No other prisoners have asked for market feeds to be delivered to the brig."

"No? How odd."

He chewed on a bite of food while he tried to think of another question that would lead her to answer his unspoken one. The food had been lukewarm to start and was cold by this point, but he barely noticed. His mind wasn't on the meal.

"The recycling stint was what gave me seed money for my first real business. I'd learned early on, you see, that working for someone else didn't suit me." She paused for effect, or so the twinkle in her eyes said. "I discovered that when I was selling pet hair detangling devices door to door."

He thought it was a joke at first, but nobody would make up something like that, would she?

"It was for a pet grooming company. I'd never had a pet in my life, unless you count the stray cats that wandered all over the back streets of Calimar, but I was working on commission and did my best to detangle every cat, dog, gerbil, and furred lizard in the city, thus to show off my product. It wasn't the worst thing I'd done, but the company was very strict about the sales pitch you had to give and it was…ludicrous. Pay was by commission only and usually late. I never worked for anyone else after that. My first business success was in that industry though, building a system for people to find lost pets. I should tell you, lest you think my whole life has been silly, that I was fifteen, sixteen at this time. I had a couple of more serious businesses later on. I didn't get into the medical industry until I met Lauren, who helped me with some of my own issues. I'm sure you don't want the details, but let's just say that she made me a believer with her microbiota transfer solution, and I agreed to help figure out a way to finance her research into the ancient alien gut bugs. I'm, ah, talking a lot, aren't I? Is this what you had in mind with your questions?" She shrugged, looking sheepish, but at least she had lost some of that nervousness. Her rambling didn't bother him the way it might coming from others. He wasn't sure why. He usually preferred silence, but the solitude of command did sometimes grow old.

"Perhaps not exactly," he murmured. "I'd been wondering what crime you committed against Felgard."

It was the wrong thing to bring up. Her sheepishness vanished, replaced by irritation. "I haven't committed *any* crimes. That's what I've been trying to tell you people. I could be researching and trying to figure out *why* he wants me, but I've been locked away without access to the net." She threw him an accusing look, and he had a feeling she had remembered her destroyed ship. She pushed her plate away, clearly ready to leave.

Viktor caught her wrist. It was silly when she was angry with him, but he didn't want to let her go—or escort her back to the brig, as the case would be. A look of raw fear entered her eyes, as if she thought he would strike her, and he let her go immediately. "Ank—Markovich." Why couldn't he remember not to use her first name? "If you'd—"

She stood, almost stumbling over the chair, righting it, then rushing to put it between them, even though he hadn't taken a step toward her. "Captain, I know you're busy and have work. I thank you for dinner, but if you're done asking questions, I'd like to go."

Viktor sighed. "As you wish."

He walked after her toward the exit, but as she was about to walk through the doorway, she stopped, turning so quickly, he tensed, almost expecting an attack.

She surprised him, not by attacking but by apologizing. "Wait, I'm sorry." She lifted a hand, palm open toward him. "I shouldn't have gotten angry. I intended…I wanted to thank you for sending our gear to us."

"All right," he said, keeping the suspicion out of his voice, but her sudden change of attitude set off his alarms.

When she had been chattering about her background, that had been her, the real her, he'd sensed, but maybe she had forgotten with whom she was having dinner and had inadvertently let her shields down. The calculation was back in her eyes now, along with that quiet fury she felt toward him. Her smile wasn't genuine, not the way it had been when she had been discussing recycling businesses.

Of course, she was attractive whether those smiles were genuine or not, and it didn't escape his attention that, because of the way she had turned so abruptly, they were standing with only a few inches between them. And she hadn't stepped back to adjust that distance, to make it less intimate. The scent of lavender and lilacs, ever so faint, drifted to his nose. He swallowed, aware of the fullness of her lips, of the sleek line of her neck running down to her collarbone. He would like to see more of that collarbone, of all of her. Get her out of that dusty, unflattering jumpsuit.

She was watching his eyes. Reading his thoughts? They weren't that original. She had doubtlessly attracted enough men to know when one was thinking of sofas, or beds as the case might be. Or dining room tables in empty rooms, late at night, with nobody else around to hear them.

Dining room tables with handcuffs on them, Viktor reminded himself. The handcuffs of a criminal. Although…more and more, he was questioning if she was truly a criminal, especially now that she'd spoken of her father as someone who had raised her with honor—something he believed because of what he knew about mashatui practitioners. But she didn't know he was wavering, and he wasn't ready yet to tell her he believed her, to risk being made a fool. Especially with that calculation glittering in her eyes. But there was indecision there too. What did it mean? That she was going to try and distract him so she could pickpocket him? He remembered the way she had watched him put away the electronic key. It wouldn't open the brig force field, but she might not know that. Or maybe she did and had a plan for that. He wouldn't put it past her to trick someone into letting her out again. The key *would* open the doors on the ship the rest of the crew members had access to.

"Captain," she said, and instead of backing away, she put a hand on his shoulder and stepped closer.

She licked her lips. Yes, she was up to something, perhaps the very something he suspected. But all he could focus on was the way her tongue moistened her lips. He could kiss those lips…and still pay attention to what was happening to his pocket.

"Viktor," he whispered.

"Oh? Are you always so familiar with your prisoners?" She was trying to sound nonchalant, but it didn't quite come off. She might be attractive, but he either made her nervous or she wasn't a very practiced seductress.

He put a hand on her waist, and she tensed. For a moment, he thought she might forget this mission she'd given herself and turn to flee. She stayed, but she licked her lips again, the pink tip of her tongue darting out before disappearing back into her mouth. He couldn't pull his gaze from her full lips.

"You're not in my command. You can use Mandrake if you prefer." He found her uncertainty more appealing than brazenness would have been, though it bothered him to know she wasn't genuinely attracted to him, that she was working up the courage to try something. It didn't bother him enough to let her go. "May I call you Ankari?" He was tired of thinking of her as Markovich. Ankari was a much more appealing name. A more feminine one.

She didn't answer right away. She peered into his eyes. Trying to figure him out in the same way he had been puzzling over her? "If you want to," she said.

"Good." Viktor massaged her through her jumpsuit, caressing her waist. When she didn't pull away, he eased his hand around to her back, rubbing her muscles and nudging her toward him, as well. Or maybe he crept toward her. He wasn't sure, but noticed when her breasts brushed his chest. There were layers of fabric between them, but the soft touch sent a charge through him, nonetheless. His groin stirred. How far would she let him go in her attempt to distract him? How far *should* he go…with a prisoner?

Nowhere. This wasn't wise.

Yet his other hand joined the first, massaging her waist, the small of her back. He inched closer to her. That alarm returned to her eyes, and she shifted one hip away from him, almost bumping against the wall. He should release her, end the game she was attempting to play, and take her back to the brig. He was already going to be spending the night imagining what might have been if he had shoved her up against the wall, kissed her breathless, and torn that jumpsuit off her. With his teeth.

But she didn't pull farther away from him. "The doctor said you had another name," she murmured.

"Huh?" he uttered, his mind elsewhere.

"Besides Viktor." Despite that concern that had flashed through her eyes, Ankari didn't remove her hand from his shoulder. She slid it to the back of his neck and scraped her fingernails through his hair.

A hot surge of blood flowed to his groin, and his trousers grew uncomfortably tight. They hadn't even kissed, and he wanted nothing more than to mash her against him and have his way with her. "She tell you what it is?" he asked, struggling to track the conversation.

"No."

"Good." He gave her a tight smile.

Ankari kept kneading the back of his neck, her fingernails grazing his skin, and it was making him want to descend upon those lips and kiss her senseless. She leaned her chest against him, her other hand stroking his waist through his shirt, her thumb slipping beneath his belt, teasing his stomach. The muscles there shivered beneath her touch, and he wanted very much for that hand to delve lower.

If it did, it would be to his pocket, he reminded himself. And he would stop her when she reached for it, but then this encounter would end. He should end it now, before it came to that. His hands drifted from the small of her back down to cup her butt. He should turn her around and prompt her to start walking back to the brig. But she was tilting her face up toward him, displaying those full shining lips that he wanted so much to taste.

"I get Spero," Viktor said, the words surprising him.

Her hands stopped moving, and she stared at him. Why had he said that? All he knew was that he wanted her to not hate him. For this to be something besides some onerous task for her. If that was possible.

"What?" she breathed, her lips inches from his own.

"I know you were young, but I get how it must have shaped your life growing up. I'm from Grenavine." He could have explained further, but he didn't think he had to. There were only two worlds that had been destroyed in the system. Everybody knew about them.

She didn't respond, didn't move, barely blinked. He wasn't sure why he'd told her that; he didn't tell anyone. But he wanted her to know that *if* she wasn't a criminal, if this all had been a mistake or some play by Felgard to get her business, he would be sympathetic to her plight. He just needed time to figure it out. After this next mission was over, they would have days in space and a stop for repairs before reaching Felgard's planet, plenty of time for research. So long as she didn't do something foolish in the meantime. No, escaping wouldn't be foolish from her perspective—wouldn't he be trying to do the same thing if he were the captured one?—but it was clear that more people than just he knew about her bounty and would be watching for her.

He ought to tell her these things, not simply think them. Yes, that would be useful, but some of the calculation had gone out of her eyes at his revelation, and she was looking at him with…concern? Wonder? Understanding? Whatever it was, it wasn't loathing, and the new expression tugged at something inside him the way the other one hadn't.

It could still be a ruse. That knowledge didn't keep him from opening his mouth and welcoming her when she melted against him, her lips reaching up to his. They were warm and full, eager and sensuous. All he had hoped. He inhaled deeply, the scent of her shampoo, of her skin—of *her*—making him heady. He tasted her, nibbled at that bottom lip she had been licking all night, understood the draw…

Her earlier hesitancy disappeared, and her hands slid across his shoulders, down his arms, and around his waist. She rose on her tiptoes, deepening the kiss, her mouth hungry, excited by him. She leaned into him, rubbing against him. Raw heat coursed through him, every part of him rigid where she was soft.

He pressed into her, stroking her body, exploring it more brazenly than before. His finger brushed the corner of something in the pocket on the side of her thigh, and he would have laughed if his tongue and lips hadn't been otherwise occupied. So *that* was what she had been nervous about. Afraid he would discover that she had pilfered a tablet? It wasn't his; he could still feel the weight of his in his own cargo pocket. He would have to watch for the key though. That was so small that he wouldn't miss it if light fingers made it disappear.

Right now, her fingers were a little higher up, more interested in slipping under his shirt and stroking his abdomen and waist. A very acceptable place for them. He let his own fingers go back to roaming. The jumpsuit was problematic. He wanted to touch silky flesh, not rough fabric.

As they kissed, Viktor followed the curves of her body with his hands, eliciting a soft moan of pleasure when he grazed the side of her breast. He found the fastener beneath her collar and slid his finger down it. The garment peeled open. He thought about pulling it all the way off her shoulders and dropping it to the floor, but that would require her to stop touching him while she lifted her arms out. He didn't want that. A conundrum. He settled for this new access. Only a lightweight camisole lay beneath the jumpsuit, and she groaned when he stroked her through it.

A ruse? Or was she genuinely enjoying herself? It seemed that way, but he couldn't forget that he was an obstacle to her, one she had come here tonight to deal with. He ought to check on that key—her hands had drifted lower—but she seemed distracted from her mission. She had forgotten to keep that outside hip away from him, and her whole body was molded against his now, his heat mingling with hers like magma in a volcano.

He growled deep in his throat, needing less clothing between them. One of her hands paused on his belt clasp, and her lips stilled. She lifted her eyes toward his, a question there. As if she needed to ask. He lowered his lips to her neck, again breathing in the scent of her warm skin, tasting her, the lingering dust from those ruins making him think of sharing a shower with her later, but now…He tugged the suit off her shoulders even as she fumbled with his belt.

He had to help that jumpsuit along, pushing it off her arms and down past her hips. She stiffened when his hands neared that pocket again. He almost snorted—as if he hadn't already noticed the cargo inside. She caught his wrists.

"I'll get it," she whispered.

He had removed enough of the jumpsuit that it would fall to the floor on its own, anyway. He slipped out of her grip, pulled her hands back to his abdomen, hoping she would go back to taking *his* clothes off, and gave her a long, hard kiss, willing it to drive thoughts of subterfuge and theft out of her mind. But there was a stiff uncertainty in her stance that hadn't been there before.

"You can have the tablet," Viktor said, his lips refusing to leave hers as he spoke. She understood anyway; he felt it in the spark of surprise that went through her body. "Not the key," he added.

Would she resent him for that? For realizing what she was up to?

After a thoughtful moment in which he tried to kiss all such notions out of her mind, she returned his kisses again. She stroked his tongue with her own, running her hands across his back, running her fingernails across his flesh, and setting him on fire. A relaxed ardor guided her movements, as if she was relieved she no longer had to worry about that tablet. He wished he had said something before. Her hands returned to his belt and finished unclasping it. Yes.

His comm chimed.

No.

Blast all the suns in the galaxy, who was bugging him *now*? Viktor wanted to ignore it, wanted to have this moment—this *hour*—but some plucky young soldier would be sent to find him if he didn't respond.

"What?" he growled, hoping the sound of his displeasure would drive whatever bridge minion was contacting him to make it a *short* message. Ankari's mouth had found his own neck now, and his trousers were sagging from his hips, her hands pushing them lower. All he wanted was—

"It's Striker, sir. We have a problem."

It was his team down on the planet, not someone on the bridge. They wouldn't have been patched through to him directly if it wasn't important. Viktor released Ankari's shoulders, pressed his hands against the wall behind her, and struggled to focus on something else besides unleashing the cannon. That was hard when her face was still buried in his neck, her tongue tracing interesting patterns there, her teeth occasionally coming out for a nip.

"What is it?" Viktor asked, hoping his voice didn't sound as husky to his soldier as it did to him.

"Tank and Rawlings are missing. And…so is the shuttle."

"*What?*"

"They were on guard back at the shuttle while the rest of us were searching the forest. It's real thick and jungley down here, so the sensors don't work very good. But we captured two of Sisson Hood's scouts, questioned them, and found his camp. We were coming back to the shuttle to tell you to bring everyone down for the invasion, but all that's left are some laser scorch marks on the ground and some charred up trees. It's hard to believe any local thugs could have taken down our men, but…there's nothing left here. Just some smoking wood. We're lucky we had all our field gear with us. I'm calling on the sat-comm. I already talked to Commander Garland about tracking the shuttle, but the chip was either removed or damaged. According to the bridge, the whole craft has just disappeared."

Ankari had stopped nibbling, pulling back to listen and watch his… collarbone. It was good that she had stopped distracting him, he supposed, but the faintly stunned what-was-I-thinking expression that replaced the passionate one of moments before was less good. He kept himself from delivering a promise of "later," not certain if she would be excited by that or not.

"We could use some backup, sir," Striker went on. "Since we took those two scouts, Hood's going to realize he has missing men sooner or later. And then there's our own missing men."

"I'll get Thomlin on research and get the rest of the strike team and come down," Viktor said. He shook his head, berating himself for not warning everyone about that bounty hunter. But Goshawk didn't have a very big crew. It would be surprising if he was behind this. Maybe there were others. That was an alarming thought. A whole legion of bounty hunters sent out here to retrieve…

He looked down at Ankari, but her chin had drooped to her chest, and she was avoiding his eyes. He stepped back from her, though he couldn't resist brushing his fingers against her soft hair as he did so.

"Thomlin," he called into his comm. "We need to have a talk. I need some intel, and I need it fast. We need to finish up and get to Felgard's without delays." He looked at Ankari, wondering if he should warn her that there were more parties looking for her, but there wasn't time. Striker was right; he needed to get down there with a team immediately. "Send Cutty to the mess hall for…the prisoner too." He hated calling her "the prisoner," especially when he had been so close to turning her into his lover, and when he was doubting more than ever whether she truly deserved to be anyone's prisoner.

Not surprisingly, her mouth hardened and some of the anger returned to her eyes at the words. Damn. He would try to make it up to her later. Somehow.

CHAPTER SIX

Ankari followed the yawning, glaring, and sighing Corporal Cutty through the corridors without thought of escape this time. She was too busy running that strange dinner meeting through her mind over and over again, trying to figure out what that kiss—*more* than a kiss, she admitted, with a hot flush swallowing her anew at the memory—had meant and why the captain— *Viktor*, he'd said to call him—had been asking all of those questions about her past.

Was it possible he had started to believe her at some point and had been trying to figure out if she was indeed a legitimate entrepreneur and not some sleazy villain? As much as she would like to believe that, she doubted he could be thinking along those lines when she had been pickpocketing, conniving, and seducing his crew since she arrived. Well, she hadn't exactly seduced Striker, but Viktor might think she had been trying to seduce him, especially since her hands had started wandering around of their own accord, and she had been about to do a lot more than the kiss that she'd originally had in mind to distract him. Good, law-abiding citizens doubtlessly weren't supposed to resort to such tactics. But it wasn't her fault she had been kidnapped. And she needed to escape. Especially with him in such a hurry to finish his mission here and tote her off to Felgard.

That had stung when he had told his man he wanted to get to the finance lord as quickly as possible. When just the moment before, he had been kissing her and acting like he cared. Why had he told her about Grenavine, leaving her to assume that he, like her father, had lost every- thing—*everyone*—there? To win sympathy? Why? It wasn't as if she had been balking at his touch. She had been trying to keep him from brushing against her pocket, yes, but she had been all over him too. And the pocket…it hadn't even mattered. He'd known! Had he known all along? Made out the shape of the tablet in her pocket in the gym? All night, she had been so afraid he would figure it out, and he had known. And he hadn't even cared. That was the confusing part. If he wanted nothing more than to reach Felgard and collect his money, why give them back the research equipment and why let her have the tablet? Why give her access to all the information she sought? He must not be thinking that she could learn what she needed to escape, but why bother giving her anything at all?

Cutty stopped to talk to someone at the bottom of a ladder. Men in helmets and battle armor were running through the corridors, gear and guns in their hands. They must all be going to join that assault team, to get their men back, and to do whatever they had to do on that moon. And get paid to do it.

They were, after all, mercenaries. Men who were paid to fight. Men for whom money mattered more than allegiance to any particular nation or idea. Ankari reminded herself that the captain was one of these people too. Whatever he'd been in the past, he was fighting for pay now. Presumably the more pay, the better. Maybe that was why he was letting her team continue with their research. He thought he could cash in somehow on the work they left behind, or maybe he thought he could get copies of everything before handing them over to Felgard. Even if Dr. Zimonjic had scoffed at Lauren's ideas, that didn't mean someone wouldn't pay a lot for the research they had done.

Yes, that had to be why he was doing more than keeping them locked up with nothing to work on. And maybe that was why he had been asking about her businesses too. Trying to figure out what she might be worth and if he could get even more out of the deal than what Felgard was offering. And if he could get in her pants along the way, even better, right? She might have initiated that kiss, but he had been eager enough to return it. That shouldn't have surprised her, but it had. And it had excited her too. She had lost control—and at one point, almost forgotten her goal entirely. She couldn't remember the last time she had been so engrossed in anyone.

She rubbed her face—it was still hot and flushed from their kissing. Her whole body was. She hadn't even realized she was that attracted to him until all that lean, hard muscle had been molded against her body, his hands rubbing and teasing her, his lips scorching her flesh wherever they touched, making her insides heat up like a sun until she was throbbing with the need to get even closer, to wrap her legs around him, to feel him inside of her, to ride him like a Goran dragon.

"Come on, woman," Cutty said, grabbing her arm. "They're going to need me on that mission, and I'm not missing the shuttle down because you're dawdling."

Dawdling? He was the one who had stopped to chat. She had just been… entertaining herself with her memories. Damn, she might still hate Viktor for blowing up her ship and trying to drag her off to her death, but she would be ridiculously disappointed if they never got to finish what they had started.

Not here though. Not on his ship. She had to escape. Maybe she could look him up once she had cleared her name and dealt with Felgard. She would wait until she was filthy rich from her business success, and then maybe she would call him up, offering to hire him to be her escort. She snorted. Would a mercenary ever get into the gigolo business? It would be a lot safer than getting shot at. Maybe she should ask Cutty if he had ever considered the line of work.

He palmed open the force field and shoved her inside without waiting for her to walk in of her own accord. No, she wouldn't ask him about gigolo activities.

He slapped the force field closed again, then ran off without a word.

"Looks like we're not going to have a guard tonight," Ankari mused. If they were going to get off this ship, this would be their best opportunity.

The lights hadn't been dimmed, and Lauren and Jamie had been lying on the floor, with their arms flung over their eyes, but they sat up now.

"Are you all right?" Jamie asked. "You were gone a long time."

"I'm fine." Ankari pulled out the tablet and tossed it to her. "I'm hoping we can escape soon, so find that technical manual and start speed reading, please."

"Oh. Good."

Ankari wanted to check to see if her friend had mailed her back, too, but figuring out how to pilot one of those shuttles had to be the priority at the moment.

"Ankari…?" Lauren was scrutinizing her.

"Yes?"

"You look like you've been kissed hard and dropped off before you were ready to go home."

"I—what?" *Did* she? Ankari hadn't had time to do much more than zip up her jumpsuit before that prompt corporal had shown up. Her hair had been a mess to start with, and she hadn't been wearing any makeup that could have smeared. Viktor hadn't left bite marks anywhere, had he? She remembered nibbling on *him*…

"Girls can tell," Lauren said, further shocking Ankari because Lauren had always seemed oblivious to people's relationships.

"Who *was* it?" Jamie asked. "The captain? Is he falling for you? Is he going to help us?"

"Not exactly." Ankari recovered her equilibrium, glanced back to make sure nobody had popped up at the security desk, then pulled the electronic handcuff key out of her pocket. "I'm not sure he'll be talking to me again when next we meet."

Viktor might have forbidden her to take it, but it had been so easy when he had been pulling her jumpsuit off. With luck, he would be too distracted by his mission to think to check for it. Maybe he would even change into some of that battle gear and leave his trousers on the ship, so he couldn't check for it until he returned. At which point, Ankari and the others could be long gone. *If* they could get out of the brig.

"Is that a key?" Jamie waved at the force field. "Will it get us out of here?"

"No, but I'm pretty sure it's tied in with the doors around the ship. They all have little sensors for something besides a palm print. Lauren, any progress with that generator?"

"Not yet, but we had a guard on duty until a few minutes ago, so I couldn't fiddle with it too much. I'm not that optimistic about it shorting out the force field anyway."

"Try anyway, please." Ankari sat on the bench to think about backup plans if the generator didn't work. That was what she intended to do anyway, but her mind kept betraying her, wandering back to her evening with Viktor. From that brief dialogue she had heard, it had been clear his mission had gone to hell. Would he be in danger down there? She'd witnessed his impressive hand-to-hand combat skills, but how useful would they be in some jungle with laser fire streaking all over the place? And when had his safety started to matter to her?

———

The humidity dripped from the leaves and fronds, the canopy overhead so dense that Viktor wouldn't have been able to see the sky if his team hadn't landed in a clearing by a stream. A few mossy ruins surrounded an old cement slab, almost invisible because of the grass and weeds spurting from the cracks. The structures were all that remained of what had likely been a logging pickup zone once. The jungle hadn't quite taken all of the area back, but in a few years, the ruins would be impossible to find. For now, Viktor had a view of the black clouds blotting out the stars and Drang, the sister moon. One of the storms, for which the moon was known, was heading in. The thick air crackled with static longing to be unleashed, and the wind had already picked up in the five minutes he had been on the ground.

"Because this night needs to get more complicated," he muttered.

"Sir?" Sergeant Hazel stood a few feet away, decked out in battle armor and watching his back.

Viktor examined the scorch marks on the tree he was standing next to, his Eytect sensor tugged into place to give him night vision for his left eye along with local weather conditions—as if he couldn't tell a storm was coming. The tree's papery bark had been scored by laser fire, parallel lines. "Double-barreled blaster," he said. "MK-45 or 48."

"Fleet issue, but there are a lot of those available in surplus stores," Hazel said, her gaze roving the trees all around.

The three shuttles that Alpha, Charlie, and Delta squads had come down in sat in the clearing, each with a well-armed pilot waiting inside. Striker and the rest of the fighters had already tramped off to the east to deal with Sisson Hood and his band of merry outlaws. Viktor itched to join them, but not until he had his missing men and his other shuttle back.

"In other words, it could be anyone." Viktor faced the clearing, eyeing the churned mud around the landing pad. "But I've only seen evidence of hand weapons so far. Nothing that would have come from a ship." He raised his voice to address the third soldier skulking around the clearing with them. "You find any tracks yet, Tick?"

"'Bout fifty million left by our own people, Cap'n." Sergeant Tick tossed a baleful look over his shoulder. He'd asked Viktor to keep the men in the shuttle until he could have a good look around, but with that storm rolling in, Viktor hadn't wanted to delay the core mission. He *had* made sure the squads funneled out of the clearing in a single file, so as to minimize the disturbances.

"Fifty million? From forty-five people?"

"Forty-five people with real busy feet," Tick said around a wad of that caffeine gum he was always chewing. He grinned, his balefulness forgotten in less than ten seconds, like usual. When it came to tracking, he liked a challenge, anyway. "Lot of critter traffic too. All agitated with this storm coming, I reckon. This the planet with the dinosaurs?"

"It's a moon," Hazel said.

"Fine, this the *moon* with the dinosaurs? It was nice of those aliens to terraform so much of this system for us, but they did get a might creative when they were adding the wildlife."

Viktor had seen the "dinosaurs" on a previous stop here—there was a zoo in the capital city. They were predators that had reminded the early settlers of velociraptors from the Old Earth fossil record. They had been known to kill men wandering in the jungle alone, but he doubted any would be out in this weather. He was more concerned about humans armed with laser rifles than feathered dinosaurs with pointy teeth. "Just let me know if you find sign of our men or our shuttle thieves."

"Working on it, Cap'n."

Viktor stalked around the clearing, too, poking under fronds and searching for broken branches or other signs that someone had pushed through the dense undergrowth. He hadn't grown up with wolves or bears or whatever

Tick was claiming this month, but he'd taken all of the prerequisite survival training courses as a part of his recruitment for the Crimson Ops.

"If there weren't any ships firing, someone had to have come on foot," Hazel said, following him. She would probably figure out the solution with her head before either Viktor or Tick found enlightenment looking at the ground. "So someone came in on foot and surprised our people."

"Except that shouldn't have happened. Standard operating procedure is for the pilot to wait inside the shuttle, in case someone needs a fast pickup. The shields are impenetrable to hand weapons. Heavy artillery might make a dent, but there's no evidence of that." Viktor waved at the ground. He didn't need Tick to tell him that nothing heavy had been dragged around out here.

"So someone would have had to convince Tank and Rawlings to open the door," Hazel said. "They're not that stupid. Well, maybe Tank. But Rawlings wouldn't have gone for that unless it was someone on our own team needing help, and Striker didn't say anything about that."

"Just that the shuttle and our men were gone when he came back with prisoners."

"What?" The wind had kicked up, and Hazel had to lean closer to hear him.

Viktor repeated himself in a louder voice and added, "It's possible one of those two intentionally let someone in."

Hazel stiffened. "Sir? What do you know?"

"That those women we have in the brig are worth a lot of money to Felgard and that a surprising number of people know we've got them." Granted, Viktor only knew about the bounty hunter right now, but that was one more person than *should* be aware of who he was keeping in his brig. "Someone also removed the tracking device inside the shuttle. A stranger shouldn't know where to look for that."

"It could have been damaged in a fight. I can't imagine Rawlings selling out."

"No thoughts on Tank?"

"He's dumb and greedy. I suppose it's possible."

"Yeah." Anger simmered inside Viktor at the thought of such a betrayal, but he kept it on a side burner. It was too early to start accusing men of mutiny. If Goshawk hadn't contacted him, he wouldn't be thinking along these lines at all. He would assume the trouble had originated down here. "It might not have anything to do with our prisoners. It's possible Sisson Hood got wind of our visit ahead of time and that this was something his men launched."

Viktor walked around the clearing again. He spotted one of the "critter" prints Tick had mentioned, a three-clawed mark that was probably right for those raptors. It was heading in the direction of a mountain range ten miles away. With the towering trees all around, it wasn't visible from the ground, but Viktor had spotted the ridge on the way down. There had been lights over there, too, but his map had promised there was a Buddhist temple in that direction, rather than anything so inimical as an enemy camp. Bandits didn't usually camp out on mountains with lights blazing so anyone could find them.

Tick had disappeared into the trees, a few meters away or a few hundred. The thick foliage had already swallowed the illumination from his flashlight, so it was impossible to tell. Maybe he was onto something. If they found footprints, they might trace them back to the source, but it would need to be soon, before the rains started and obliterated everything. The problem was Viktor was more concerned about where the shuttle had gone than where the thieves had come from. Was it already back at some headquarters where his men were being interrogated? Or up on someone's ship? Or maybe the men had already been dumped, and someone was taking the shuttle away to rip it apart and sell it for pieces on the black market. If this had something to do with stealing the prisoners, maybe the shuttle was heading up to the *Albatross* right now with a strike team ready to invade his ship.

Viktor halted, the simmering anger threatening to boil over into hot fury. Why hadn't he thought of that right away? It was such an obvious possibility.

He was about to stomp back to the parked shuttles when Tick yelled from the trees. The wind made this voice sound distant, but he was probably within fifty meters. "Got a trail, Cap'n."

Viktor pushed through fronds and branches, with thorns clawing at his battle armor. The clearing quickly disappeared from sight, and he had only his ears to rely on to find Tick. It would be easy for someone without equipment or a good sense of direction to become lost out here. Rain spattered on the leaves high overhead. It wasn't dampening his shoulders yet, but it would start dripping through to the jungle floor soon.

He stepped around a vine-strangled tree, and Tick's flashlight beam came into view.

"Take your time, Cap'n, no rush." Tick grinned again, his big white teeth flashing in the darkness. They were the same age and had even crossed paths a time or two back on Grenavine, but Tick always seemed twenty years younger. Must be the gum keeping him perky. "These the tracks you were hoping to find?"

Tick pointed at a clear boot print, many clear boot prints. A trail of them wound back into the jungle, heading in the direction of those the mountains. At least six sets. Most of the prints were facing toward the shuttle clearing, men on their way to the ambush point, but a couple were following the same trail and heading the other way.

"Didn't spot 'em closer to the landing site, 'cause they took to the trees here." Tick pointed up to the branches, highlighting a couple of snapped branches with his light. "Probably knew someone with my fine tracking skills would be out later, so they didn't want to walk at the end. Might've had some short-range hover packs."

"These prints." Viktor crouched and pointed. "They look like they're on top of the others—made after. You agree?"

"Yup, that's right, Cap'n. You do a fair bit of tracking for a kid who grew up in the gardens."

"They made us go out and hunt from time to time." Viktor didn't talk much about his time in the fleet, even with the oldest members of the crew, so he didn't bother mentioning where he'd truly learned to hunt. "So. At least two tracks leaving the landing pad. Not *everyone* left on the shuttle. I don't suppose you can tell if these tracks might belong to our men?"

"Not just from the prints—we haven't got standard uniform boots, and I haven't taken a look at Tank's or Rawling's treads lately, but let me walk along a spell. Might be able to pick out their gaits. Tank rolls along like he's on a horse, you know." Tick headed off, flashlight toward the ground.

Branches snapped and leaves rattled behind Viktor, announcing Hazel's arrival. He showed her the tracks.

"We following them, sir?" She glanced toward Tick's receding back.

Good question. Viktor was tempted to hop in one of those shuttles and fly back to the ship on the chance that their stolen one was already heading that way, but that would leave one of his teams stranded down here if his people got in trouble and had to retreat in a rush. Besides, all he had was a hunch so far. And Bravo squadron was back on the ship. It wasn't as if the *Albatross* was adrift and waiting for someone to board it and take over. He had known there might be trouble while he was gone, more trouble than a handful of pilots and engineers could be trusted to handle, no matter how capable they were in combat.

"Yes, but I want to let the ship know first." Viktor tapped his comm unit. "Garland, any change in status?"

The wind whistled in his ears, nothing else.

"I can't get him, either, sir," Hazel said after trying her own comm. "They have some weird storms out here that affect the ionosphere. Must be interfering."

"So glad we paid for that state-of-the-art communications equipment last year." Viktor pushed through the damp leaves, rain droplets spattering his armor and face, and headed back to one of the shuttles. Its comm equipment was more powerful. Lightning flashed in the distance, and he winced, the Eytect unit a hair slow in washing out the sudden brightness. He tugged it off and stuffed it into his pocket. All of his equipment was unreliable tonight.

When he stalked inside the shuttle, Lieutenant Sequoia, his boots up on the console, looked up from an old-fashioned book he was reading. "Problem already, sir? You look grouchy."

"That how you guard my shuttle?" Viktor pushed the boots to the side and jabbed the comm.

"*Sound* grouchy too." Sequoia shifted his book to reveal a laser pistol and waved to a hologram displaying the area around the shuttle, presumably demonstrating that he was paying attention to the surroundings. Another Grenavinian, he had been with the company since the beginning, too, and was a good pilot and a reliable man, but he had zero career ambition and even less interest in commanding others, so he wasn't always the model soldier.

"If someone steals this shuttle while you're in it, I'm sending you to remedial pilot school with Commander Thatcher."

Sequoia's face grew pale, and he lowered his boots to the deck. "I… would rather have my pay docked, sir."

"Yes, I know." Viktor jabbed the console again. "Garland, come in. You there?"

"Here, sir. What's—" The speaker interrupted him with a crackle and hiss.

That didn't sound promising, either, but at least Viktor had gotten through. "Hazel, Tick and I are going to follow some tracks. The rest of the crew is approaching Hood's hideout. I want you to keep an eye out for our missing shuttle. If it shows up out of the ether, ask some pointed questions and make sure there aren't any unauthorized visitors on it, do you understand?" Lightning flashed beyond the viewport, and the first spatters of rain landed on the craft's nose. "Garland?"

"…breaking up, Captain. I heard that you're tracking and…about shuttle?"

Viktor raised his voice, as if that could somehow make his words cut through the storm interference more easily. "If that shuttle shows up, make sure nothing fishy is going on before you let it on board."

"…understand, sir. The shuttle…already here."

"What?"

"…a few minutes ago."

"Send a team down to check on that, Garland. I want to know what happened. I want a full report."

More static answered him. The rain picked up outside.

"Should I fly up to check on things?" Sequoia asked.

"No. Not yet. Garland should be able to deal with any problems small enough to fit in a shuttle. If there's even anything to deal with." Viktor might have missed half of Garland's words, but they hadn't sounded alarmed. Maybe Tank and Rawlings had already resolved their trouble and were reporting back to the ship. Still, why wouldn't they have come back down to pick up the men they had marooned down here first instead? "Just…don't let anyone in who's not supposed to be in."

"No, sir, wasn't planning on it. Especially not given how grouchy this weather is making people."

Viktor gave him a flat look and started for the door. He glanced back before leaving and caught Sequoia reaching for his book. Sequoia stopped, smiled innocently, and crossed his hands in his lap over the pistol instead. Viktor returned to the comm for a moment.

"Commander Thatcher," he called to the shuttle next door. "Are you there?"

"Of course, sir," came the prompt reply.

"Lieutenant Sequoia is lamenting how little he has to do over here. Would you mind running through some navigational math problems with him? To help him stay alert."

Sequoia's mouth sagged open, an expression of horror forming on his face.

"*Certainly*, sir. Given the potential fluctuations in the ionosphere from the coming storm, it would be an apt time to review linear equations useful for navigating magnetic fields. Lieutenant, shall we begin with a discussion of the Lorentz force?"

Viktor smiled, as much at the enthusiasm in Thatcher's voice as at the look of betrayal Sequoia launched at him. "Not a good idea to call your captain a grouch," he said and jogged outside, trusting he wouldn't find boots on the console again anytime soon.

Hazel was waiting, stoic in the face of giant raindrops splashing onto the cement landing pad around her. There were already impressive puddles. Viktor was tempted to forget the prints and go help the rest of the team, so the company could complete its core mission more quickly, but the storm would wash those tracks away before long. "We're going to follow them for a couple of miles, see if we find anything useful, and if not, we'll cut over and join the others."

"Yes, sir."

Viktor eyed the ever-darkening clouds. He hoped the storm—and the communications—would improve soon, but he wasn't counting on it.

CHAPTER SEVEN

Zzzzpt.

The hair on the back of Ankari's neck stood up, but the force field didn't flicker, or show any sign of disturbance at all.

Lauren sighed. "It's not fair to hire a microbiologist and then expect her to blast her way out of spaceships. I didn't study that in school."

"Technically, I didn't hire you," Ankari said. "I offered you a share of the company."

"What's the difference?"

"You get paid less and you're expected to do more."

"I knew I should have read the fine print on that contract."

"But," Ankari said, lifting her hand into the air grandiosely, "when we get bought out or make an IPO on the galactic stock exchange, you'll become a very rich woman." She caught a whiff of her armpit while it was up there next to her nose and grimaced. "I need a shower." She wondered if Viktor had noticed. He was used to running around with sweaty soldiers. Maybe she had been an improvement, even with her three-days-since-the-last-washing fragrance.

"A cold one?" Jamie asked. "Because of your need to cool down after your steamy kissing with the captain?" The girl was decidedly intrigued by Ankari's evening dalliance.

"No, I've recovered from that. I just want to wash myself for hygienic reasons." And so she would smell better the next time she was entangled with someone. "How's the research going?" Ankari pointed at the tablet. "Can you fly the shuttle yet?"

Jamie prodded the display dubiously. "Fly it? I think so. As long as a lot of difficulties don't come up."

"I notice she didn't say anything about landing it." Lauren pulled open the side of the compact generator. "Ugh. So many circuits." Strange that she wasn't daunted by things with trillions of cells, but a few colored wires could make her cringe.

"Let me see if I can help." Jamie scooted onto the floor next to her.

Ankari grabbed the tablet. She had been tapping her feet, eager for her turn so she could see if Fumio had responded to her mail. When she logged into her account, the lack of new messages made her slump back against the wall. It had been twenty-four hours since she mailed him. She couldn't believe he hadn't responded; he never checked out of the virtual world. It was odd that she didn't have any other messages, either. At the very least, some greedy finance outfit or another usually sent daily offers for lines of credit with exorbitant interest rates for her various businesses.

Ah, but wait. The messages were starting to trickle in now. That was more lag than usual. Odd.

She tapped on Fumio's name, and his face came up. She opted for a text version of the video since the security cameras were presumably still rolling, even if the crew was too busy to have anyone standing guard tonight. She also wasn't entirely positive she would want the other women to hear the unfiltered news if something catastrophic—even more catastrophic than their current situation—was on the horizon.

Ankari, sweet cakes, it's good to hear from you, Fumio's message read, *but you're right: you're in an alarming predicament. Felgard placed a bounty on you and your business partners two weeks ago, a legal one, not just a sub rosa version for the entrepreneurial criminal element. You're lucky the police didn't stop you and arrest you in some port along the way. Or maybe you've been off the grid. You certainly haven't mailed me in ages, and you know how interesting I am to talk to. Regardless, the story that he's offering is that you and your colleagues broke into one of his electronics facilities, stole information from the data banks, and killed his favorite guard on the way out. Or maybe it was his favorite dog. I don't remember. There's a rule about wanted posters being rushed through the channels when someone gets murdered. I, of course, know this is all a lie because he didn't have any video or any concrete evidence—there's some doctored-up stuff, but anyone with more than three brain cells could see through it. Also, the last I heard, electronics weren't anything you were interested in. Nor, pardon my assumptions, could I see you successfully breaking into a top-security electronics lab.*

Ankari was shaking her head as she read, confused by the whole story. It seemed so random. If Jamie and Lauren hadn't been listed on the bounty as well—her company was mentioned by name, too—she would have assumed some *other* Ankari Markovich had crossed the lord's path.

But Felgard, being a lord of finance, doesn't need to produce the sort of evidence mere mortals do to get the law to issue warrants for arrest. Up until two days ago, there was a one hundred thousand aurum reward for your capture. You and your cohorts are wanted alive, if you didn't already know. That recently went up to two hundred thousand, and there's a note here about you being held by the Mandrake Company. Mercenaries, but I guess you already know that. I looked them up, and they're a scary group, especially the captain. Ex-Crimson Ops. Be careful out there. It's not clear why Felgard increased the reward, if you've already been captured by someone, and all I can assume is that Mandrake Company decided it wasn't going to give you up or tried to get more money out of the lord. I don't fully know how things work in that world, but it sounds like Felgard has, in listing your captors, given the system an open invitation to pay a visit and try to steal you out from the mercenaries. Either way, I hope you're safe. If you escape them and need help, I can meet you on Orion Prime. Do you need me to? Let me know. I already tried to hack into the net and get the wanted poster removed, but because it's going through the government system, it's particularly well protected. I'll keep working on it, but I think you're going to have to see Felgard and work things out with him. Standing by, Fumio.

Ankari didn't know what stunned her more: that someone was willing to pay two hundred thousand aurums to have her—her, Jamie, and Lauren—delivered to his door or that the captain hadn't been willing to give her up. Of course, that was just Fumio's speculation. Maybe Viktor simply hadn't liked the terms he'd gotten from Felgard when they had spoken.

"So…interesting news," she said. Maybe she shouldn't say anything. Would this worry the others unnecessarily? Maybe, but they had a right to know.

"You downloaded a program for opening cell doors?" Jamie asked.

"No. Is there such a thing?"

"I'm not sure."

"The bounty on our heads has been increased to two hundred thousand," Ankari said. "And everyone in the system knows where we are." She waved to indicate the mercenary ship.

"What?" Lauren stared at her.

"*Why?*" Jamie added.

"We're going to have to take that up with Felgard. He really wants us. All of us. It must be related to our business, but I'm perplexed since we haven't done trials on anything more interesting than mice yet."

"Yes, but those mice had some amazing results," Lauren said. "Anyone who read the paper I published last month would have seen the potential."

"That's the one you told me about that was printed in *Specialized Gastroenterology Quarterly*, right?" Ankari asked. "The peer-reviewed journal that three people read?" She supposed it was possible that Felgard was a subscriber, but it seemed unlikely for someone outside of academia to keep up with such publications. Of course, journalists occasionally scanned them for news stories.

"Yes," Lauren said, "and it's more like three hundred people, thank you."

"What was the name of the article?"

"Increasing Genetic Potential, Health, and Longevity Through Ancient Alien Microbiota Transplants."

That was less obscure than a lot of the titles of articles Lauren had published. Ankari could see it catching a reporter's eye. Anything to do with the long-dead aliens was always a hit with the popular press. She plugged the title and author name into the news searcher and waited, drumming her fingers on the side of the tablet. Why *was* there so much lag tonight?

When the results came up, she groaned. "Lauren, did you seriously not know about this? Because you're cited." She turned the tablet toward her partner. A Chao Yu had published an article called, *Alien Gut Bugs as Potential Life Extender and Cure to Deadly Ailments*. It had been syndicated in no less than five hundred news outlets. That had been just under three weeks ago. And Felgard's bounty had come out two weeks ago. Coincidence? It hardly seemed likely.

Lauren's face grew ashen as she looked at the tablet. "None of you saw this earlier?"

"I don't read the news," Jamie said.

"I do—" the financial news, mostly, "—but we were busy packing and bartering for used science equipment then. And then we were out at the Bartoka Ruins for almost a week, and I don't know. We've been so busy." Ankari tapped on one of the articles to skim it. She doubted her name was mentioned, else someone in her circle of friends would have forwarded it to her. No, she wasn't in there, and neither was Jamie nor the company, but it wouldn't have been hard for someone to research Dr. Lauren Keys and find out where she was currently employed. And the name of their company, Microbacteriotherapy, Inc. could certainly sound promising to someone who had read the sensationalized article.

"This is all my fault then," Lauren whispered, looking around at the confines of the cell.

"No, it's not," Ankari said, "but if a feeling of guilt helps you get that generator working in a way that drops the force field, I'm willing to glare at you with condemnation."

Lauren didn't manage a smile. Her face was bleak. "We can try it now, but I don't think it's going to do anything." Her shoulders slumped.

Inspiring.

"Try it," Ankari said. "If it's not going to work, we'll have to think of something else." What that something might be, she had no idea. Since nobody was guarding them, there was nobody to seduce or stab with a syringe, not that she had one anymore.

Lauren and Jamie bent over the generator. Ankari leaned forward on the bench, her hands clasped, her eyes on the force field, hoping…

A deep hum came from the depths of the ship, and the lights flickered. Ankari straightened. "Was that you two?"

"I haven't pressed the button yet." Lauren sounded bewildered.

The lights flickered again, not only in the cell but in the entire security area. Ankari jumped to her feet. She tapped the field, and it buzzed at her, sending an unpleasant shock through her body. It was still up, but had it been when the lights had gone out? She waited, ready to test it if the power cycled again.

Darkness fell. Ankari swiped her hand through emptiness. The field was gone.

"Come on. Grab your stuff. Hurry." Ankari snatched up her own bag, not certain how long they had—or what would happen to someone caught in the middle of the force field when it reactivated. She lunged into the corridor. Bangs, thuds, and grunts of "ow" sounded in the darkness behind her, then she was being jostled as the others bumped into her.

"Are we all out?" Ankari asked.

"Yes."

As Ankari was feeling her way toward the door, the lights came back on. She expected some announcement, some explanation, but the ship's communications system remained silent. They needed to get out of the brig and to the shuttle bay as quickly as possible, but she stopped at the desk, hoping she might find a weapon inside. She didn't know what was going on out there, but she had a feeling it had to do with the three of them. And their two hundred thousand aurum reward.

The desk drawers held two sets of handcuffs and a number of unopened food bars. Ham log, turkey log, mixed meat log. Maybe Ankari needed to start a new business in supplying mercenary outfits with more appealing shelf-stable food items. She stuffed them in her pack anyway.

Without warning, the ship shuddered. It wasn't enough to throw Ankari off balance, but she did put a hand on the wall, not certain what was coming next.

"Did we hit something?" Jamie asked.

"Or did something hit *us*?" Lauren added.

"I don't know, but leaving is sounding like a better idea all the time." Ankari slipped the electronic key out of her pocket. This was one of the few rooms she had seen that had a lock on the inside as well as the outside, doubtlessly to put extra obstacles in the way of escaping prisoners.

The door opened before she reached it. She looked down at the key in confusion. Had it transmitted a code?

Then a number of hulking men in the corridor stepped into view, none of them familiar. One thrust a gun through the doorway. Ankari jumped back, kicking at it in midair. More by chance than skill, she struck it, knocking the weapon from the man's hand. The hulking figures surged forward. Ankari slammed her hand against the palm lock, hoping something would happen.

The door slid back shut. The palm panel flashed, "Incorrect match. Access denied."

Good.

Thuds sounded at the door, followed by the whine of a laser weapon firing.

"What the hell—" Lauren asked, crouching behind the desk. "Who are they?"

"If I knew, I'd tell you." Ankari snatched up the fallen gun and pointed it at the door, trying not to feel like someone planning to halt a waterfall with a measuring cup.

More shots fired. Wisps of smoke wafted from the lock panel.

"Anyone have any ideas?" Ankari asked.

"Go back in our cell and hide?" Lauren said.

"Throw egg logs at them?" Jamie asked.

"I need to hire some security people," Ankari muttered.

"Or get the captain to retire and work for you," Jamie said. "He looks like he could knock down some thugs."

"Too bad he's down on the moon." Ankari joined the others behind the desk. She doubted it would stop laser fire for long, but it was the closest thing to a barricade the room had.

More shots fired, then someone shouted. Or was that a cry of pain? If those people were trying to sneak into the brig to steal the prisoners, they were being rather noisy about it.

Something thudded against the door, then a scrape followed, almost like a metal fork on a metal plate. More smoke flowed from the panel. Ankari waited, her finger tight on the trigger. She planned to shoot anything standing in the doorway and prayed she could hit them all before they hit her.

But then it grew silent.

"What happened?" Jamie whispered.

As if Ankari knew. As smart as her two partners were—Ankari had seen their IQ tests—they were out of their element when the fights started.

Rhythmic thuds sounded next. Footsteps? Running footsteps? They came close to the door, but then passed it, fading to nothing again. After many long seconds passed without a noise, Ankari lowered the gun and stepped out from behind the desk. The smoke still rising from the lock panel didn't entice her to touch it, not that her palm had done anything anyway. Remembering the key, she waved it next to the wall. She didn't expect anything—even if it would have worked once, those men must have melted the innards with their shots.

Surprisingly, the panel gave a sickly bleep, and the door slid open. Ankari aimed the gun into the corridor, but immediately knew there was no need. At least six unmoving men lay on the floor, their weapons fallen at their sides. They were all in black, and as she had thought at her first glance, she didn't recognize any of the faces. Intruders. How had they gotten on board?

"Should we tie them up somehow?" Jamie whispered.

"There were those handcuffs," Lauren said. "But only two pairs."

"There are probably another ten pairs in that Striker's cabin."

"I don't think we need to worry about that," Ankari said, numbed by the unmoving figures, the open unseeing eyes. "Looks like the Mandrake Company men took care of them." She forced herself to step into the hallway and pick up laser pistols for Lauren and Jamie. One of the bodies didn't want to release its weapon, even in death. She let him keep it and found another one.

Lauren and Jamie accepted them, all the jokes gone from their lips as they realized the men were all dead. By now, Ankari had a good idea of the layout of the ship, so she led them straight to a ladder that would take them up to the middle deck. She paused when more laser fire sounded, echoing from somewhere above her.

"Maybe we should wait for Viktor's men to clear out the roaches," she whispered.

Lauren and Jamie had squeezed into the bottom of the ladder well with her.

"Who's Viktor?" Lauren asked.

"The captain."

"Oh." Whatever Lauren thought about the first-name basis, she didn't mention it. She was too busy flinching at noises.

Ankari climbed the ladder and was about to crawl out of the well when a door opened somewhere down the corridor.

"We get all of them?" someone asked.

"Better have, or the captain will flay us. Don't know why Tank sold out, but if Rawlings was in on it, he's going to be dead when Mandrake gets a hold of him."

The voices were coming closer. Ankari scooted down a few rungs, waving below her to warn the others.

The ship shuddered again. It didn't sound like it was in danger of flying apart at any second, but Ankari gripped the ladder tightly.

"Can't believe that little cruiser is picking a fight with us." Footsteps accompanied the words now.

Ankari hoped the men would continue on to another ladder and that they needed to go up to the bridge and not down to the brig.

"It's just trying to distract us, I bet."

"As if we wouldn't notice these rats with guns running around our ship."

"I don't get it though. Why were they here?"

For me, Ankari thought, leaning farther away from the corridor and the light spilling into the ladder well.

"Because the captain's gone, and they think they can take the ship? I don't know."

The men continued past the ladder, and Ankari released the breath she had been holding. She listened intently until their words and their footsteps had disappeared, then peeked into the corridor. There weren't any bodies on this deck, but those men had been fighting with someone. Tank, that had been one of the men Striker had mentioned as missing, hadn't it? Along with a shuttle? Ankari probably should have been paying more attention to that conversation, instead of letting herself be distracted by the tendons in Viktor's neck...

"This way," she whispered to the others. She had a feeling they were going to find more bodies in the shuttle bay. She hoped they found a shuttle too.

Voices drifted down from the deck above. Those men had to be searching the entire ship, looking for more intruders. They would doubtlessly have no trouble dealing with escaped prisoners if they came across them.

Ankari waved the key in front of the shuttle bay door pad and clenched her fist when it opened. The bodies she had expected were there. Two more men in black lay in front of the single shuttle in the open bay. She didn't see any of Viktor's men. Good.

"Everyone in," Ankari said, waving for the others to join her so the door would shut again, then she jogged down the stairs. The layout of the space was similar to that of the cargo bay, minus the gym equipment. There were a few control panels along the wall at the bottom of the staircase. "Think we can gain access to the bay doors from inside the shuttle?" she asked Jamie.

"You'd think so."

"Your technical manual didn't say so?"

Jamie gave her a flat look. "It was for the shuttle, not the shuttle *bay*."

They stopped in front of the door on the back of the sleek black shuttle. It was open, and there were three more bodies inside, two of them wearing the same black and killed with laser fire. Smoke still wafted from some of the clothing. The third man was bald and wore a leather jacket more in line with the civilian clothing Viktor's crew favored. His throat had been slit.

"Any chance we can leave them...those...here?" Lauren extended a finger toward the bodies.

Ankari might have thought the question callous, but Lauren truly looked disturbed at the idea of climbing into a shuttle full of dead men. Admittedly, Ankari wasn't that enthused about the idea, either. "If you'll help me move them. Jamie, want to get up there and see if you can start this?"

"Starting it should be easy. Figuring out what to press to get the shuttle bay doors to open might be more of a challenge."

Good point. Ankari doubted she could simply wave the key at them.

"All those bodies are going to be blown out into space when the bay doors open," Jamie said. "Just so you know."

Ankari and Lauren stared down at the dead man they had been about to move. She didn't feel good about flinging corpses into space, but..."That's probably what the captain would do with them anyway."

Lauren grabbed the legs, leaving Ankari to take the body under the armpits. She had seen dead people on the streets as a child, but she had never touched a dead man before. It chilled her to think how easily a life might be taken. Had these people truly made this ultimate sacrifice just to try and collect a bounty? Viktor's mercenaries made similar sacrifices for money. Most of them must not believe they would be killed, but either way, Ankari found this willingness to fling oneself into battle for such trite rewards hard to understand.

Without talking, she and Lauren moved the bodies into the bay and sat down behind the cockpit. Jamie tapped a button, and the shuttle door closed, sealing them into the gray oblong can. There were seats for sixteen people and the pilot, but it still felt claustrophobic. Unlike the cargo haulers she was used to, these were lean, aerodynamic vehicles intended solely for moving troops.

"I'd be worried that she has the technical manual open on the console beside her," Lauren murmured, "but she flew us most of the way to the ruins like that."

"I'm sure she'll have this mastered in no time," Ankari said.

"They're going to know on the bridge that we're here as soon as I depressurize the shuttle bay," Jamie said. "Are we—"

The white lighting beyond the view screen dimmed, and red lights flashed. A series of warning bleats went off. Clinks and clanks came from beneath the shuttle, something securing them so they wouldn't be blown out as soon as the bay doors opened? Or were they already being released into space?

"Er, ready?" Jamie finished.

Ankari snapped her harness. "Ready."

"Me too," Lauren said.

A couple more clunks sounded underneath them, and the craft lifted. The view on the screen switched from what was visible out the front to what was visible out the back. The departure process must have been auto-mated, because Jamie wasn't touching anything.

"Bridge to shuttle bay," a male voice growled over the comm, "you don't have permission to depart."

"What do we say?" Jamie whispered.

Ankari was tempted to respond with something sarcastic, but the bridge might have a way to stop them and bring them back inside. They had equipped their science freighter with tractor-beam technology for col-lecting samples; a mercenary ship might have it too. For collecting wayward shuttles.

"My vote is for nothing," Lauren said.

"Let's go with that for now," Ankari said. They had already left the shuttle bay and were maneuvering away from the ship. Jamie still hadn't had to do anything and was staring down at the console with a perplexed expression.

"Shuttle One," a calmer voice said, though it didn't have any less steel in it, "this is Commander Garland. Identify yourself or prepare to be fired upon."

"They're not going to fire on their own shuttle, are they?" Jamie whispered.

A warning light and alarming beep came from the console.

"What's that?" Lauren asked.

"Either the ship is powering their weapons, or the shuttle stores are out of egg logs," Jamie said.

Ankari pushed her hands through her hair. "Maybe we can buy time enough to get out of their range." Good idea, but how? "Uhm."

"Shuttle One, this is your last warning. Return to the shuttle bay now or—"

A blast of red light shot past a porthole. Ankari stared at the view screen, certain the shot was meant for them, but it skimmed past their nose without striking the shuttle.

"That hit the ship," Jamie said, frowning at a display. "And it came from another ship."

"Them again?" Garland asked someone—his voice was distant now, as if he had turned from the comm. "Enough with the warning shots. Blow them out of the sky before they can get back into those clouds. And—" The rest of his words were lost, with Garland or someone else cutting off the comm.

"I'm not entirely sure what's happening," Ankari said, "but we have to take advantage of the confusion. Get us down to Sturm, Jamie."

"I am. Actually I'm *not*, but we're going anyway." Jamie waved toward the view screen, which had changed as they rotated around, thrusters igniting to take the craft away from the *Albatross*. A glimpse of a black disk-shaped ship occupied the corner for a moment, then it weaved away, avoiding laser fire. The big round moon came into view next, its dense verdant green visible, even though they were heading toward the dark side of it. An angry band of reddish gray clouds smothered the lower half of the landmass the shuttle was pointed toward.

"That's all the wild side, I think," Ankari said, punching up Sturm on the tablet. "Mostly loggers, miners, and a few outposts over there. That's probably where those raiders are hiding out and where the captain and his people went. I'd much rather disappear into a city than a jungle. Anchortown is...that way." She pointed toward the horizon where a halo of sunlight promised dawn.

"I'm sure it is," Jamie said, "but I don't have any control of the shuttle."

"What?" Lauren asked.

"I haven't since I shut the door. Everything's been automatic. At first, I thought it was part of the mercenaries' automatic launch sequence, but something else must be going on."

Ankari stared at the ominous mass of storm clouds they were heading toward. As they drew closer, white spots flashed in them—lightning.

"I think I'm beginning to see why that other ship was firing," Lauren said. "They wanted us to get away, because they knew we were going... wherever they want us to go."

Ankari sank back in her chair. Lauren was right. If those men who had come to the brig had intended to kidnap her and the others, they must have planned to leave in the same shuttle they had come up in. So, Ankari had led her people into a trap. Why wouldn't the shuttle be flying toward the other ship, though? The ship that was apparently harrying the *Albatross*?

Even as the thoughts raced through her head, something streaked past to the shuttle's right. With thrusters firing orange, the disk-shaped ship blasted down into the moon's atmosphere. It was hard to tell if it had been damaged or if it was simply fleeing now that its task was done.

Maybe the plan for the bounty hunters, or whoever was after Ankari's team, was to meet up on the moon below. To meet up exactly where the shuttle had been programmed to land. Ugh.

"We walked into a trap, didn't we?" Jamie asked.

"If so, it should just be a variation of the same trap we were already in," Ankari said. "Except this time, we have weapons. Maybe we can shoot our way out, surprise the bounty hunters. They'll be expecting us to show up in handcuffs and with the rest of their allies, not on our own."

"Maybe we can *shoot* our way out?" Lauren raised her eyebrows, reminding Ankari exactly how combat-ready most of her team was. She couldn't claim to be an expert marksman, either.

"Captain Viktor was actually hospitable, for a captor," Jamie said. "What if our new captors aren't?"

"They have to keep us alive if they want the bounty," Lauren said.

"That doesn't mean much."

"Can we stop giving up and throwing ourselves to the ground in front of these people before we've met them?" Ankari asked. "Jamie, see if you can figure out how to disable that autopilot. If we can gain control of the shuttle, we're free women."

"All right." Jamie hunted around the console, then opened a panel underneath it and peered inside.

Ankari crouched to help her look, though she had no idea what she was looking for. It was better than watching the moon approach below them, that storm and whatever fate awaited them getting closer and closer.

A shudder ran through the shuttle, and she pitched to the grated floor, her back thudding against a chair.

"Is that Garland?" Lauren asked. "Did he shoot?"

"I think it's the storm," Ankari said. They had descended into the clouds, and the flashes of electricity they had seen from above were all around them now. Great branches of white light streaked across the view screen. Wind railed at them, and the craft shuddered and heaved.

"Is that better or worse?" Lauren hadn't left her chair. She was strapped in—wisely so—her fingers like claws as she gripped the armrests.

All sense of gravity or a controlled entry disappeared, and the ship plummeted straight down. Ankari was thrown across the small cabin, striking a wall and more chairs, pain erupting in her hip as it slammed against something hard. She tumbled onto the floor and wrapped her arms and legs around the bottom of a seat. Terror welled in her throat, along with the certainty that they were going to die. This hadn't been what she had meant when she said they would be free women.

Then the shuttle caught itself, correcting the fall with a lurch that would have heaved Ankari up to the ceiling if she hadn't been holding on so tightly. As it was, something popped in her shoulder. She barely noticed.

The craft leveled out and seemed to be flying mostly horizontal again, but still on a downward course. Always downward and toward its inevitable fate. They were under the clouds now, but the wind continued to beat at the craft. The engines ground and whined, struggling to keep them in the air. Maybe it was Ankari's imagination, but they definitely didn't sound as hale as they had in space.

"Is everyone all right?" she croaked. She released her chair bottom, but only so she could return to her seat and strap herself in. Lauren hadn't moved, but her face was whiter than a skeleton. Jamie pulled herself out from under the console—she must have wedged herself in there somehow.

"Not really," Jamie croaked, "but I did find this." She lifted out a small black rectangle with wires sticking out of it. It looked more like something that might be jury-rigged from junk found in a spare parts bin rather than a sophisticated piece of technology. Jamie dropped it and climbed into the pilot's seat, strapping herself in. "Let me see if…" Her fingers pressed buttons and threw switches. She glanced toward where she had kept the tablet, but it had flown off to who knew where.

"Any luck?" Ankari asked. The roiling storm clouds made the night darker than pitch, but the vague outline of a mountain range was visible ahead, along with the undulating jungle below, trees and leaves waving under the harsh wind. She tried to decide whether it would be worse to crash into trees or into the side of a mountain…The trees might cradle them and keep them from being smashed into the ground. The mountains appeared less yielding, but the shuttle was determined to head toward them.

"I think I have control back," Jamie said, "but it's not doing much good. We took some damage and—"

The shuttle lurched, as if they were a ground vehicle and had driven over a huge speed bump. Ankari would have been thrown to the deck again if she hadn't been strapped in. "We're a little close to the trees, I think."

"There's no place to land." Jamie's strained voice didn't fill Ankari with hope. "We're going to crash."

Another bump came from below. Branches scraped against the hull, and rain pelted the top of the craft. A bolt of lightning struck a tree right ahead of them, and the sky flashed a brilliant white for a moment, revealing the craggy silhouette of a black mountain rising from the jungle. They were closer to the range than Ankari had realized. She gripped the armrests. There was little else she could do, except pray the shuttle had devices built in to protect its crew in a crash landing.

After another lurch, something shorted out, sparks flying from the open panel beneath the console. An acrid smoke flowed into the air. The view screen snapped out, and darkness descended on the cabin.

———

Rain fell from the broad plant leaves in waterfalls. Viktor was already drenched, so it hardly mattered, but the worsening visibility was making it harder to follow the trail. The mud was turning to a river of dirt, the prints obscured, but Tick led the way without hesitation.

"You'd think those two men would have taken shelter at some point and that we'd catch them," Sergeant Hazel yelled, her voice at the top of its range so she could be heard above the heavy rainfall.

Viktor merely shook his head, not in the mood to yell. His clothing was sticking to his body beneath his armor, and his balls were swimming in a pond. He was in the mood to shoot people.

"There's a rise ahead," Tick called back. "We can get a look around, get our bearings."

The trail they were following was a meandering mess, but Viktor's Eytect promised they were still going in the direction of the mountains. Still, given the unreliableness of his equipment tonight, he wouldn't mind a look at the landscape. He found it hard to believe men would have walked ten miles through the jungle to ambush that shuttlecraft. They had to have a closer camp. Striker hadn't been on the ground for that long before he had called up, reporting the shuttle missing.

Tick led the way to a basalt outcropping sticking up out of the trees. It was mossy with a few plants managing to find purchase, but the greenery faded halfway up. Lightning streaked across the sky, making Viktor rethink their climb to higher ground, but he continued up nonetheless, passing Tick along the way. At the top, the jungle stretched in all directions, and he grimaced, not seeing much in the way of clearings or potential spots for camps, nothing large enough that provided a break in the canopy anyway.

The wind gusted so hard, it threatened to knock him off the rock. He spread his legs, bracing himself, and squinted through the rain toward the mountains. Not much there. He couldn't see the lights he had picked out on the way down earlier.

The wind shifted directions, bringing the sounds of artillery weapons firing in the distance. His men attacking. It must be, though they hadn't brought any big weapons, preferring swift infiltrations to drawn-out sieges.

"How much farther should we follow the tracks, sir?" Hazel had heard the weapons, too, and she doubtlessly wanted to be with the rest of the company, the same as Viktor did.

"What do you think, Tick? How much longer can you track in this?"

"I can track forever, Cap'n. You know that."

Viktor frowned down at him, wanting a more serious answer. The rivers of rainwater flowing down the animal paths weren't going to leave the tracks visible indefinitely.

Tick chewed thoughtfully on his wad of gum before shrugging and answering. "I can keep on it a while longer. Lots of broken branches, not just footprints. Someone hacked through with a machete in spots."

"Sir, look." Hazel pointed past Viktor's shoulder at the same time as lightning flashed through the sky, one bolt striking a tree not far away.

She wasn't pointing at the lightning, but at what was flying through it. A sleek black shuttlecraft, its hull gleaming with moisture as it streaked through the sky like a bullet. Its running lights were out, and it skipped off the treetops, the pilot struggling to maintain altitude. He had to be looking for a place to land. But he *who?* Who was flying the shuttle now?

"That the same one that's missing?" Tick yelled as the wind picked up again.

"Yes." Viktor had caught the nomenclature on the side during the lightning strike, not that he had expected any of the other three shuttles to randomly fly overhead. Not when two of the pilots were busy doing math problems with each other. But if this shuttle had been up at the ship, what was it doing back down here? He wished his conversation with Garland hadn't been so garbled.

Viktor stood on his tiptoes, straining to keep track of the craft. It was heading toward the mountains. First the tracks and now the shuttle. *Some*one had a base over there. Maybe that temple wasn't full of monks after all.

"He's not going to make it," Tick said.

Viktor shook his head, annoyed by the whole night and annoyed that he was about to lose a perfectly good shuttle.

He'd no more than had the thought when the craft slammed into an ancient tree rising higher than the surrounding canopy. It caromed off like a marble smacking into a wall, then dropped, disappearing into the jungle.

"Let's go." Viktor scrambled down the rock hill.

The shuttle was only a couple of miles away, but if the terrain between here and there was anything like the terrain they had been tramping over thus far, they wouldn't be able to take a direct route.

Viktor jumped the last six feet, spattering mud in all directions as he landed. A screech emanated from the trees, making him pause. Answering cries came from the jungle. They made the hair on the back of his neck rise as some primordial warning system went off in his mind. Danger. An ancient danger. He'd heard the sound before and recognized it. Those raptors Tick had been talking about. A pack of them. He had assumed they would be bedded down for the storm, but the shuttle crash must have roused them. Predators always knew to take advantage of wounded prey.

More bloodcurdling screeches came, one from nearby. Something rustled in the leaves. Viktor's rifle, strapped across his chest, was always close at hand, and his finger found the trigger in the darkness. He flipped the night scope to illumination.

By the thrashing of branches, he tracked the creature's movement. It wasn't heading toward them, but in the direction of the crash. Maybe the raptors could smell blood even two miles away.

"They better keep that shuttle door closed," Tick said, squishing into the mud next to Viktor. "The critters sound hungry."

Nobody pointed out that the three of them didn't *have* a shuttle door to close.

"Eyes open," Viktor said, though Tick and Hazel were experienced and hardly needed the warning. He led the way into the jungle, not worrying about the tracks now. The screeches of those raptors would tell him where they needed to go.

CHAPTER EIGHT

Ankari remained conscious for this, her second crash of the week. Her head slammed into the back of her seat and the harness dug into her shoulders, chest, and legs. Maybe consciousness was overrated. It was utterly dark in the shuttle, and all she knew was that they were dangling in the air—in the trees probably—the nose pointed down. She knew that because only her harness was keeping her from dropping out of her seat. With the power and view screen still out, she couldn't tell if they were three feet above the ground or three hundred. Rain pummeled the hull with such power that it sounded like they had landed under a waterfall.

An unearthly screech came from somewhere below them. The wind? Some animal? Ankari wished she had been able to finish reading about Sturm. For now, getting out of this shuttle had to be the primary concern, especially if there were people out there who had been waiting for it to land.

"Lauren? Jamie? Are you alive?"

A groan came from below her, toward the nose of the craft.

"I'll take that for a yes," Ankari said. "For at least one of you. Jamie?" She was the one who should have been in the cockpit.

"Yeah." Jamie groaned again.

"Lauren?"

"How can you be so calm?" Lauren demanded, her voice somewhere between a rasp and a soft screech. She was probably afraid someone—or something—would hear them if they yelled. That was a possibility.

"I trembled, cried, and lost control of my bladder while we were crashing," Ankari said. "I'm past that now." Not exactly true, but she was willing to tamp down desires to scream frantic curses if there was a chance staying calm would get them out of here before anyone with guns found them.

"Really?" Jamie sounded less panicky than Lauren. Good.

"More or less." Ankari didn't think she had peed on herself, but only because things had happened to quickly for her to succumb to total and utter fear. "I'm going to unstrap myself, try to find our packs—" not to mention the pistol that she had dropped a few eons ago, "—and see about opening that door. It doesn't look like we're getting emergency power, so I'm hoping there's a manual override."

"There is," Jamie said. "I saw it when we came in."

"Good."

"We're hanging," Lauren said. "Jostling things around might not be a good idea."

Another screech came from outside.

"Staying here sounds like an even worse idea," Ankari said.

"If we stay in here, whatever's making those noises won't be able to get to us."

"Maybe, but the bounty hunters or whoever planned all of this will. They probably saw us crash."

Lauren grumbled but didn't object further.

"Once I get the door open and we can see around, we can judge things better." Ankari's feet fell toward the nose as soon as she released the leg half of the harness. This was going to be a challenge. How was she supposed to climb up to the door at the back of the shuttle when they were dangling nose first above the ground? She would worry about collecting their gear from the bottom—nose—first.

She unfastened the rest of her harness, though she didn't want to let go until she had something to stand on. She probed in the darkness with her foot and tapped something.

"That's my head," Jamie said.

"Oh. Am I close to the—" The cracking of wood came from outside, and the shuttle plummeted. It crashed to a stop again almost as soon as it started, but that ten-foot drop and lurch was enough to send Ankari's heart into her throat. "I might pee myself yet," she whispered.

"Not when you're above me, please." Jamie's humor sound strained, but at least she was trying.

Ankari brushed the console with her foot, found a place to stand, and let go of her harness. She wobbled but crouched and caught her balance. She patted around, located one pack and—yes, the laser pistol. One of them at least. "You two still have your weapons?"

"I stuck mine in my jacket." Clothing rustled, and Jamie added, "Still there."

"I don't know where mine is. I wasn't exactly thinking about it when we were crashing out of space and into the treetops." Lauren gulped, clearly trying to control herself, but that frantic edge to her voice worried Ankari.

Best to get out of here. Lauren would calm down once they were standing on solid land.

Another screech sounded. Then again…

Ankari tugged a pack over her shoulders, found another one, and pushed it toward Jamie. She found the third and, having no idea whose was whose, strapped it over her chest. Climbing with all of that wasn't realistic, but she couldn't abandon their research without trying. It was all they had left of the company and their mission.

Another branch snapped. Ankari grabbed Jamie's chair, trying to brace herself this time. The shuttle tottered and tipped but didn't fall straight down. The tail lurched sideways, smacking against something—the trunk of a tree? The jolt nearly shook Ankari free from the chair, and she lost the pistol again. She wished they would finish crashing already. Unless they were dangling over a chasm, in which case, this was better than plummeting to their deaths.

The shuttle caught on something again. Its new position was nearly horizontal, and Ankari took advantage. She groped around and found the pistol, this time stuffing it into her jumpsuit, and clawed her way over chairs—the aisle was somewhere on the side of the shuttle at the moment—to reach the door. She patted all around it, trying to find an emergency release latch. If she knew for sure she had her own pack, she would be tempted to root around for the flashlight, but it was probably down at the bottom anyway.

"It's up top and to the right." Thumps and curses came from behind her. Jamie was making her way toward Ankari. "Or at least that's where it is when the shuttle is facing the right direction."

Ankari located it and tugged, trying to figure out how it opened. She fell over as the latch released abruptly. "Found it," she said, catching herself against the wall. Or maybe that was the floor.

The sucking hiss of a seal being broken accompanied a draft of humid air thick with the scent of vegetation. The door opened outward with a clank. Normally it would land on the ground, so someone could walk down it, like a gangplank, but in the wet dimness outside, the ground wasn't visible. The door simply extended out into the air, like a *plank* rather than a gangplank. They could walk off into nothingness…

The shriek they had heard earlier rose above the wind and rain once again. It sounded much louder without the hull to block the noise. Much closer.

"What's making that noise?" Jamie asked.

Ankari inched out on the door to peer over the side. Vines, leaves, and branches crisscrossed beneath the shuttle, and she couldn't see much of the ground or tell how far down it was. Strange chirps and rustles came from somewhere below them. An answering screech came from a different direction than the first.

"I don't know, but there are a bunch of them," Ankari said. "Lauren, are you ready to go? I don't think staying here is a good idea." She looked outward as well as down, wondering how close to those mountains they were and if anything there would offer a safe haven. Or would it be full of bounty hunters?

"I don't think going out *there* is a good idea," Lauren said. It didn't sound like she had left her chair, or even unfastened her harness.

"She may be right," Jamie said. "We could stay here until dawn. Until the storm passes. I can't imagine bounty hunters would be out in this anyway."

"With two hundred thousand aurums waiting to be plucked from the sky?" Ankari squinted into the gloom. She thought she had seen a light out there somewhere. Maybe they were close to an outpost. But no matter how she leaned and turned her head, she couldn't spot it again.

"They'll probably figure we'll be here in the morning."

A screech sounded, and foliage rattled in the tree nearest to them. Ankari leaned back inside. The noise had come from lower than the shuttle, but not as low as the ground. Could the creatures making all that noise climb? Not a comforting thought.

"Aren't the days and nights here long, though?" Ankari thought she remembered that factoid about Sturm. "Something like four Novus Earth days for a complete revolution?"

"I don't know. I don't suppose you have that tablet? We could look up the world and what's making those noises."

"I haven't seen it since it went flying off your console."

Light glinted in the distance again.

Ankari jerked her head in that direction. "Did you see that?"

"See what?" Jamie asked.

Ankari pointed toward the ground and out a ways. A hundred meters? She wasn't sure. There was so much foliage that she couldn't imagine any of them could see far. But the light came into view again. No, that was another one.

"There are at least two lights," Ankari said.

"I see them now," Jamie said. "They look like flashlights. Maybe they'll scare the animals away, so we can get out."

A rattling of leaves to the left was their only warning before a shadow leaped out of the darkness. Ankari grabbed Jamie's arm and jumped back, jerking the pistol up with her free hand. She had no idea what was attacking, but she didn't hesitate to fire.

A red laser beam sprang from the pistol, but it cut through empty air. The creature twisted, landing on the open door, the crimson streak illuminating it for an instant. A meter high and two meters long, the feathered animal looked like a cross between a bird and a reptile with a big blunt head and rows of razor-sharp teeth.

Ankari fired again, but it seemed to anticipate her action, leaping up to evade the shot. It landed, then lunged into the shuttle. Ankari stumbled back, but not fast enough. Something sharp raked her arm. Claws? Fangs? She couldn't tell, but it hurt.

The creature lunged toward Jamie next, and she hollered in pain. Ankari couldn't fire again, lest she hit her friend. She kicked out, trying to strike a moving shadow. She caught something, but it was more solid than it looked, heavier than a bird. The blow barely moved it. Something bit into her shin, and she cried out, scurrying back and looking for cover. In the dark, she slammed against a chair instead.

For a moment, the creature's strange silhouette was visible against the rainy night outside the door. Its head darted in, fangs striking for Jamie, who'd turned her backpack toward it as a shield. Ankari wrapped both hands around the pistol grip and took a long second to aim this time.

She squeezed the trigger, holding it down for an extended blast. She struck the creature full in the side. It staggered back, its screech turning into a squeal of pain. It spun toward her, but she kept firing until it crumpled to the floor.

Before Ankari could blow out a relieved breath, the leaves shook, and two more of the creatures leaped out of the trees and onto the shuttle door.

"Find the other guns," Ankari ordered, though she didn't know if Jamie was fit to fight or if Lauren had taken off her harness yet. "I need help."

"—hear something," came a voice from the jungle floor. "...crashed over there. *Up* there."

Whoever the speaker was, Ankari didn't recognize him.

The creatures spun toward her, and she had something more pressing to worry about. She flexed her finger to shoot the closest one, but the shuttle tilted in that direction. Too much weight on the door? Ankari clutched at the wall, searching for a handhold. The shuttle kept tipping, slowly, groaning as it went. Branches cracked outside, and leaves rained down along with the water.

The creatures cried out in their high-pitched shrieks, and their claws scrabbled on the metal. One leaped off the door, choosing the nearest tree instead. Ankari shot the other. It was a glancing blow off the thing's tail, but the creature squawked and leaped away.

The floor continued to tilt, and Ankari lost her footing. She might have slid right outside, but someone caught her arm.

"You can't leave," Jamie whispered. "You're the only one with a gun."

"I thought yours was in your shirt." Ankari braced her foot on the side of the door to keep herself from falling out. The craft wobbled and groaned, but stabilized again, albeit with a thirty-degree tilt to the floor now. Maybe that would keep the fanged birds out.

"It was. I tried to get it out, and that winged freak slapped it out of my hand. I'm bleeding from a dozen spots. Can you take me home now?"

Beams of light streaked up from the jungle floor, probing the foliage. Searching.

"I don't think so," Ankari murmured. "Lauren? We've got to get out of here, or we're going to be captured."

"I'd rather be captured by humans than eaten by those dinosaurs," Lauren said.

"Dinosaurs? Is that what they are?" Ankari asked.

"Not exactly, but they were similar enough to the velociraptors from Old Earth that someone called them that. I remember reading about them once. In a tourism brochure." Her voice was squeaky with disbelief, or maybe that same panic that had been wrapped around her since they crashed.

"I guess it's better to be mauled by a velociraptor than a bird," Jamie whispered.

Twigs snapped outside. The lights were getting closer. At least six beams. Maybe eight. There was a whole squad of people striding up to the ground beneath the shuttle. Laser rifles fired down there, and the screeches of the creatures intensified. They sounded more angry than afraid.

"Stay or go?" Jamie whispered.

Lauren had a point, and Ankari hesitated. Even if these people were bounty hunters, as long as the team was wanted alive, they shouldn't be in danger of being killed. But if they wandered out into the jungle, they would have to deal with those raptors and whatever other predators made this side of the moon their home.

Still...

"I can't stand here and let them capture me," Ankari said. "I've got a gun and food in my pack. I want to take my chances with the jungle."

"I'll come," Jamie said.

"Lauren?" Ankari could leave her, but the business was nothing without their microbiologist, and she hated the idea of splitting up anyway. Surely they were stronger together.

More shots fired below. Someone yelled, a yell that switched to a bellow of pain in the middle.

"Fine," Lauren growled, bumping and cursing as she picked her way past the chairs. "You two are crazy though. I want you to know that."

"Maybe I'll give you a bigger portion of the company if we survive," Ankari whispered with a smile. "We're going to have to climb down, but if we can use the trees, walking along the branches for a while first, they won't be able to see us from below."

"I'm not a squirrel," Lauren said.

"At least you're not injured," Jamie said.

"Come on, troops." They would squabble all day without moving if Ankari didn't prod them along.

She eased closer to the door. The tree they were perched in groaned. Ankari looked around the corner and found a branch that appeared sturdy enough to accept her weight. She stepped out on it and tried to find something to grip with her hand. There was a vine. When she touched it, it moved. A snake. It hissed with displeasure. She jerked her hand back, afraid it was something else that wanted to kill her. The snake merely curled up out of sight and slithered away.

"Going this way," Jamie said from the other side of the door. She must have found a more promising perch, because she soon disappeared into the darkness.

The rifle fire had stopped below. Afraid the men wouldn't be distracted anymore, Ankari hurried along her branch, grasping at smaller ones for support, until she reached a thick trunk covered in ivy or whatever creeping foliage was native to the moon.

"Lauren?" she whispered. Rain was still smacking the leaves, but the wind had dropped off, and she worried about her voice carrying. "There's room this way."

Two flashlight beams swung upward, finding the shuttle. Ankari squeezed around the trunk of the tree, putting it between her and the searchers below. She found a new branch to stand on and sank low, trying to stay hidden by the foliage but at the same time wanting a view of the people on the ground.

Their flashlights didn't do a lot to illuminate their faces, especially with the beams directed toward the treetops, but she grew more certain that they weren't men from Viktor's ship. If they had been, she might have given up and gone down, choosing to fight another day in exchange for a way out of the jungle. But these men, clad all in black, reminded her more of the troops that had invaded the *Albatross*.

More flashlight beams combined, brightening the hull of the ship. "Well, now, there's a pretty girl. Looks like you had a rough landing." Neither the voice, nor the snickers that followed it, sounded friendly.

Someone else spoke, his voice utterly hard and cold. "Where are the men who were with you, woman?"

"You might as well come down," someone else said. "It's not like your shuttle is going anywhere." More snickers.

"You want me?" Lauren asked. "Come up and get me."

"If I climb all the way up there, I'll want a reward from you."

Lauren didn't say anything. She gave a long look in the direction Jamie had gone, then disappeared back into the shuttle.

"Go get her," the man with the hardest voice ordered. "And keep your eyes open. There's supposed to be two others too. Not to mention the rest of our shuttle team."

Ankari fingered her pistol, wondering how many would climb up. If all of them did, she might be able to pick them off, but if she started shooting, they would shoot back, and she didn't know how much protection this tree would offer her. She leaned her forehead against the wet leaves. "What do I do?" she whispered.

Only two men started up a tree. The others waited on the ground, keeping their lights on the shuttle and the nearby foliage. Ankari tried to make herself smaller in her spot. If she and Jamie got away, maybe they could sneak in at a better time and rescue Lauren. For now, Ankari dared not stay so close to the shuttle, not if she didn't want to be spotted. Careful not to make a sound, she eased along a mossy branch, trying to reach the next tree.

Leaves rattled as one of the climbing men drew closer. Ankari made it to another trunk and stepped behind it. Her heel slipped off, and she had to grab for a branch. Leaves shook right beside her, and a twig snapped. She winced, looking back.

The climber paused and stared in her direction. She froze, hoping the darkness and the foliage hid her. She wasn't silhouetted by flashlight beams the way he was...

She rubbed the trigger of her pistol again. She could shoot him, right there, when he was looking in her direction, but what then? There were eight or ten more people on the ground, and, like Lauren had said, she was no squirrel that could scamper off into the canopy without ever touching the earth.

The man continued his climb, turning his back on her, and reached the shuttle. He stepped onto the open door, lunging for the side since it was still tilted so drastically. Between one blink and the next, some final branch broke and the shuttle fell out of the trees. Ankari couldn't stop herself from gasping and stretching out a hand, as if she could halt its fall. The man yelled. Lauren yelled. And then the shuttle smashed to the ground.

CHAPTER NINE

A human scream pierced the dark jungle, a different pitch than that of the raptor screeches that had been assaulting Viktor's ears. This was no animal; it was a woman. Ankari? Could she have ended up down here? Kidnapped from the ship and stolen away in that shuttle? He fumed at the notion that Bravo squad hadn't been enough to keep intruders from boarding the ship and kidnapping people, and he slashed harder with the long serrated knife he was using on the foliage. He needed a damned machete—or a herd of ravenous goats.

Excited screeches erupted up ahead. If he were in a cleared field, Viktor could have seen the raptors and whatever they were attacking—the shuttle crew, he feared—but here, he couldn't see more than five meters in any direction. He, Tick, and Hazel hadn't even seen any of the noisy predators, though they had been listening to the bloodthirsty cries as they cut their way through dense foliage. The animal trail—and the tracks—they had been following before had veered off in another direction, so they had to slash through vines, clamber over massive logs, and push through ferns that towered over their heads.

A laser weapon fired, several of them, and Viktor halted, lifting his knife in the air to stop the others. "I'll go straight in, Tick you take left; Hazel, right. We're getting our shuttle back and our prisoners, if they have them."

It irked him that he didn't know who *they* were. Some team Goshawk had put together? Someone else? He'd tried to contact the ship again, but hadn't been able to get a working link. He was beginning to think it might have less to do with the storm and more to do with another ship jamming communications. He had checked in with the rest of his team down on the moon, at least. They had been busy with the fighting but had reported that they could handle the situation without him.

"It sounds like there are more of them than there are of us," Hazel said.

Viktor gave her a flat so-what look.

"Just pointing it out," she said.

"We can take them," Tick said with a wink. "But like usual, I'll let the cap'n run in and macerate the meat up a bit before I jump into the fray."

Hazel grunted, then cut away from them, using her own knife to slash at the foliage. Tick disappeared to the left. Viktor continued on, straight toward the commotion. Though the wind might drown out the sound of vines and branches being cut, he slowed down anyway, just enough to be certain he could push through without making much noise.

A great crash came from a hundred meters ahead, like a building falling over, or maybe a tree slamming to the earth. Cries of pain, both human and animal, followed on the heels of the noise.

The first person came into view, standing in mud and trampled vegetation, his back to Viktor. Wearing all black armor, he wasn't anyone familiar. A rifle in his hands was aimed toward someone crawling out of...

Cold fire raced through Viktor's veins. That was his shuttle and one of his prisoners. Both were damaged and caked with the mud, an absolute mess. Someone grabbed the girl—it was the biologist, Keys—and hoisted her to her feet.

Viktor ought to wait for Tick and Hazel, give them time to circle in from the left and right, but his rage, the *audacity* of these people, made him want to charge straight in. He kept his head about him enough to stalk closer in silence, knowing he should assess the odds before announcing his presence with a barrage of laser fire. There were more than ten men out there, all armed, and they were staggered, some half-hidden by the snarls of undergrowth. He might not have accounted for everyone yet.

His eye on the closest man, Viktor dipped into the pouch of throwing knives he wore on his belt. Without lowering his rifle, he hurled the weapon left-handed. It flew through the air and found the bare flesh between the man's helmet and his armor, sinking into the back of his neck, severing vertebrae. He crumpled to the mud without a sound. He was on the outskirts of the group, and nobody seemed to notice. A laser-scorched raptor laid near him, one of several creatures on the ground, most unmoving, a few twitching as they died.

"What'd you do with our men, girl?" her captor growled. Blood dripped from her temples, and her jumpsuit was torn.

Where was Ankari? And the young engineer? Viktor couldn't tell if there were more people in the shuttle. The door had been half torn off and, judging by the logs and splinters of wood everywhere, the craft had hit every branch on the way to the ground.

"And where are your friends? We need all of you for Felgard's bounty."

Keys looked too dazed to answer, but the man didn't care. He growled, drew back his arm, and slammed the back of his hand into the side of her face. She flew away from him, landing in the mud.

Viktor choked down the urge to charge in recklessly again, but he wasn't going to dawdle, that was for damned sure. He crept forward, another knife in his hand. He almost threw it at the man hurling the woman around, but he was in the center, and everyone would see it land. He chose another man on the outskirts, targeting the side of his neck.

"Don't ugly 'em up too much, boss," one of the bounty hunters said. "You said we could have our fun with 'em before dropping them off."

"Better find the others then," someone else said with a laugh. "Gets a bit crowded with just one girl."

A frustrated screech came from the jungle, a raptor annoyed it had been denied its prey.

"Aw, shut up," one of the men yelled and fired into the trees.

Taking advantage of their distraction, Viktor threw his third knife. The black-painted blade arrowed across the clearing without anyone glimpsing its passing, and it slammed into the man's neck. This thug, too, fell without a sound.

Viktor moved parallel to the group, trying to find another man on the outskirts that he might pick off while he waited for signs that Hazel and Tick were nearby. He kept the big wet fronds and leaves between him and the enemy, careful not to stir the foliage.

"Watch where you're firing," someone growled from the trees behind the shuttle. "Some of us are out here working. Finding prizes."

Two new men in black squished through the mud, one of them holding another woman in front of him, shoving her so that she would have stumbled if he weren't gripping her. That was the engineer, Flipkens, her pale blonde hair a snarled mess. Blood stained her torn clothes in several spots, and her eyes bulged with fear as she was forced to join the cluster of men.

Viktor picked out his fourth target, a grizzled brute who had noticed he'd lost sight of one of his comrades, the first person Viktor had downed. He was walking in that direction.

"Nice," someone purred. "She's prettier than the other." The big man strode forward to paw at Flipkens's hair, then run his hand down her chest. "We'll have us some good fun before dropping 'em off."

The terror in the girl's eyes and the leers on the faces of the men were too much. Anger overrode wisdom, and instead of hurling his weapon at his chosen target, Viktor flung the blade at the man pawing Flipkens. The knife struck true, landing in the bounty hunter's eye. Nobody failed to see this attack, and the men spun in his direction, raising their rifles.

Viktor was already on the move. Their lasers cut through nothing but leaves. Using a tree for cover, he fired into the camp, short accurate shots rather than indiscriminate blasts at anything that moved. Though anger might fuel his body, sending barely restrained energy coursing through his muscles, he kept his mind calm and analytical, as he'd been trained to do. He fired, ducked and moved, found a tree or boulder for cover, then fired again. The bounty hunters hustled for the protection of the jungle. Viktor had no problem shooting them in the back, so long as they weren't near the women. Fortunately, Keys and Flipkens had been smart enough to fling themselves on the ground once the firefight started.

"He's over there," someone yelled. "Get behind him, go."

Viktor shot two more men before the rest found cover behind the trees. He could hear them tramping through the brush, trying to find a path to him. He let his rifle fall about his chest on its harness and yanked out daggers. He could have waited for the men to approach him, but he went on the hunt himself. He picked his route more carefully, not making a sound as he chose logs over mud and took to the trees to keep him from squishing noisily on the damp ground.

A bounty hunter leading with his rifle crept close below him. Viktor dropped down behind the figure, yanking his head back as he dropped and slicing a knife across the man's throat. That had been the one who had struck Keys. Good.

He cut down three more bounty hunters without them ever knowing he was there. He grabbed a fourth man, ready to take him down, too, but caught a whiff of strawberry gum at the last moment. Tick was whirling toward him, rifle in hand, but Viktor caught the weapon.

"It's me," he breathed. "Fall in."

Without a word, Tick followed him, moving just as soundlessly in the jungle. They killed a trio of men hunting together, then a pained cry came from the clearing.

"Mandrake, I know that's you out there," someone growled. "You kill any more of my men, and I'll make sure you don't get that bounty, either."

Viktor and Tick slipped through the brush, finding the trampled ground around the shuttle again. A burly man with a short gray beard stood with his back against the side of the craft and Flipkens pulled to his chest, a dagger to her throat.

"That's Captain Jarlboro," Tick whispered.

Viktor recognized him too. Not Goshawk after all. Another mercenary captain. How many people were after these women?

"Meet up with Hazel," Viktor whispered. "Clear out the rest of the woods. I'll deal with him."

The Keys woman was on the ground, inching toward a fallen merc. Inching toward the laser rifle that had fallen beside him, rather. Good.

"I'm not screwing around, Mandrake." Jarlboro tightened the blade against Flipkens's neck, and she gasped with pain. "Get out here. You want to make a deal, I'm listening, but you touch any more of my men, and I'm—"

A shot fired from the captain's side, from the trees behind the shuttle. It slammed into his helmet, and he staggered to the left, but his hand tightened on the dagger. Knowing that shot hadn't done serious damage, not through the helmet, Viktor charged. He sprinted the intervening ten meters, launched himself off a log, and rammed into the other captain, tearing the girl away before Jarlboro could cut into her. The merc tried to turn the dagger on him, but Viktor twisted his torso away and slammed his own blade into the man's gut. The fine mesh armor kept the point from piercing, but Jarlboro still grunted at the power of the blow, his shoulders jerking forward. Viktor shoved his head back, exposed his throat, and sliced through the jugular. Blood sprayed him, and he shoved the man to the side.

"I don't make deals," he told the dying man.

As he spoke, he was already turning to face the clearing again, to check for more danger while the shuttle protected his back. The sounds of fighting came from the trees, and he almost started for it, but he remembered the shot that had distracted Jarlboro. He looked that way, expecting Sergeant Hazel to step out of the shadows, but it was Ankari who walked hesitantly toward him, a laser pistol clenched in her grip, her face ashen but determined.

For an instant, something between shame and uncertainty rushed into his chest, an unexpected feeling, a wish that she hadn't seen him killing people and that he wasn't standing over a body with blood painting his armor.

Viktor pushed the feeling away and lifted a hand toward her. "Come check on your friends while we deal with the others." Please. He should have said please. She wasn't one of his soldiers.

But she came, giving him a worried look he couldn't decipher as she passed, then she dropped to her knees in the mud to check on her engineer. A twig snapped nearby, and Viktor jerked his rifle in that direction, holding his fire in case it was one of his people. The tip of a barrel pointed through the brush. *Not* one of his people. He fired, and the branches rattled, something slumped to the ground, then was quiet. He trusted his aim. Jarlboro's men would likely lose their eagerness to fight when they realized their captain was dead, but it was dark and confusing out there. That information might not have percolated through the unit yet.

Viktor touched Ankari's shoulder, refusing to acknowledge that it stung when she flinched. "Take them in the shuttle for now. Please."

She looked up at him, maybe surprised by the word. Admittedly, it wasn't one he used often or that flowed off his tongue. He patted her shoulder, then stepped past her, facing the trees.

"Your captain is dead," Viktor called. "Surrender or disappear if you want to live."

A fern shivered on the other side of the clearing, then a clang sounded as something struck the side of the shuttle. Guessing what it was instantly, Viktor pounced. He would only have a second. In the dim light, it was tough to spot the small grenade, but he'd heard it land. There. He snatched the explosive and hurled it back where it had come from, hoping it wouldn't clank off a tree and bounce back.

It parted the leaves and exploded with a blinding flash of light. Wood snapped, and trees heaved. Dirt and debris rained down all around the shuttle. Ankari had helped Flipkens inside and was going back for the biologist. Viktor grabbed the woman first, dropping his weapons to lift her in both arms and carry her inside.

A short burst of laser fire came from the spot the grenade had been thrown from. A moment later, Sergeant Hazel walked out of the brush there, her rifle at her side. Broken twigs and leaves stuck out of the fasteners on her armor, but she appeared uninjured.

"He didn't want to surrender," she said, her voice deadpan.

"A mistake." Viktor laid down Keys, then sighed as he looked around the dim interior of the shuttle. There was as much mud on the floor of the craft as there was outside, and it had more dents in it than the rusty, perforated tanks on the fleet artillery range.

"Yes."

"Tick, you out there?" Viktor called over the sound of water running off leaves and splattering to the soggy ground. The rain had slowed earlier, but it was picking up again. The wind too. He had a feeling they were in the eye of the storm, and that it would continue to gust and rain all night.

"Yup, we got all but two, I think. I was trying to get a count of how many we were dealing with when you blasted in there, blowing holes in people." Tick stepped out of the trees behind the shuttle. "Want me to track the ones that took off? They're heading for the mountains, it looks like."

"No." Viktor eyed Jarlboro's body. "I doubt they'll trouble us again."

"There might be more," a soft voice said from behind him. Ankari came to his shoulder, a battered and mud-splattered tablet in her hand. She brought up a message and handed it to him warily. Her calculating feistiness was nowhere to be seen on her face. Was she not sure where she stood with him at the moment? Or simply worn down by the events of the night? Even in the poor lighting, he could tell she hadn't had a pleasurable last few hours. None of them had.

Viktor wanted to give her a hug, to cradle her against his chest and protect her, but wasn't sure if she would want it, so he simply accepted the tablet. "Sweet cakes?" he asked, reading the greeting aloud.

Ankari snorted softly. "He calls everyone that. Everyone female, anyway."

His humor faded as he read further, about the increased bounty and that Felgard had apparently let everyone in the system know where to find the women in question. "I'm going to kill him," Viktor growled.

"Felgard?" Ankari watched his face, the faintest expression of hope dawning in her eyes. She had to be wondering if she still had prisoner status.

"Listen, I'm not—"

Lightning flashed, and Tick and Hazel ran inside as the rain went from hard to torrential.

"Glad you didn't send me to track anyone, Cap'n," Tick said, shaking off like a dog and spraying water everywhere. "My gun would rust out in that. I might too." He looked curiously at the women, Ankari standing at Viktor's side and the other two slumped in chairs. "This all that came down?"

"I don't know," Viktor said.

"Oh, thought you might have, uhm, made inquiries."

Viktor snorted, though he was glad Tick had chosen those words instead of interrogated.

Sergeant Hazel slapped at the auxiliary lighting panel, but nothing responded. "Fine, I'll find the first-aid kit in the dark," she grumbled, waving her flashlight around the interior. How *had* those vines gotten all the way up to the front? They were plastered across the control panel.

"You injured, Sergeant?" Viktor asked.

"Not seriously, but your prisoners are. Wouldn't expect a man to notice such trite things as blood flowing from a woman's head."

"It *is* dark in here," Viktor said. "Must be your maternal instincts that let you sense such things."

Tick snorted. "Hazel? She's about as maternal as a chicken. Chickens eat their own eggs, you know. Which is a real threat to mercenary rations. Can you imagine where we'd be without egg logs?"

"Not even remotely." Viktor caught Ankari and Flipkens looking back and forth at each other and wondered what they thought of their blood-covered saviors—or maybe they still saw Mandrake Company as their captors—tossing jabs at each other. He groped for a way to explain that Tick and Hazel came from his home world and had been with him since the beginning, but then Tick and Hazel would be wondering why he was explaining himself to people he hadn't yet to claim as anything other than prisoners. Hazel had been there when the team had captured the women, but Tick had never met them, so he supposed introductions were in order. "Tick, this is Keys, Flipkens, and Markovich. Ladies, Heath 'Tick' Hawthorn. You ever get lost out in a jungle, he can help you find a way out. I believe you've all met Sergeant Hazel."

The sergeant had Flipkens holding her flashlight so she could apply a bandage to Keys's cut temple. She had taken Ankari's rifle and made sure her comrades weren't armed, either. Practical, but it reminded Viktor that the rest of the crew would continue to think of the women as prisoners unless he said something to the contrary, and with such a huge reward attached to them, he didn't know if he dared do that.

"Which is the one that knocked out Striker?" Tick asked. "'Cause I'm already predisposed to liking her."

"That's Markovich. The feisty one," Viktor said. Ankari looked at him, brows raised, so he added, "She's being quiet tonight. Might need some of your gum to perk her up, Tick."

"We all might, sir," Hazel said, "if you're planning to have us march farther tonight."

A distant screech sounded. If they stayed here, they would have to post guards all night. That was doable, but they had come far enough that they ought to only be a couple of miles from that Buddhist temple. That might make a desirable refuge, assuming it wasn't already giving refuge to bounty hunters. He imagined the expressions on the faces of Jarlboro's survivors if Viktor and the others strolled in after them. Refugees or not, the temple would be dry, something he wouldn't mind being about now. Unless they could get one of the other squads to pick them up, it would be twice as far to walk back to the landing site.

He tapped his comm. "Striker, report."

Lightning flashed outside. He wondered if he would get a response.

A burst of static came over the comm, but Striker's voice was clear enough when he spoke. "Just about done cleaning up, sir. We didn't find Sisson Hood himself yet, but we're hoping he's in the compound here, already dead. There are a lot of bodies around. His men were dug in here good and put up a fight. This was definitely his lair. There's some women locked up back here that are all roughed up. They identified him. There's lots of loot too. I, ah, suppose we'll be giving it back?"

"Yes, we're getting paid in aurums for our work. No need to make off with people's silverware and antique andirons." Viktor grumbled to himself. They needed Hood's head.

"It's more like nice weapons and some diamonds pulled out of the mines, but understood, sir. We do have quite a few injuries and a couple of men who need to get back real quick to see Doc Zimonjic. Where are you? How much longer will you be? Should we wait?"

"We found the missing shuttle. No sign of Tank or Rawlings." Viktor looked at the women, wondering if they had run into the missing soldiers.

"One of your men…" Ankari pointed upward. "Your people killed everyone in that boarding party, it looked like, but one of your men was in the shuttle, already dead, I think."

Viktor growled at the situation. He hadn't meant it to be an audible snarl, but Ankari stepped back. He lifted a hand in apology—and hoped she read it as such. He would get the rest of the story out of her later, but it could wait until they reached the temple and they could talk in private. "The shuttle's not operable," he told Striker, "at least not at the moment. One of the mechanics will have to take a look when it's lighter. And drier."

"You want us to swing over and get you on the way up?"

Yes. Going back to the ship now sounded quite appealing. But there was still the matter of the missing men and the tracks Tick had been following before the shuttle crashed. Not to mention that the other shuttles would struggle to find a landing spot that didn't involve smashing every branch in a tree on the way to the ground.

"Go up, drop off the sick, take care of everybody, and send a shuttle back down to pick us up at the temple in the morning. Send Bassman and

Chen with spare parts. I'll show them to the other shuttle. I expect it to be made operable again."

"What temple, sir?" Striker asked.

"There's a Buddhist monastery in those mountains. It's on the map. Thomlin will know where it is."

"You're sure you'll be all right down here in the storm?"

"We're fine. Out." Viktor faced the others. "Who's up for a walk?"

Nobody groaned out loud, but the women's shoulders all slumped. Even Hazel's might have drifted downward a hair.

"Hand out the gum, Tick. Two miles, people, that's it."

———

If one more vine smacked Ankari in the face, she was going to let out a screech that would put those raptors to shame. With every step, her feet sank into the mud, and with every third one, she had to yank a stuck foot out of the mire. The caffeinated gum the tracker had shared had helped for the first hour of the march, but its effects had worn off, leaving nothing but weariness dragging down her limbs. Thorny branches clawed at her clothes, which were plastered to her body, the water adding at least ten pounds to their weight. She was still carrying two packs, because Lauren, despite the sergeant's first-aid ministrations, could barely walk.

Ankari tripped over another root and only kept herself from sprawling by grabbing a branch. The branch turned out to have thorns that sliced into her soggy palms like barbed wire. She yanked her hand free, cutting skin in the process. She kept herself from whimpering—or screaming—barely. Mostly because she, once again, had no idea where she stood with Viktor and his team. At first, she had been relieved, almost delighted, to see him charging out of the jungle to demolish the other mercenaries. But watching him slit throats and shoot men with the chilling accuracy of a computer had reminded her how deadly he was—and how uncertain she was of how he would feel toward her group. Once again, she'd escaped—using the key she had plucked from his pocket—and this time, they had succeeded in stealing his shuttle...and crashing it. When she had stepped out of the trees, his stare hadn't *seemed* angry—in fact, he had almost been gentle, but she didn't want to make assumptions or mistake weariness for amiability.

"You all right?" Sergeant Hazel asked from behind her, touching her shoulder.

"Yes, sorry."

It was at least the fifth time Ankari had apologized. Viktor and his tracker were up ahead, cutting a path through the jungle, and it wasn't as if the group could have moved quickly under any circumstances, but she couldn't help but feel her and her team's clumsiness was slowing everyone down. Jamie and Lauren were just as tired as she, not to mention more badly wounded, and they kept giving her looks back over their shoulders, silently asking if they could sit down and mutiny. It was probably only the continuing screeches from the jungle that kept them moving. Nobody wanted to be left alone with those raptors roaming about. The creatures hadn't ventured close and attacked again, but Ankari believed that had more to do with her well-armed escort than any lack of interest in munching on humans.

Ground down by the events of the night and the awful weather, Ankari didn't notice at first when they turned onto an actual trail, one where the vines and branches had been cut back. It was still muddy, but it wasn't as difficult to navigate.

Viktor put away his big knife and waited for the women to pass, then fell in beside his sergeant. It was the first time the route had been wide enough for anyone to walk side by side. Ankari kept her eyes focused on the ground ahead, but listened, hoping to hear something useful—or at least that their destination was close.

"Less than a mile to the temple," Viktor said. "We spotted some fresh tracks though. We're not the only ones headed that way."

"Would the monks give refuge to mercenaries on the hunt?" Hazel asked.

"They'll give refuge to anyone. They only ask you to leave if you're fighting in the temple." Viktor raised his voice. "Markovich, you want me to carry those packs for you?"

Ankari wasn't expecting the offer, or for him to acknowledge her, and she managed to trip again, this time without the help of a root. She found her balance before planting her face in the mud, but Viktor caught her by the upper arm, too, making sure she would remain upright before releasing her.

"Thanks." Ankari's shoulders burned and her backed ached, so she would have loved to give him the packs, but she made herself offer a stoic, "I'm fine," instead. All right, it might have sounded more long-suffering than stoic, but that was all she could manage.

"How come you never offer to carry my stuff, sir?" Hazel asked, amusement in her voice.

"You're a highly trained soldier in superior physical shape. Also, you glared lasers at me the one time I opened a door for you."

Hazel snorted. "I have no memory of that."

"Any sign of anyone following us?" Viktor asked.

"Just the storm clouds."

"They are persistent. Keep an eye out."

"Yes, sir," Hazel said.

Viktor jogged a couple of steps to walk beside Ankari. "Miss Markovich, I'd consider it a kindness if you'd tell me how you and my shuttle came to be down here on the moon. I'm quite certain I left you in the brig. Again."

Ankari could feel his eyes upon her, but she stared at the muddy trail instead of meeting his gaze as she mulled over possible answers. He had asked quite politely, but would that politeness remain if she told the truth? At the moment, he might think some of those thugs had kidnapped her from the brig. But if she lied and was later caught—there had to be video coverage of what had been happening on the ship—then she would only be delaying his ire.

"Someone was attacking your ship, and when the power went out in the brig, we let ourselves out," Ankari said.

"The *power* went out?" Viktor looked back at Hazel.

"Just for a few seconds. Some men in black were waiting in the hall-way, and we figured they'd come to get us, but we delayed them briefly, and then your people charged through, mowing them down. After that, they forgot to come in and check on us—there were still some other intruders on your ship—so we let ourselves out of there too. There was another fight at the shuttle bay, but we were hiding in the ladder well, so didn't see any of that firsthand. Afterward, we slipped inside and invited ourselves onto the conveniently unguarded shuttle. Jamie closed the door, and we had plans to find ourselves a nice city down here to disappear into. But there was some device attached under the control panel—Jamie could tell you more about that—and it caused the shuttle to be on autopilot. It was determined to come down here. We tore out the device, but too late to do anything. The storm hit us hard, and we couldn't find a spot to land, not that we had the control to manage to land anyway."

She sneaked a glance at him, wondering how he felt about all this news, and the revelation that her team had been responsible for crashing his shuttle. She refused to feel *that* bad, considering he had destroyed her own ship, but she found herself reluctant to say things that would anger him.

It might have been the shadows, but his face was hard to read.

"We got a glimpse of the ship attacking yours as we were flying away," Ankari added. Maybe he would be interested in that and would forget about the shuttle. "It was disk-shaped. It didn't seem big enough to seriously damage your ship. More like it was trying to distract them so the shuttle could escape." She decided not to mention the part where they had realized they had walked into a trap. He would connect the dots by himself, anyway.

"Did the boarding party come in through an airlock?" Hazel asked. "Or up in the shuttle from the moon?"

Ankari shrugged, though she belatedly realized the sergeant was talking to Viktor.

"Garland would have had all of Bravo squad standing next to that airlock if a ship tried to attach or send people over in suits. They must have come in the shuttle. With someone there to guide them in and talk to Garland, make him think there was no trouble." Viktor's voice had grown soft, dangerous. Ankari wouldn't have wanted to be the "someone" who had helped the other side. "Markovich said someone—Tank, probably—was in the shuttle and had already been killed."

"So he betrayed us, then was betrayed himself?" Hazel asked. "What happened to Rawlings then?"

"I don't know." Viktor touched Ankari's arm. "Did you see a runty fellow with shifty eyes and a missing finger at any point?"

"I only saw the bald one and the people in black, but we were hiding from everybody. Also, most of the men we had time to take a good look at were dead, thanks to *your* men."

"All right. I'll have to wait for morning to get the full report, unless the temple has a decent comm station. Looks like you were coming down here one way or another tonight, Markovich."

Ankari nodded glumly. "Given what we experienced in our five minutes of shared company with those people, I think I'm glad we took the route we did."

Viktor looked toward Lauren and Jamie. "Jarlboro's outfit always had a less than savory reputation."

"Guess your Striker should have joined them then."

Viktor looked down at her, a hint of sadness in his eyes. "Perhaps so," he murmured.

Belatedly, Ankari got the impression he had been hoping she would point out that his outfit was more...savory. And she wished she had caught that before she'd spoken flippantly. She didn't know what her status was with him, but he and his team had cut their way through the jungle and risked their lives against those other mercenaries to save the lives of her and her partners. Sure, they might have been protecting their investment, but the result was that Ankari and the others weren't being mauled by horny brutes who couldn't even keep their hands to themselves in the pouring rain in the middle of a predator-filled jungle.

"I'd rather be completely free and not anybody's prisoner, but I appreciate that we're not with them now," Ankari said. She couldn't quite manage a thanks-for-saving-us-Viktor. "I also appreciate that you haven't thrown us up against the trees and beaten us senseless for escaping and crashing your shuttle."

"Well, it looked like that had already been done."

Ankari grunted. That was the truth. She wondered how bad she looked. Bad enough that he wouldn't want to strip her out of her soggy jumpsuit and engage in another round of kissing, she assumed. Which was, of course, fine with her, especially if he *was* just protecting his investment out here. He might be polite about it, but in the end, she was still his prisoner. Still, he'd been furious at Felgard when she had shared Fumio's letter with him. Maybe there was some chance she might convince him that she could make a better offer. She just had to figure out how to do that. Two hundred thousand aurums. She'd never come close to earning that kind of revenue from any of her companies, unless one counted gross sales, and she didn't. Gross sales couldn't pay off a mercenary.

"Sir?" Tick stopped and raised his hand.

The wide trail had turned into a road, and the foliage opened up ahead. The towering mountains had come into view, rising sharply with little in the way of foothills to ease the climb. The rocky spurs and cliffs were made of a dark stone that didn't support many trees or other shrubbery. If not for a pair of lights part way up a steep slope, Ankari would have missed the temple; its outer walls were made from the same dark rock as its surroundings. The ground had been cleared around the base of the mountain, including a broad cement landing pad kept clean of encroaching foliage. She wasn't sure how they would climb the steep hill to get to the temple, but the idea of getting out of the rain was nearly enough to send her sprinting ahead of the group to try.

"Trouble?" Viktor asked when the rest of the group caught up with the tracker.

Tick handed him a compact pair of binoculars. "Hard to say. The doors in the wall are open though. Like someone might have just gone inside. Or like they're expecting guests for some reason." He lifted his eyes toward the black sky. Yes, this wasn't exactly good weather for visiting. Neither flying nor walking had proven healthy.

After a moment, Viktor lowered the binoculars and looked back at his bedraggled group. "You want to stay here while Tick and I have a look?"

He was probably talking mostly to Sergeant Hazel, but Ankari heard herself saying, "No," before she could think better of it. She held out her hand, grimacing at the rain spattering her waterlogged skin. The screeches hadn't sounded for the last few minutes, but she was willing to risk the temple, even if they had to fight another battle before a dry spot might be found.

"Hazel?" Viktor asked.

"I'd rather stay together, sir," she said.

Viktor must not have had a strong opinion either way, because he shrugged and waved for them to follow him when he strode into the open.

Both he and Tick kept their rifles at hand and watched all around them. There weren't any craft sitting on the landing pad, nor was there any sign of life, apart from the two lights.

From a distance, Ankari hadn't been able to see the road crisscrossing the steep slope in switchbacks, but it led them up the hillside, closer and closer to the temple. The structure itself was mostly guarded from view by the surrounding wall, but a few rooftops were visible, and she had the impression of different tiers of buildings, each nestled onto ledges and built right up against the cliff. Her legs soon burned from the climb, and her interest in the architecture waned. She decided to let the men remain vigilant while she fantasized about dropping her packs and changing her clothing. Maybe finding a bed. Some blankets. Sleep.

The animal noises of the jungle faded until only the sound of the rain remained, pounding down on the mountain. Lightning flashed, highlighting the backs of Tick and Viktor. Lauren and Jamie, too tired to speak, followed behind Ankari, and Hazel guarded their rear. Because she was right behind the two men, Ankari heard their murmured conversation.

"Should be a monk up there on night guard duty." Viktor pointed to a tower poised on a corner that looked out over the jungle.

"You been here before, Cap'n?"

"Not this particular temple, but others. Most are laid out similarly. Similar protocols."

"Like leaving the front door shut in a storm?"

"I'm not familiar with that one."

The road ended at wide steps that climbed steeply straight up toward the door, which was propped open, with lanterns mounted on the wall on either side of it. Flame appeared to burn in the fixtures, fluctuating with the winds beating across the mountainside, and Ankari wondered if it was truly fire or some effect achieved with more modern technology. The place *did* look like an ancient habitat that could have predated the colonists who reached the galaxy fifteen hundred years earlier.

The thick wooden door proved more ajar than wide open, with a head-sized rock on the ground keeping it from banging shut. Rifle leading, Viktor stepped inside first. Nobody shouted or shot, and Tick went after him. Ankari stepped past the rock, keeping her back to the wall in the small, irregularly shaped courtyard that opened up. It was more like a walled balcony, rather than a courtyard, with the cliff rising on two sides and a building on the third, a simple rectangular structure, though a more interesting pagoda sat on the next section of the ledge, behind it. The only entrance to the temple appeared to be in the closest building.

While the rest of the group funneled in, Viktor and his tracker trotted around the courtyard, looking for signs of what, she could only guess. A fight? The flagstone floor wouldn't hold footprints.

When Hazel came in, she took up a position beside the door, so she could watch Viktor but also monitor the route behind them.

Lauren slumped against the wall, and Jamie crumpled to the ground beside her. Ankari stood next to them, not wanting to get in the mercenaries' way.

"I'm so tired," Jamie said, keeping her voice low. "And wet. I really hope we can rest here."

"Is it horrible that I'm missing the brig on their ship?" Lauren asked, her eyes closed.

Ankari, taking her cues from the men, didn't let herself relax beyond levering the packs off her shoulders. She wished she still had her pilfered laser pistol. Maybe she should have put up a fight when Hazel had taken it, arguing that she and her friends might help if there was another attack.

Viktor and Tick stopped to bend their heads over something near the front door. There weren't any lights on in that first building. Viktor pushed open the front door without having to turn a knob or latch. It certainly hadn't been locked. Maybe the structure had been abandoned.

The two men disappeared inside.

"Someone's looking for Jarlboro," Hazel said, gazing through the gap between the door and the wall.

"What?" Ankari stood on tiptoes to peer over her shoulder. "Oh."

The running lights of a ship burned bright against the dark clouds. They outlined a disk-shaped vessel, one Ankari had seen before. "That's the one that was attacking your ship."

"Jarlboro's *Golden Coin*. I wonder who's going to inherit it."

"Someone who plans to take it off to some planet with tropical islands with white beaches, while ignoring bounties, I hope."

Hazel quirked a lip. "I don't know. Your bounty would buy a lot of those fancy drinks with umbrellas." Her eyes weren't exactly gleaming with calculation, but she definitely gave the impression that this scenario pleased her.

"How much of a cut do *you* get?" Ankari asked, morbidly curious. She remembered Striker talking about his two percent.

"Two percent, same as most of the senior crew members."

"What do the normal crew members get?" Maybe they would have less incentive to turn her in if they didn't get a share.

"Salary and a smaller percentage. There are over a hundred people in the outfit."

"How much does the captain get?"

"He's supposed to get three percent, but I've never seen him buy anything with it except weapons upgrades and new equipment for the ship. He'll *probably* be buying a new shuttle this time." Hazel slanted her a cool look.

"Some reward."

"I'll say, but the man doesn't even own furniture. He doesn't seem inclined to hoard material goods, nor does he ever talk about buying property and retiring somewhere." Hazel's gaze returned to the sky. "Wherever that might be," she whispered, her words clearly only for herself. "I've yet to see a world that can replace home."

The disk-shaped ship was flying back and forth over the jungle. Over the crash site, maybe. Walking through the undergrowth had been disorientating, and Ankari couldn't be certain.

"The monks are gone," Viktor said from behind her.

Ankari jumped.

"Come in and get dry," he added, then picked up the packs before she could, slinging both of them over one shoulder. He looked like he was thinking of picking up Jamie, too, but she staggered to her feet with the help of the wall. Lauren stumbled toward the door, where Tick stood, holding it open.

"Gone?" Hazel asked as the group crossed the courtyard.

"We didn't look throughout the whole temple, but there's no sign of them in the first three buildings," Viktor said.

"Where would they have gone? And why?"

"I think these are the monks who tipped off Intel to Sisson Hood's location. They might have feared retaliation. And if Hood slipped through our people's fingers, they'd have a reason to fear it." Viktor clenched his jaw.

Ankari bet he wished he had been with the rest of his unit rather than hunting for missing shuttlecraft and escaped prisoners. She frowned down at the flagstones. Even though she didn't regret trying to escape—and she'd have to try again as soon as her friends were up to it—she did regret... something. Inconveniencing him maybe. Or that their situations meant it was never going to make sense for her to kiss him if she wasn't trying to steal something at the same time.

She rubbed her eyes, wondering why her thoughts had gone there. As weary and battered as she was, kissing should be the last thing on her mind.

"Markovich?" Viktor asked softly.

She was the last one standing outside in the rain. She shuffled inside, glancing up at his face and finding his thoughts difficult to guess, though there seemed to be a glumness about him. Again, she told herself he was tired and she couldn't read too much into what she thought she sensed. For all she knew, he was thinking about his three percent. And new shuttles.

CHAPTER TEN

Viktor prowled the halls of the temple, searching for clues as to where the monks had gone. He had appointed himself first watch, letting Tick, Hazel, and Ankari's group find rooms where they could dry off and get some rest. He had set sensors and cameras that were linked to his tablet on the walls and near the doors, so he would know if anyone approached the temple—or tried to leave. There was food in the kitchen, including bread that hadn't gone stale, so the monks hadn't been gone long. The living quarters had closets with robes and undergarments, so he didn't get the sense that anyone had packed up for an extended journey. In a big room with a granite Buddha statue sitting cross-legged on a dais, a few candles were lit. They were fat candles and could burn a long time, but he figured their presence meant someone had been here within the last twelve hours.

After his first circuit of the temple, he checked his tablet—the sensors were set so that nobody approaching from the outside should notice them—but nothing had changed, so he allowed himself a moment and walked into the shrine room. His family and seventy-five percent of the people on Grenavine had followed Novus Druidism, but there had been a few Buddhist sects on the planet, so he had been in the temples before. He lit a new candle and stood in front of it, his head bowed. Perhaps he might receive some enlightenment if he pondered his problems here, amongst the faint smell of melted beeswax.

The escaped Sisson Hood was a concern, as was the missing man he had yet to account for, but the women were foremost in his thoughts, Ankari in particular. What was he going to do with them, now that he had this new knowledge, that bounty hunters and mercenaries might be descending upon him in droves until he got rid of them? The logical thing to do, for the safety of his ship and crew, was to take them to Felgard and drop them off as quickly as possible. But that was no longer the right thing to do, because he no longer believed they were criminals or that the bounty on their heads had been righteously placed there.

If he was honest with himself, he hadn't believed that since he had seen Ankari using mashatui against Striker. Honor and integrity were always so closely linked with that ancient art, with practitioners indoctrinating it in their students at the same time as they taught the moves. Even if there had been a doubt, Ankari's words and actions had further implied that she wasn't a criminal. Perhaps not the pickpocketing—he smiled ruefully—but he accepted her explanation of growing up on the streets and learning those skills as a matter of survival. And it made sense that she would use every talent she had in order to escape from what could only be an unpleasant situation with Felgard. Perhaps even death if Felgard discovered that their research wasn't a solution to whatever problem he sought to solve. Or even if it *was* the solution. Someone who would set the galaxy to hunting people for nothing but personal gain—and who had essentially double-crossed Viktor as well—couldn't be trusted to let them walk free once he had what he needed.

No, Viktor no longer wanted to turn Ankari's team in.

The problem was that the crew *did*. Everybody knew about the prisoners and had plans on how to spend the bonus money. If this were the GalCon Fleet, and those men had sworn oaths and there were military laws to ensure discipline in the ranks, he could simply tell them that he had changed his mind, knowing they couldn't leave his command short of deserting, a situation that, as he well knew, came with a lot of baggage. But mercenaries were fickle men. He could probably explain things to the old gang from Grenavine, but the rest? He risked losing people over this, if not starting a mutiny. Not to mention that if he let the women go and the bounty was still on their heads, he wasn't doing them any favors. If his own crew didn't go after them, someone else's would, that was evinced by the risks Jarlboro had taken in attacking an outfit that was bigger and better armed than his own.

Viktor looked from the flickering light of the candle up to the Buddha's face where it hugged the shadows near the ceiling. As in every depiction he had ever seen, the statue emanated calm and serenity. It was strange, he acknowledged, that a mercenary should look to the Buddha for advice, but he supposed he hoped some enlightenment might come to him in this place.

It didn't.

He picked up his tablet to check the sensors, cycling through the cameras and pausing on the one watching the hallway to Ankari's room. Maybe he should talk to *her*. It wasn't his way to confide in anyone, some notion that a captain should be inscrutable and unflappable, he supposed, but perhaps two could find a solution where one failed.

Viktor left his candle burning and returned to patrolling the temple. He hadn't yet solved the mystery of the missing monks when Tick relieved him from watch duty, but at least he had an idea of where to start with his other problem.

———

Ankari woke up and immediately snuggled deeper into her blankets, wanting nothing more than to return to sleep. Darkness lay beyond the small window, and rain pattered on the tile roof.

A soft knock sounded at the door, and she blinked blearily in that direction. That must have been what had woken her to start with. It couldn't be time to get up yet. She didn't want to give up her bed or her blanket. Neither was luxurious by galactic standards, but after the hard bench in the *Albatross's* brig, their comfort could not be underrated. Maybe her caller would go away if she didn't answer. Except it might be Jamie or Lauren, wanting to have a meeting to figure out what they were going to do. As if she knew.

When the knock came again, louder this time, Ankari reluctantly pushed the blankets from her shoulders. A cool draft stirred against her legs. She was wearing some monk's robes, and there were a lot of air holes. It probably made sense for the humid climate, but it made her feel a little naked, even if the flowing garment hid most of her body. Not that it mattered for Jamie or Lauren. She touched her jumpsuit and undergarments, which were hanging from hooks to dry, but they remained extremely damp. She had washed them—and herself—before falling into bed. The temple didn't have many modern amenities, but a shower room was fortunately one of them.

The door opened as she was reaching toward the knob. The flicker of lantern light brightened the hallway outside.

"Ankari?" a soft voice asked.

Ankari froze. It was Viktor. And he was using her first name. She couldn't imagine what he wanted. No, that wasn't true. She could imagine what he might want just fine. But she didn't want it. The memory of their kiss flashed into her mind, countering her thought and heating her body with a flush that pushed all thoughts of sleep from her mind.

"Can I come in? I need to talk to you. In private." Viktor poked his head around the door, looking not at the bed but directly at her.

She didn't remember making a noise, but he had known somehow that she was standing there. She licked her lips. "All right." It came out as a whisper.

Talk. Was that truly all he wanted?

Viktor stepped inside, shutting the door behind him. He had changed out of his battle armor and wet clothing, and stood before her in clean black trousers and T-shirt. He must have showered, for the mud and grime—and blood—were gone from his body, and his short dark hair was clean and combed, his face shaven. For the first time since she had met him, he wasn't armed, at least not visibly. Jamie hadn't misspoken; he *was* a handsome man, especially with the grim-faced soldier left somewhere else for the moment. She swallowed, again aware of her bare legs and the unflattering monk's robes. Her hair was probably a tangled mess, too—she had gone to bed with it wet.

Not that it mattered. For talking.

"Uhm." Ankari spread a hand toward the simple wooden desk chair. It was the only place to sit in the room, aside from the bed, and she wasn't going to invite him to join her there.

He rejected the desk with a flick of his fingers, only resting his lantern on it, then he leaned against the wall. Oh, right. His no-sitting thing. She folded her arms across her chest. She would stand, too, then.

"I have a conundrum," Viktor said. "Several of them, and you're at the center of most of them."

"I hope you're not looking for sympathy, because *you're* the one who picked me up." Ankari decided not to complain about her destroyed ship again, since she might have cost him a combat shuttle. It was probably worth more than her rainbow junker with its shag carpet in the lounge. Albeit, the scientific equipment might make it a draw.

"Not sympathy. Just...tell me what you want to do about Felgard."

"Avoid him?" Her voice rose in a question, because she wasn't sure what he wanted to hear. It was as if he was giving her some kind of choice, but that couldn't be right.

Viktor gazed into her eyes. "I no longer believe that you're a criminal."

Her reflex was to snap that it was about time, but she kept her mouth shut, realizing the simple words might contain more than their literal meaning. Dare she hope that he no longer wanted to turn her team in?

"But because my whole crew knows I have you, letting you go when there's such a sizable bounty on your head would be...problematic. I'm sure you don't care if I'll have a hundred well-armed soldiers with their hackles up, especially if I let you go voluntarily, but it's a problem for me. Also...I'm not convinced that letting you go would be doing you any favors, when there are so many dangerous men after you."

Ankari listened, barely breathing, barely daring to hope that he was contemplating releasing her instead of turning her in. Most people wouldn't care whether someone deserved a bounty or not when that much money was on the line. Was it possible he actually *cared* what happened to her? She couldn't imagine what she had done to win that regard—she wasn't *that* good of a kisser, and she had been a pest to him from their first meeting—yet his words intimated that her life or death mattered to him for some reason.

"I don't know if I have a solution when it comes to mutinous mercenaries, but they wouldn't *have* to know that you let us go voluntarily. You could just look the other way, couldn't you?"

His lips twitched into a wry smile. "So they'd think me incompetent? I'm not sure that would save me from their ire."

"I've escaped a couple of times," Ankari pointed out. "They couldn't be all that surprised if it happened again."

He snorted but didn't deny it.

"As to the rest…I appreciate that our welfare seems to matter to you, but I don't expect anything from you. This is our problem, however unfair it was of the universe to dump it on us, and we'll have to figure something out. Find a place to hide out. Maybe we can create fake identities." She had little experience with such things, but if they found their way back to civilization, a real city, she would feel more confident in her ability to take care of herself.

"And spend the rest of your life hiding?"

"Maybe Felgard will forget about us." That sounded overly optimistic, but after a couple of years, maybe…

"Even if other passions catch his fancy, as long as he leaves that bounty out there, the rest of the galaxy won't forget about you."

Ankari closed her eyes. He was right. She had never met this Felgard, but she already hated him. As long as that bounty was out there, her life would never be hers again. Her dreams for her business, for other businesses, for taking her family off Novus Earth and giving them the safety and security they'd never known…Nothing would come to fruition. Sooner or later, she would end up in another bounty hunter's brig.

Moisture gathered behind her eyelids. "I guess we'll have to confront him somehow. Figure out what he really wants and hope it's not…despicable. Or impossible." If Felgard had read that sensationalist article, he might very well expect them to be able to do something they couldn't, not yet. Maybe not ever.

Ankari lowered her chin, not wanting to open her eyes or admit to the tears there, not with Viktor watching on. This wasn't *his* problem.

"In sending the galaxy to my door," Viktor murmured, surprising her because his voice was closer than it had been, and because she hadn't heard him move, "Felgard has made an enemy of me. If I were given the opportunity, I would shoot him for this."

Ankari blinked a few times and did a quick rub of her eyes before looking up. Viktor was still a step away from her, but he was close enough that she could smell the soap he had used to wash, the clean scent of his shaving cream. He lifted an open hand. An offer. What exactly was he offering? To go with her to confront Felgard? Why?

She took the step toward him, sensing that was what he wanted, and asked, "How do I give you this opportunity?"

"That's something we have to determine, but I find myself wanting to help you, to protect you." His hand found its way to her back, and he drew her into a hug.

Even though this new turn surprised her, Ankari didn't resist. The defiance had seeped out of her; there was no reason for it now. If he spoke the truth, he was no longer the enemy. He might even be an ally. She laid her cheek against his chest, feeling the warmth of his body through his T-shirt. After the constant angst of the last few days, it felt good—incredible—to lean against something. No, to lean against him.

"That's strange," Ankari murmured, "considering all of the things I keep stealing from you."

He chuckled softly, a pleasant sound, one she hadn't heard before, one she immediately liked.

"I know," Viktor said, lifting his other hand to the side of her head and stroking her hair. "But in a world where people are constantly trying to kill me, having a woman sticking her fingers in my pockets isn't as much of an invasion as you'd think."

His own fingers worked their way through her hair, combing it away from her face, grazing her scalp and sending delightful shivers down her neck. The kiss from the day before—or had it only been the evening before, a part of this endless night?—returned to her thoughts. He had asked her to suggest a solution to their mutual problem, though, not to rub lips with him. She should concentrate. She definitely shouldn't be admiring the curve of his pectoral muscle beneath his shirt, or the way his nipple poked against the fabric. The urge to rub her face against his chest, to nibble at him through the shirt…it was silly and should be ignored. He had said something, hadn't he? About fingers in his pockets. That only made her think about her fingers and letting them wander. Not to his pockets, but to other places. Wait. Solutions. That's what they were supposed to be working on.

"You probably just feel guilty because you blew up my ship," she said. Hm, that wasn't a solution.

"I *am* feeling contrite about that at this point." Viktor rubbed her through the robe, strong fingers kneading the muscles of her lower back, muscles that were sore and tight after that slog through the mud, and she groaned softly, hot pleasure radiating through her. "This would be a good time to ask for a favor," he murmured, his voice close to her ear, soft and secret, just for her, "if you're so inclined."

A favor? After he had just told her he wanted to help her deal with Felgard? She was more inclined to want to do *him* favors. Would he appreciate that? She tilted her head back to gaze into his eyes, to search them for an answer. He returned her regard, his green eyes half-lidded, gentle. The last time he had looked at her like that, before they had kissed, he had whispered that he was a Grenavinian, and that he, too, had lived through the destruction of his world. Maybe that had something to do with why he was here, why he wanted to protect her. It had been, what, eight, ten years since Grenavine had been destroyed? He would have been an adult, a soldier in the fleet then. She had been so young when her own world had been destroyed that it couldn't have affected her the way losing his affected him, but if he saw some common link between them, someone worth saving... how could she complain about that? Of course, if his tender feelings had more to do with her heritage than her, she should probably object.

Maybe it had something to do with the exquisite massage he was giving her, but she didn't want to object to anything about him. She wanted to make him care about her based on her own merits.

Ankari lowered her chin, his chest filling her vision again. She slid her hands up his back and buried her face in his shirt, feeling the contours of hard muscle through the fabric, drinking in the clean manly scent of him. Her cheek brushed against one of those erect nipples, and she gave in to her earlier urge. Her lips parted, and she teased it with her tongue, then her teeth. The hand massaging her scalp stilled, and he took a deep breath, his hard chest rising against her, the fabric of his shirt rasping against her face. An interesting sensation, but she wanted to touch him, to taste him, without the material in the way. His lower hand kept kneading her muscles, pressing her against him as he did so, against something else that was erect, straining for escape. They hadn't even kissed, but the feel of him responding to her touch filled her with desire, a longing to feel more of him against her. In her.

He wasn't wearing a belt, so she freed his shirt from his waistband easily, running her hands along his warm, smooth flesh, alternating between rubbing him and scraping her nails along his ribs, over a knot of scar tissue from some past battle. Her memory of him in the jungle came to mind, a panther springing from log to tree, bringing down lesser predators as if they were hapless kits. She pushed his shirt up, wanting to see the great predator before her in the flesh. He rumbled with pleasure, almost a purr. Or a soft roar. He pulled his shirt over his head, tossing it on the desk. Before it landed, she was crouching, kissing his abdomen, the smell and taste of him intoxicating her. She ran her hands up his back, rising and finding that nipple she had teased before, licking and sucking, then grazing it with her teeth.

"Ankari," he murmured, almost a groan. He bent down to nuzzle her hair, inhaling deeply.

Hearing him whisper her name, hearing the ache of desire in his voice, rather than the frustration that could have been there after all the trouble she had caused him, it made her want to please him. Not to prove her worth or anything else to him, just to make him enjoy his time with her. But he kept distracting her with his strokes and massages, making her forget her original intent. She wanted to kiss him hard and hot on the mouth and demand that he take her over to that bed.

Instead, she found the buttons of his trousers, unfastening them even as she kissed and nibbled her way to his other nipple, sucking it, promising more to come. She slid his trousers over his hips. This time he *did* groan when he whispered her name, digging his fingers into her hair, arching toward her. As she kissed her way lower, past the dark hair sprinkling his chest, down the ridges of his abdomen, she lowered a hand, stroking his straining shaft, feeling the blood pulsing against her palm. Her body ached and throbbed in sync, aroused by his groans, his touch, and the sight of him. She dropped to her knees, the soft wool of a sheepskin rug touching her skin, making her realize how alive her body felt, how much any touch, however slight, roused her flesh.

She grasped the base of his shaft with one hand and gripped his firm backside with the other, then leaned into him, her tongue darting out, licking his heated flesh. His head fell back, his muscles taut. A bead of sweat snaked down his abdomen, and she sensed the tension in his body, how much he wanted to grab her and bear her to the floor beneath him. But he wanted this too, she was certain of it, and she smiled as she ran her tongue along his engorged length. When she found the tip, taking him in her mouth, he snarled a "yes" that aroused her further. As she drew him deeper, the hot taste of him raking across her tongue, she lowered one hand between her legs, finding a gap in the robe, pleasuring herself even as she quickened her pace with him. He pumped against her, filling her mouth, though she could tell he was trying not to be too forceful, too rough. She scarcely would have noticed. She couldn't get enough and worked him faster, deeper, trying to take more of him in, craving all of him. She lifted her gaze, watching his magnificent form as he arched into her, his sweat-slick skin gleaming by the lantern light, the corded muscles of his arms flexing beneath his tattoos, his fisted hands as he kept himself from grabbing her head, forcing himself against her. Her hot core pulsed beneath the frantic movements of her hand, and she found her release before he did, but she didn't slake off, still reveling in the trembling of his body, his ardent desire straining into her.

"Ankari," he whispered in a warning, touching her head, letting her know to pull away.

She only lifted her hands, grabbing his hips, pressing into him, enjoying the taste of him, wanting to feel his pleasure coursing through her. He came with a roar that brought that image of the panther rushing into her mind again. Later, she might be ashamed, knowing she had found the thought of him prowling through the jungle and dealing death arousing, but for now, she merely curled her hand around the back of his leg and rested her head against his thigh. Spent.

Viktor bent down and gathered her in his arms. He stepped out of his trousers and walked to the bed. She might have been amused that she was still wearing the shapeless robes, but supposed she hadn't needed to undress further, not for this. She wanted more of him, but another time would be fine, when they had both slept. She draped her arms around his shoulders and looked into his eyes, hoping for the promise that there would be another time.

His eyes reflected the flame of the lantern, the warmth in their depths making her belly shiver. He sank onto the bed, pulling her into his lap, and kissed her temple gently. Tenderly. He nuzzled her ear and her neck. His warm breath whispered across skin moist from his kisses. Her body responded to him, her nipples tightening, and heat stirring in her depths again.

"Aren't you tired?" Ankari murmured, knowing he didn't need her now, not yet.

He smiled against her neck, kissing his way down to her collarbone. "Just showing my appreciation." He hesitated, lifting his gaze to hers, a question there. "Unless *you're* too tired for appreciation."

"No." Thoughts of sleep had already wandered out of her head, and she couldn't help but speculate wildly on just *how* he might show that appreciation. "I think I'd wake from the dead for this."

"Good. But I intend to keep you alive." His voice was husky, almost a growl, and it made her shiver, knowing the panther wanted to be her protector.

Their lips met for the first time that night. If he minded the taste of himself on her, he didn't show it. His hand found the gap in her robe, warm, calloused skin coming to rest on her bare thigh. He had scarcely touched her, but she scooted closer, kissing him hard, demanding more. His hand slid upward, his thumb finding sensitive flesh still damp from earlier. Her breath hitched as he grazed her, and he smiled against her lips.

"No underwear beneath that robe, eh?"

"It was wet." She thought about making a dirty joke, but her eyes were too busy rolling back in her head as he stroked her with his thumb.

He leaned her back onto the bed, his lips never far from hers. "Because of the rain or me?" he teased, his eyes crinkling with humor, humor that she doubted many people got to see from him. She treasured it, cheesy line and all.

"Yes," she whispered, and pushed open her robe, wanting him to be able to touch all of her, to—

A beep came from the pile of clothing on the floor.

"No," she protested, not wanting any disturbances, not until morning. Not ever.

He gave her a long kiss, and she thought—hoped—he might ignore it, but at the second beep, he sighed and climbed out of bed. She watched him go, so disappointed that it was all she could do not to replace his missing hands with her own, especially as she admired his powerful form, the shadow and light of the lantern playing over the rises and dips of his musculature.

"What?" Viktor asked, his eyes on her body, as well, the swell of the breasts she had bared.

She hoped someone was just checking in, maybe wondering why he wasn't in his room, that it was nothing major, that he could return to bed and touch her with more than his eyes.

"We've got company, Cap'n," came the tracker's voice over the comm.

In an instant, his eyes hardened, and he was the captain again, grim and forbidding. Ankari found the expression far less intimidating than she would have an hour ago, but she lamented its return, knowing it meant he would leave before he spoke the words.

"Be right there." Viktor grabbed his shirt and trousers, dressing in a flash. "Lock your door," he said, kissing her before he jogged for the hallway, leaving the lantern on her desk. He paused with his hand on the knob, giving her a long backward look, and promised, "Later."

"I'll be here," Ankari whispered.

CHAPTER ELEVEN

Viktor stopped in his quarters to grab his mesh vest, his optical sensor, and his weapons, then ran to the end of the hall, meeting Tick in the open room. He would have much preferred staying with Ankari for the night—or the week—especially after her…exquisite attention, but ignoring a threat could mean death for all of them.

"Your sensors picked up something outside, Cap'n." Tick might have knocked on his door first and might have wondered why Viktor hadn't been in his room, but he didn't say anything about it. He only held out the tablet, which Viktor had handed to him when he took over guard duty.

"A person?" Viktor asked.

"Nothing showed up on the camera. It could be a glitch—the storm's been wreaking havoc on our comm equipment, after all—but I thought you'd want to be alerted." For once, Tick wasn't chomping on his gum. He eyed Viktor warily, like he knew he had interrupted something and wondered if he should have kept his mouth shut until he had more evidence. No, there were too few of them down here to take chances.

"Yes. I'll check the sensor." Viktor tapped the tablet. The one with the alert was out front, on the wall overlooking the stairs. "Wake up Hazel. Have her watch the women, then come find me."

Tick resumed chewing his gum and nodded with relief. "Yes, sir."

Viktor jogged for the front door, watching the shadows as he passed meditation and meeting rooms. Most of the candles around the shrine had gone out, though the one he had lit still burned. He cycled through the cameras and sensors before going outside, wanting to know if any images had been captured. The alarm by the gate beeped intermittently and irregularly, reporting an audio anomaly. According to the cameras, nothing had come up the steps, but he'd had limited equipment with him and the units were sparsely set. It was possible that someone had walked along the wall, approaching the camera from behind, though the person would have had to know it was there, and he had camouflaged all the units well. Was it possible his earlier search had missed someone hiding in the temple? Someone who might have watched him from the pagoda tower?

Rifle at the ready, Viktor stepped outside into the courtyard. A fine mist hung in the warm air, but the majority of the rain had stopped. The sky was lightening a hair, the first promise of dawn somewhere behind the mountains. He lowered his sensor over his left eye, surveying the courtyard with the enhanced vision. It parsed the shadows and gave him readouts on the temperature, humidity, altitude, and other conditions. When a shutter flapped open in the wind, it gave him a noise and motion detection alert, though his own human senses had already registered that particular movement.

Convinced nothing lurked in the courtyard, Viktor padded across the wet flagstones. Hazel had shut and locked the outer door, and it remained in that state. Instead of opening it, he jumped, caught the lip of the stone wall, and pulled himself up. Settling in a crouch, he observed the jungle and the landing strip far below, as well as the road winding up the mountainside. He didn't see a soul, nor was anyone on the steep stairs carved into the cliff. He twitched his eye to activate the binocular function of the optical sensor and took a slow survey of the horizon. If Jarlboro's ship was still out there, it wasn't within ten miles.

A soft thump came from below, something heavy bumping against the wall. He scooted to the edge and peered down. He had seen death thousands of times and been ambushed so often, it took a lot to give him a start of fear, but his heart rate *did* jump up a few notches at the appearance of a body when he hadn't expected one, one that wore a Mandrake Company patch on its shoulder. He couldn't see the soldier's face from the top-down view, but recognized the hair and the missing finger on the left hand. Rawlings. He hung from a hook on the wall, one meant for plant baskets, not corpses. When the wind blew, the body wobbled, bumping the stone occasionally.

That was what the sensor was complaining about. But how had Rawlings gotten there without something showing up on the camera?

Viktor had anticipated the possibility of a shuttle coming down from above, and he had set a camera to monitor the possible approach routes from the sky. Was it possible some small craft had slipped through? Or...

He twisted to look at the cliff rising behind the temple. Inhospitable, craggy, and vertical, its thousand feet of height didn't recommend it as a possible route into the compound. Still, *he* could have made the descent with minimal gear, and he couldn't rule out the possibility that others might have come down that way, if they had been properly motivated. He couldn't imagine them doing it while carrying a body, which suggested that Rawlings might have been alive at the time and climbed down with them. Coerced to do so? Or willingly assisting them to reach their goal? It hardly mattered now. Viktor couldn't kill him again for betraying the company.

A hint of movement on the cliff toward the back of the temple drew his attention. Using the eyepiece, he enhanced his vision. A thin rope came into view.

Cursing, Viktor leaped into the courtyard. He would warn Hazel before going hunting. Or maybe he would just set traps and lie in wait around Ankari and her friends. He had just told Ankari he wanted to protect her. As much as he wanted to annihilate these people for threatening his company and trying to steal his prisoners, it didn't make sense for him to run off on his own, especially when the shuttle should be coming back for them soon.

As soon as he opened the door, a feeling of concern—of dread—washed over him. It was quiet inside. Too quiet.

How long had he been out in the courtyard? Less than five minutes the clock on the Eytect told him, but Tick should have woken Hazel and joined him in that time. Maybe Rawlings's body had been placed as a distraction, meant to give the intruders the time they needed to get in without dealing with Viktor.

He kept his snarl silent as he raced toward the sleeping quarters, cold fury burning in his veins. He sprinted around a corner only to halt abruptly, freezing like a statue when he spotted a limp body on the stone floor. Tick. A second figure was slumped unconscious against the wall a couple of steps farther on, someone in a thin, black form-fitting suit with a hood pulled over his head. It was different from the black clothing Jarlboro's men had been wearing. For one, it didn't register at all on the display of his eyepiece. It was as if the person wasn't there at all, and nothing more than a deep shadow hugged the wall.

Beyond the two men, several of the hallway doors stood open, including the ones leading to Hazel's and Viktor's rooms, as well as the one to Ankari's room. With thoughts of her filling his mind, he almost rushed straight in that direction, but he crouched to touch Tick's throat. Viktor had lost numerous men over the years, but when he lost those from his home world, those who had been with him since the inception of Mandrake Company, it hit him hardest.

Tick didn't stir at his touch, but a soft pulse beat beneath his skin. Only unconscious. Viktor would return to tend to him, but for now, he raced down the hall, pausing only to look in Hazel's room. The covers were rumpled, but the bed was empty.

He ran for Ankari's room next and only instinct kept him from charging inside, some warning niggling at the back of his mind. The lantern he had left on the desk was out. The window hadn't been open before; it was now. Water dribbled from the wooden frame, and the wind whistled inside, smelling of moisture, the jungle, and…blood. There was a pool of it on the floor underneath the window. A feeling of numbness came over him, and he stepped toward it without thinking.

The warning tickling his mind rose in intensity. He jumped to the side, putting his back to the wall. At the same time, a black boot swung down, knocking his rifle from his hand.

Viktor leaped back to face the opponent falling from the ceiling. He punched, but the figure twisted in the air, evading the attack. Viktor yanked his dagger and a throwing knife free, as angry at himself as he was at his assailant. By now, he should have anticipated a threat from above; he shouldn't have been staring at blood and worrying about Ankari.

In the darkness, Viktor didn't see the laser pistol being aimed at him, but he knew it was there from the way the fighter crouched, his free hand guarding the weapon. Viktor hurled his throwing knife and threw himself sideways. The whine of a laser sounded, followed by shards of stone being blasted free from the wall, but the pained grunt of his opponent filled the air, too, and he knew his blade had done at least some damage.

It wasn't enough to slow his attacker. The lean man, hooded and clad in black like the figure in the hallway, leaped across the room. A blade flashed, cutting toward Viktor's face. Already on his feet, Viktor threw a hard block, knocking his assailant's arm up so he could rush into the opening with his own dagger. The point would have stabbed through flesh, but some thin armor lay beneath that sensor-thwarting clothing, and it deflected his blade.

A knee came up, ramming Viktor in the chest. He roared, scarcely feeling the pain, and tackled the other man. They went down in a flurry of blows, thrashing on the floor, each trying to find an advantage. Nails clawed at Viktor's eyes even as he tried to pin his attacker. He squinted his lids shut, denying those probing fingers access to sensitive organs. He found the leverage he needed to roll the man onto his stomach. Viktor leaned into his back. An elbow struck his chest, but it didn't have much power behind it, not when the man's face was smashed into the floor.

The smell of blood reached his nostrils—they must have rolled close to that pool beneath the window—and it incensed Viktor. He roared and tore through the man's last defenses, finding his skull with both hands. With adrenaline surging into his muscles, Viktor gave a great twist. Bone crunched, and a shudder coursed through his foe's body.

A soft clunk came from above him. Viktor reared back from the fallen man, yanking another knife free, ready for another opponent. But it was Sergeant Hazel, crawling through the window, coming in from outside. Where had she been? Up on the roof? The windows looked out over the cliff. She landed on the floor with a grunt.

"What happened?" Viktor wanted to interrogate her about Ankari and the others, but noticing the way she strained to sit up and lean against the wall, grabbing her shoulder, he rushed to her side, bumping something with his foot. The lamp. It skidded and hit the base of the wall. "Are you all right, Hazel? Are there more men?"

"Not out there," she said. "That's why we went."

Another person slid through the window and landed on the floor, robes swirling at her feet.

Viktor was fairly certain it was Ankari—her movements were much more lithe and athletic than those of her friends—but he turned on the lamp and stuck it on the desk before going to her. She was busy helping someone else inside, anyway, the engineer.

Sergeant Hazel held up the hand she had been clutching her shoulder with, and blood dripped from her fingers. "I could use some first aid, sir. A glug of whiskey, too, maybe."

"I can find at least one of those things, if our attackers are all down. Two men, is that all you saw?"

"I only saw one," Hazel said. "The one who threw a knife in my shoulder. Tick jumped him, and then I think one more came after him. Do you know if he's…" She looked toward the door. "I wasn't sure whether to help him or guard the prisoners. Since I was injured, I thought I'd at least get them somewhere safe—" Her gaze shifted to the window. "Safe-ish, then come back."

"Tick is alive." When the microbiologist appeared in the window, Viktor added, "Looks like we all are." He met Ankari's eyes, wanting to rush over and give her a hug, but she didn't appear injured, or even all that rattled—what was a climb on a roof after all they had endured that night?—and he had to make sure his soldiers were taken care of first.

"We need to get them dropped off at Felgard's as soon as possible, sir," Hazel added, bending over and clasping her hand to her shoulder again. "Our company can't survive all these attacks indefinitely."

"We'll figure it out." Viktor gave Ankari a nod before leaving to check on Tick and find the first-aid kit, wanting to make sure she knew he had spoken truthfully to her and still meant to find a way to help her with Felgard, not simply turn her in.

She nodded back, her expression wry but not afraid or displeased.

After digging into his gear and pulling out bandages, a scanner, and a medical repair device, Viktor went first to Tick, since he had no idea what his injury was—for all Viktor knew his back could be broken. While he was checking his old friend, Hazel's voice drifted out of the other room, a weird note in it, "Sir?"

Viktor tensed, expecting more trouble. "What?"

"You got a picture of what Sisson Hood looks like?"

"There's one on my tablet."

"Because I think you may have just killed him."

Huh. "I suppose that would explain why Striker and the rest of the team didn't find him in his hideout." And why these men were running around in hoods.

"Abandoning his people for a more lucrative prize?" Hazel asked. "Not particularly true to the legend."

After identifying a concussion—and a fist-sized lump on Tick's head— Viktor left the repair device fastened to Tick's skull, so it could work, then toted the rest of the gear into the room, pausing only long enough to tug the hood off the other fellow crumpled in the hall. He was dead—a laser shot had burned off half his throat—but his face was still identifiable, and Viktor thought he was familiar too. He would have to check the database of wanted posters.

"At least we'll be paid well for this diversion," Viktor said, stepping into the room to help Hazel, who had lain down on the bed.

"That is good." Hazel closed her eyes. "I'm more than ready for shore leave. A nice one. Not a few nights at some dented tin can of a town with more gambling halls than restaurants."

"Most of the men *like* those places."

Hazel mumbled something unintelligible. Viktor unrolled the bandages to dress her wound while he waited for the repair device to finish on Tick. There was a lot of blood loss, and he'd need more supplies from the others' first-aid kits—but this would be a stopgap.

"Need any help?" Ankari asked, sitting on the end of the bed. Her monk robes were almost as wet and grimy as her other clothing had been, and a fresh smear of dirt smudged her cheek. It was hard to stay clean when one had a bounty on one's head.

Viktor nodded. "Apply pressure here, please."

Hazel's eyes opened. "Sir? Did you just say *please?*"

"Yes."

Hazel's gaze flickered back and forth between Viktor and Ankari. He didn't think he was giving moon eyes to Ankari or doing anything that would suggest they had spent time together in a non-platonic-prisoner-captor sort of way, but Hazel sighed and shook her head.

"We're not going to get that two hundred thousand, are we, sir?"

Ankari's brows rose.

Viktor didn't have a good answer, so he didn't respond. He gave Hazel a sedative. That probably wouldn't work for the rest of the crew. Oh, well. He would figure out something.

———

Sleep was elusive after the attack. Ankari kept trying to think of what she might offer Viktor—more importantly, his *crew*—that could mitigate the loss they would feel if two hundred thousand aurums didn't flow into the company's coffers. She had this vague notion that she might *hire* the company, but she wasn't exactly rolling in gold nuggets at the moment and none of the mercenaries had been intrigued by the idea of a share of her "pre-revenue" business yet. Still, now that she knew about that free publicity she was getting from Lauren's article, they might be able to make some money based on current acceptable practices. The reproduction of the complete alien microbiome was years out, but they could certainly perform already established medical procedures and improve the health of individuals plagued with persistent diseases and infections. She could vouch for the efficacy of that herself.

Ankari shifted her weight, the hard stone of the floor digging through the blanket she was resting on. Lauren and Jamie were next to her, having no trouble snoring. Sergeant Hazel was sleeping on the bed, and Tick was recovering in the chair. Not, he assured them, sleeping, though his head kept listing to the side, until he twitched alert again, his eyelids leaping open. His gum fell out during one of these episodes. He didn't notice.

Viktor was sitting on the floor near the door, his eyes closed, his rifle in his lap and his tablet at his side. One lid peeled open every few minutes to check the alarms, so Ankari didn't think he was sleeping. If they had been alone, she might have crawled over and snuggled against his side. Or in his lap, though she would have had to compete with the rifle.

There were rooms and beds enough for everyone, but nobody had suggested they split up again. If more attackers came, Viktor was the only one still largely uninjured and capable of fighting at full capacity. Though even he must be tired by now. When his sensors chimed, he rose without a word and walked out of the room. Tick's head jerked up, and he smacked his lips a few times, yawned, then grabbed his rifle and left too.

Viktor hadn't seemed all that alarmed. Ankari hoped that meant he recognized whoever had shown up on the camera. Maybe his shuttle was circling and looking for a place to land.

Since she wasn't sleeping anyway, she left the room and padded after the two men, the stone floor cool against her bare feet. The warmth of the thick air kept it from feeling unpleasant, but she hoped her socks and underwear would be dry before it was time to leave.

Voices came from a chamber ahead. Were Viktor's men already inside? Ankari stopped at the mouth of the hallway, expecting to see people wearing jackets with Mandrake Company patches. Instead, a file of at least twenty men and women in monks' robes shuffled through the room, heading for other hallways.

A lean, brown-skinned man in his sixties or seventies had stopped to talk with Viktor and Tick. He had wispy white hair that stuck out in tufts, and he might have appeared reverent and wise, if not for the tattoo collection peeking out from underneath the rolled sleeves of his robe. Some of them depicted images more lurid than anything Ankari and Viktor had been doing the night before. She gaped at a pair of men performing erotically—and acrobatically—with a woman on her hands and knees and wondered if: a) that was illustrating consensual sex; and b) exactly what kind of temple this was. True, the tattoos were old and faded, perhaps from a long-forgotten and much rougher time in the man's life, but there were ink removal procedures one could pursue...

"...of course we seek to avoid violence and the taking of life whenever possible," the tattooed monk was telling Viktor, "but I do appreciate you ridding our moon and our temple of that murdering, raping, con artist, Willow. I was very tempted to return to my more belligerent ways in regard to him, but apparently I am not the—what was it Xueqin called me?—the ass-kicking, kill-happy bastard I once was."

Ankari blinked, trying to imagine the spindly man happily killing much of anything, and she was also confused as to who Willow was. Hadn't that been Sisson Hood that Viktor had taken down? Maybe the other man had also been some infamous villain, though that name hardly sounded like something that would drive fear into enemies.

"It should not please me to see mutilated corpses in the trash heap," the monk continued, "but there is a certain satisfaction in knowing a villain's crimes will not continue."

"They weren't mutilated," Viktor said. "Just dispatched."

"Yours was mutilated a bit, Cap'n," Tick said helpfully.

"His neck was broken."

"That'll mutilate a man."

"Just because you shot yours…"

The monk smiled cheerfully during this conversation. Ankari wondered if she should walk out and join the men instead of eavesdropping from the shadows.

"I do appreciate you cleaning up the blood and moving the bodies, however mutilated, out of the temple, Willow," the monk said. "Some of the younger inhabitants who were born into this way of life are disturbed by such unpleasantries."

"How odd," Tick said. "Cap'n, you know your prisoner is spying on us, right?"

"Yes."

Ankari flushed as all three men rotated to face her.

"Maybe you should punish her," Tick said, smirking.

Ankari wasn't sure if that was an inside joke or an innuendo or what. The tracker didn't sound serious, and Viktor only snorted.

"I was just wondering who Willow was," Ankari said. When in doubt, deflect the attention off to someone else.

Tick's smirk deepened. "Right, who's that Willow fellow? Going to share that with her, Cap'n?"

"No. Tick, it's dawn. Get on the comm with the ship and make sure someone is coming to get us. Ling, have we earned some breakfast?"

"Yes, of course. All we have to offer is yours."

"So rice and vegetables?" Viktor asked.

"Fruit also."

Tick elbowed Viktor. "You can mash it all up in one of your drinks."

"Wonderful. Ankari, breakfast?"

Tick's brows rose, but he walked off to do Viktor's bidding without comment.

"I believe you are already familiar with the temple, but the kitchen may be found in that direction." The monk extended his arm. The motion made the bodies in the erotic tattoo wiggle. "I must contact the government and inform them that Sisson Hood and his bandits are no more." He inclined his head toward Viktor, then walked in another direction.

"Do your friends want to eat?" Viktor asked Ankari.

"They were sleeping when I left. I'm inclined to let them rest. I can bring them something." Besides, she was more interested in the conversation she might have with Viktor in private. Presumably, he didn't have sex on the mind if he was leading her to a cafeteria, but that was fine. She needed to run her ideas by him. "I've been thinking about a solution to your problem." It seemed presumptuous to call it *their* problem, even though he had stated an interest in working together to deal with Felgard.

Viktor gave her a sidelong look as they walked down the hallway the monk had indicated. "It's only been three hours since I mentioned that problem. You were busy climbing on the roof during one of those hours. And climbing on…something else during another." His eyes glinted.

Since a pair of monks was walking out of the dining room doorway as they entered, Ankari kept her grin sly and secret, but seeing that humor on his face warmed her heart. And other things, as well. "Which left me another hour for mulling."

"All right. Tell me in a minute." Viktor waved her to a table, then disappeared into a small kitchen.

None of the monks was having breakfast yet, so she didn't know what he would find back there. Ankari sat down on a bench at the rectangular table, leaving it up to him whether to sit across from her or next to her. He returned soon with cups of coffee and two bowls of instant oatmeal. He considered his seating options, then leaned his hip against the end of the table. Ah, right. The standing habit. One that left her staring at his crotch. Hm.

Ankari stood, picked up her bowl, and leaned against the table beside him, giving him a little smile.

"Huh." His grunt sounded pleased. At least he shifted his weight so their shoulders were touching as they stood side by side, eating oatmeal and gazing out at the world—or at least the rest of the dining room—from their feet.

"You've read that letter from my friend," Ankari said. "What wasn't in there was some information Jamie, Lauren, and I scrounged up on the net, that one of her academic papers had been turned into a sensational health article and broadcast all over the system. We believe that's what brought our company to Lord Felgard's attention, even if we're not sure yet why he's opted for putting a bounty out for our arrest, rather than simply contacting us about our services. Not that we actually have services yet. Even so, he might have offered to buy us out for our research too. He's a mystery for me at this point."

"Maybe throwing some money out there was easier than tracking you down and talking to you himself."

"He could have hired a lawyer or a private detective to find us for a much smaller amount. And, hell, if he'd offered us two hundred thousand for a straight-up buy out, I might have been tempted." Ankari chewed on a bite of bland oatmeal—did monks not have brown sugar?—and considered her words. Would she have? "No, that's not true actually. I think we'll be worth a lot more than that one day. Especially with the publicity. I knew the alien angle was hot—people have been fascinated since we first found their ruins in this system, after all—but I hadn't anticipated that much interest. If that's an inkling of what we can expect, the future is looking promising, so long as humans can actually get something out of those alien gut bugs."

"Is that likely?" Viktor asked, switching his empty oatmeal bowl for a coffee mug.

"The mouse trials were promising, and that was just using a few of the known bacteria. After Lauren finishes analyzing the stool samples and we get a complete profile on what the typical microflora of the time was, well, she could tell you more, but even I can see the potential just from my lay-man's understanding of her work."

"It sounds like you have a greater understanding than that."

Was that a compliment? She smiled at him just in case. It seemed the right response, for he smiled back. Strange that it should tug at her soul so. It had been scant hours since he had admitted he cared for her, that he wanted to protect her. Before that, he had been The Enemy. She had never fallen for soldiers in the past, and even though he had an appealing face—especially when he wasn't scowling—and body, she wasn't quite sure why that smile made butterflies dance in her stomach. Maybe something about the fact that it was as rare as a blue diamond. And maybe he was too. He had admitted he was wrong about her and wanted to make things right, rather than simply doing what would be easier—and far more profitable. It touched something deep inside of her. One didn't find that sort of integrity in many places in the galaxy, certainly not in a mercenary outfit.

A bleary-eyed Sergeant Hazel walked in the door, and Ankari looked away from Viktor, realizing she had been staring into his eyes for a long time. She expected him to move away from her, now that they had a non-monk witness to their closeness, but he merely gave Hazel a nod and sipped from his coffee. She had showered and changed, but her arm looked stiff and painful. She nodded back, but there was a wariness in her eyes when her gaze flickered toward Ankari, taking in her presence at her captain's side. She didn't comment, instead heading past him for the kitchen and the coffee scent drifting from it.

"There are some medical procedures that could be done now," Ankari said, figuring she should return to business while they had time. That shuttle ought to be down to pick them up soon, and how was she going to have private talks with Viktor then? Would she and the others end up back in the brig? So the crew didn't think anything had changed? "Other clinics do them, but we might be able to make a name for ourselves, thanks to the publicity. Once we prove ourselves credible, with successful microbiome transplants, we might even be able to sell future services. Take a deposit for those who want to get on the list for the alien microflora treatment. We wouldn't make any dubious promises or prey on people's hopes. We would make it all legitimate, and we'd let people have their money back at any time if they changed their minds. Anyway, you're probably wondering why I'm pouring all this in your ear over coffee."

Viktor's eyes weren't glazing over, but Ankari would be surprised if he didn't start checking his tablet soon or glancing toward the door, hoping someone more interesting would walk in.

"Aside from the fact that you might make an intriguing donor," she added, mostly to see if he was paying attention.

"A what?"

"You would have to be tested, of course, certified disease free and metabolically sound, but from what I've seen—" Ankari gave his stomach a pat, "—you probably have excellent gut microbiota."

"I…"

Goodness, had she rendered the mighty captain speechless? "It's quite amazing, really, considering the food you eat. All those dubious logs."

Of course, if he had been raised in Grenavine, he would have been born into an ideal environment. The planet had been known for its people's back-to-nature lifestyle, with farmers growing food forests that mimicked the wilderness and maintaining livestock that roamed free on mountainsides rather than being cooped up in barns. A healthy place to be a kid. She wondered if he had appreciated it at the time. Probably not. What kid did?

"Do you always discuss these topics with men you see, or am I special?" Viktor asked.

"You're special." Ankari had been in the mining business briefly with a former lover and had discussed work with him, but she hadn't ever complimented his gut bugs. He would have been too busy trying to talk her out of her fifty percent share to notice, anyway. "I just wanted to try and give you an idea as to our value. Our business's value, that is. Your people take a risk going in to see Felgard. He might not even pay you. I imagine he has all sorts of security, and he isn't afraid of mercenaries."

"He should be," Viktor said.

"Regardless, if Mandrake Company chose to work with *our* business, instead, we could give you some shares and a percentage of earnings. It would be an investment in the future rather than a simple payday."

"If you were making money now, that might be an easier sell."

"Yes, but now's the time to get in. You could have, say, ten percent just for helping us with this small Felgard problem, whereas when we're big and can afford our own huge security staff, we'd have no need of you."

"No need at all?" Viktor murmured, lowering his chin and gazing at her through his eyelashes.

The expression surprised her, both for its playfulness—such a strange word to attribute to him—and because it immediately had her thinking bedroom thoughts. "Well, I would always be open to hiring quality help, but you wouldn't get the deal I'm offering now."

"And are you authorized to offer this deal? How much of the company do you own?"

"Seventy-five percent."

He straightened, surprise crossing his face, then a more serious expression taking control. "That much? I had this notion that you and the others would be equal partners. You and the microbiologist, at least."

"Jamie only has five percent. We basically brought her on to pilot us around the system and keep that boat in the air. I thought about offering Lauren half, or closer to fifty percent, but she was just sitting in a lab, doing research and working for someone else when we met. I was the one, with my knack for crazy schemes, to suggest there might be a way to finance independent research and turn the results into a practice that could help people. Further, she had no interest in running day-to-day operations or doing the marketing or any of the things that actually make a business successful, so I offered her a percentage commensurate with the effort she was willing to make." Ankari remembered how she had been the one to climb down that ancient latrine shaft, doing the dirty work. Literally. "I'm fully able to offer your company ten percent to come on board as our...special security detachment. Temporarily, of course. I don't expect you to forget all of your other assignments and be at my beck and call. This would just be for Felgard and...any other emergencies that might come up."

"Twenty percent," Viktor said, "and you set up your labs on my ship, so we can keep an eye on our investment."

Ankari stared at him. Was he actually negotiating with her? Yes, she had made an offer, but she hadn't expected him to take it, not right here and now. She had mostly wanted to give him something to think about, an option that *might* appease his crew, the possibility that they could potentially earn more over time than they would from turning her in. Twenty percent. That would still leave her as the majority shareholder but without much wiggle room if she needed to barter pieces of the company to others in the future.

"Fifteen percent," Ankari said, "and we will gladly accept your offer of a laboratory if it comes fully stocked with the equipment we need, equipment we *had* before a certain mercenary company blew up my ship."

"How much would that equipment cost?"

"We don't need anything shiny. I can shop at the surplus medical suppliers, auction houses, and rummage sales, get good deals. Three or four thousand should get us set up nicely."

"Twenty percent, and I know an illegal medical facility we can raid for your equipment."

Ankari almost choked on the idea. Raid. As if that were a common business practice. "You're offering to undertake this raid with your ship and your men?" The men he was afraid might mutiny over her bounty not being collected? Was she insane for even negotiating with him? Was this all *legal*?

"Yes." Viktor stuck his hand out. "Deal?"

Wasn't she supposed to be the business savvy one here? Why did she feel like she wasn't getting the best of this negotiation? She should have known he was brighter than he looked the moment she'd met him and he had known what the hell aliuolite was. "Twenty percent," she said, "but I want the option to buy you back down to ten percent later on, given a five-hundred-thousand-aurum valuation of the company."

"You can buy us down to fifteen percent at that valuation." His hand was still sticking out.

Ankari looked at it for a long moment. "Just to be clear, this deal would start as soon as we return to your ship, and my team and I would no longer be staying in the brig?"

"You'll stay in your lab."

"Which won't be in the brig."

"Correct."

"Where *will* it be?" she asked, imagining some utility closet full of mops.

"I'll find a spot."

"Larger than a closet?"

"You can set up in my cabin if I can't find anything bigger." Viktor wriggled his fingers for emphasis. "Do people ever actually close deals with you?"

"Rarely." Ankari took his hand. "All right. It's a deal. All of it. You'll handle explaining things to your company?"

"Yes."

"This should prove interesting," a voice murmured from behind them.

Ankari jumped, but Viktor responded right away so he must have known Sergeant Hazel was sitting there, sipping her coffee, all along. "That's why you signed on with me, isn't it? I'm sure 'see interesting places and meet interesting people' is on your application."

"I was twenty-two at the time," Hazel said. "I thought the gum stuck to the deck of the space port was interesting."

"Then this won't disappoint."

CHAPTER TWELVE

Stars drifted by outside of the porthole in the *Albatross's* briefing room. Viktor leaned against the wall at the head of the rectangular wooden table, its warm knots and whorls a contrast to the cold gray metal of the ship's bulkheads. The old cedar boards had come from Grenavine, and Commander Borage, the chief of engineering who had been a carpenter in his former life, had assembled it and figured out a way to attach it to the deck plating so it wouldn't fly around in a rough battle. Borage sat to the right of the head of the table now, with Commander Garland waiting across from him. Sergeant Tick, Sergeant Hazel, Lieutenant Sequoia, Sergeant Aster, and Sergeant Rowan occupied the other seats, everyone silent, but everyone making eye contact and trading shrugs with each other, wondering why they had been called here. They knew the old crew had been assembled, the men and women Viktor trusted most because he had known them longest and they had all come from Grenavine, either when he had or later on, as homeless refugees drifting out of space to join the outfit when they'd heard about it. Zimonjic, who had been married for a time and had left her Grenavinian surname behind, was the only one absent, but there was an empty chair waiting for her. There were others on the *Albatross* who ranked higher, but they hadn't been invited to this private meeting. Doubtlessly, Viktor's old comrades were wondering why.

The door opened and Dr. Zimonjic entered, her pockets full of medical tools once again. She had been busy patching up Tick, Hazel, and the company's three new business partners—Viktor was about to explain that revision to everyone, everyone he felt he could implicitly trust, both because of their long service and because they had joined the company for reasons other than money.

"Sorry I'm late," Zimonjic said. "I was treating those girls, so they could be returned to the brig. Something odd happened though. Cutty said he was taking them to some new lab that's being set up on B-deck?" She looked at Viktor as she spoke, her eyebrows elevated.

"Yes." Viktor waved her to the empty seat. "There's been a change of plans."

Tick, who was chomping cheerily on his gum, elbowed Hazel. "Here it comes."

He looked like a man anticipating an entertaining show. Hazel, her face guarded, didn't respond.

"Since we captured those women—Markovich, Keys, and Flipkens— I've learned that they haven't committed any crimes—" Viktor thought of Ankari's pickpocketing of his key, but that hardly counted, "—so Lord Felgard's bounty is a rogue one. The law isn't going to touch *him* over it, but we would be walking the edge of a cliff if we turned these people over to him."

Commander Borage pushed a hand through his scruffy mop of gray hair, taking the lack of a dress code to the extreme, as usual. His face hadn't seen a razor in days, and there were enough coffee stains on his shirt that it looked like a diorama of Mondor's seventeen moons. "We've walked along that edge before, sir. You've been known to take a particular interest in figuring out how far we can push GalCon without becoming targets for retribution."

"But I haven't turned innocent civilians over to petty finance lords with some secret, illegal agenda, either." Viktor spoke the truth, but he hadn't always taken a stand on issues of morality—sometimes a man couldn't afford to out here, not if he wanted to keep his ship flying and his crew eating—and he watched the faces around the table warily, wondering if any-one would call him a hypocrite. He demanded military courtesy and respect around the rest of the crew, but these people all knew he'd always expected them to speak openly to him in private.

"The whole crew's anticipating that bounty." Borage looked around, probably wondering if he had the support of the others. He received a few nods. "We'll get more for them than we got for destroying all of Sisson Hood's men and turning his head over to the magistrate on Sturm. And, Captain, we need a lot of repairs after the Fallow Station Battle."

Viktor nodded. He knew that all too well. They were on their way to Recon and Repair at the Dock Seven space station now.

"We're out of at least a dozen spare parts in the engine room right now, what's installed is cobbled together with spit and tape, our weapons are depleted, and the fuel tanks are running near empty." Borage folded his hands on the table and studied them. "I'm not just trying to pad my retirement account here with my concerns about bounties. It's going to be an expensive repair bill."

"Retirement account?" Tick grinned. "Who told you that you've got a retirement account, Borage?"

"Well, I get this quarterly report." Borage managed a faint smile. "It all looks very official."

"Lies, it's all lies. The job's designed to kill you before you ever get to draw on it."

That drew a few snorts. Viktor couldn't deny it. He doubted he would make it to retirement. How many mercenaries ever did?

"We'll have enough," Viktor said. "We got paid for Fallow and with the bonus of Sisson Hood's bounty, we'll easily…break even."

There was no way to spin that more positively, and this round of snorts was expected.

"It'd be nice to come out ahead once in a while," Lieutenant Sequoia murmured wistfully.

That might be as good of an opening as he would get for discussing their new business partners, but Zimonjic spoke first.

"Captain, these women…do you have solid evidence that they're not criminals? I wouldn't expect you to simply take a person's word for it, but I just wanted to make sure." There was nothing antagonistic or suspicious in her expression; she looked like she simply wanted to know the answer, and was perhaps hoping Viktor might have overlooked something and that Ankari and her partners would indeed be proven criminals.

"I had doubts from the beginning, and I had Thomlin dig around. None of them has a criminal record, nor are Felgard's claims substantive." True

enough. He had been hounding Thomlin for that information since returning to the ship. He would have preferred to personally handle the prepara-
tions of Ankari's lab, but he had known he would need evidence, or as close
to it as he could get, before sharing his decision here.

"Just because something couldn't be dug up on the net doesn't mean
there isn't something there," Zimonjic said.

Tick nudged Hazel again. "Sounds like someone's bitter that one of her
syringes was stolen."

"Not at all," Zimonjic said. "But it is because of how easily that happened that I question Ms. Markovich's…wholesomeness. Just because a
criminal hasn't been caught and doesn't have a public record doesn't mean
he or she isn't a criminal."

"Nonetheless, I'm not going to punish someone without some proof
that she deserves it," Viktor said. "It's my fault for not doing more due
diligence ahead of time." Not that he ever had when browsing the wanted
posters around the system. And if Ankari were male, would he have bothered to look deeper? Maybe. But he had admittedly found her compelling.
Best to move on and not give the others time to linger on his words. "We'll
still be going to see Felgard. It'll be an incursion rather than a delivery."

Eyebrows flew up around the table.

"As you already know, Felgard double-crossed us on the bounty. I intend
to make it clear to the rest of the system that Mandrake Company is not
to be crossed." Viktor let that sink in before continuing on. *That*, at least,
would sound like him, the influence of a woman notwithstanding. "I would
have shot Felgard for that alone, but I've struck a deal with Markovich. We'll
be taking care of him for her and will receive a twenty percent share of their
company in exchange for our services." Viktor didn't mention that there
would be ongoing services and that the women were setting up camp on the
Albatross. Those details could be explained later. As could the fact that he
had tasked Thomlin with hunting around to see if any rogue bounties might
be out for the finance lord himself. Someone like that had to have enemies
or at least competitors who would be happy to see him gone—and might
pay for that to happen. Viktor could hardly bring this up when Felgard himself wasn't a criminal and his main argument for not turning in the women
was that they weren't criminals, either.

Tick's ever-present gum chewing had come to a halt, his jaw hanging slack.

"You want us to break into Felgard's compound and kill him?" Garland asked. "How many times did you get hit on the head down on that Moon, Viktor?"

"He'll have the best security money can buy," Borage said. "Not to mention powerful allies. We're good, but is this a war we want to fight? Sneaking in and trying to kill a lord of finance?"

"We won't have to sneak in. We'll walk in the front door under the guise of delivering his bounty. And Markovich doesn't demand that he be killed, only that he ceases to be a problem for her company. Since we'll own a share of that company, we'll naturally want to protect our interests."

"She doesn't *demand* that he be killed?" Borage asked. "Wasn't she a prisoner yesterday? How the hell did she turn into our employer?"

That had been a poor choice of words. Viktor wasn't used to having to explain himself. "Business partner," he corrected.

Tick and Hazel were exchanging long looks, and he braced himself for a contribution that might theorize exactly how Ankari had come to be…making demands. He hadn't been flaunting his new relationship, but he hadn't skulked around or hidden anything, either.

"Sir," Hazel said carefully—apparently she'd lost the silent argument as to who should broach the subject. "In all the years I've known you, you've never let…feelings for someone influence your command decisions. I'm—we're—concerned that might be the case now, and that it might be to the detriment of the company."

This time a lot more jaws than Tick's fell open. Zimonjic looked particularly apoplectic, even if she soon rearranged her face into a more neutral position. Viktor understood why, but he didn't know what to say to her. He never had.

"You're wrong, Sergeant," Viktor said, though he was speaking to all of those in the room, all of those staring eyes fixed on him. "I've let my feelings influence my decisions from the beginning. There are a lot of people here—" he spread a palm toward the table, "—who didn't know much about their jobs and had no military experience when I brought them on board. I chose them over more qualified individuals because we share an ancestry, roots we could trace back to the first colonists who landed on Grenavine."

Several people looked down at the table or at their hands. Viktor hated to use their common history to try to take advantage of past favors like this, but the truth was he needed a favor. Who else could he ask?

"Sometimes, you have to trust that people are worth more than their résumés," he said, "and that they can grow into the responsibility you give them."

"But, sir," Lieutenant Sequoia said, "they're not applying to join the company. They're...I don't know what they are. I'm not sure I can trust them."

"I understand," Viktor said, "but I hope you can trust *me*. I won't put the company at more risk than is necessary. I can go down with a small team and deal with this. If I get myself killed, Garland can rename the company, steer the *Albatross* off to distant stars, and likely avoid any wrath my actions might draw."

The expressions around the table ranged from sullen to glum. He hadn't expected more. He could only hope he could prove them wrong, prove that he wasn't doing this because Ankari had a talented mouth. That it was because she was like them, like him, someone worth putting trust in.

"I wanted you all to know what the plan was," Viktor said. "I'd prefer the rest of the company didn't, not until after I've confronted Felgard. There are those who might take it upon themselves to attempt to collect the bounty on their own, stealing the women and sneaking away in a shuttle once we've made orbit. Two hundred thousand is a lot more than anyone's salary around here, so I'm sure it's crossed some minds. I'll be increasing security in case anyone is considering that or other mutinous intentions."

Borage flinched at the word mutinous. He wasn't the only one.

"But as long as people believe they're getting a share of the bounty, that might be enough to keep them in line. The women will be busy in a lab rather than staying in the brig for the rest of the journey. I want twenty percent of a viable and profitable company, so that's what I've got them working toward. If anyone asks, let them believe...whatever they want. That we're using them to make us intellectual property to sell after we turn them over. I don't care what they think, so long as it's not the truth.

Not yet. I'll explain everything afterward. I believe I can make everything work out in the company's favor in the end—" Viktor hoped he wasn't being delusional in saying that, "—but it'll be easier if I don't have people second-guessing me at every step. There's much to be done before taking a team into Felgard's stronghold. I want to concentrate on that, not on damage control." He looked around the room, trying to gauge people's reactions, their feelings. Nobody was happy about this, but would they make trouble for him? Nobody spoke during his pause. "I'll consider it a favor from each of you if you help me maintain this ruse for a few days and let me know if you hear of anything troubling."

There were words that would never be spoken within a captain's hearing that other, lower-ranking soldiers might be privy to, and he knew it. That was a big part of why he had shared all of this with them. He might have clammed up, explained nothing, and gone on pretending to everyone that the women were prisoners until the end. But he needed a team to take down with him, and he would need a good pilot and some good fighters. He had all of those in this room. And Garland and Borage could keep the ship together, the crew under control, until he returned victorious. That was the meaning of the name he'd taken, after all. Any other result was unacceptable. It always had been.

He thought about asking if there were objections or concerns, but if he asked, there would be. Better just to be the captain in this, make the decisions and not invite a discussion.

"That's all I have for you right now," Viktor said. "I've got an incursion team in mind, but I'll talk to people individually about that." He hoped he could select most of it from the people in the room, but he planned to ask for volunteers, not force anyone. "Dismissed," he said.

People slowly got to their feet. Tick, Zimonjic, and Borage all looked like they had something to say, but when he made eye contact with each of them, they simply sighed or shook their heads and looked away. For the first time in some years, Viktor found himself wishing for the counsel of Doc Aglianico. His old friend had been somewhat outside of the regular chain of command and had never feared speaking bluntly or offering advice. Zimonjic was a capable medical officer, but she had never filled that particular role for him.

Commander Garland was the one to linger after the others left, standing at the foot end of the table, stroking one of the old cedar boards. His expression said he would miss those boards if something happened and he was no longer able to visit that table. It had a special meaning to all of them. Viktor knew that, but he tried not to read too much into his second-in-command's expression.

"You've always had a knack for making life more complicated than it needs to be, Viktor," Garland said.

Viktor snorted. "Tell me a new story."

"Other mercenaries don't worry about moral issues; they just worry about making money. Keeps things simple."

Viktor didn't think Garland was actually suggesting he do that—he had been a freighter pilot hauling livestock before the fall of Grenavine, not some soldier or hardened killer. Likely, he was only pointing out the difficulty of their situation and perhaps a frustration with it.

"I don't know if that's true of *all* mercenaries, but I didn't get into this for the money. You of all people should know that. It was about finding a way to stay free in an increasingly unfree universe. On a planet or a moon, they can always find you. Out here..." Viktor gazed out the porthole to the stars. "Out here, there's a chance to live freely, to make your life simple or complicated, in the manner of your choosing, in the way that suits your nature."

Garland grunted. "Good thing you don't say that poetical nonsense in front of most of your soldiers."

"Yes, you're probably right."

"I don't know what the girl means to you, and I don't care, but this deception of the crew, I think that might come back to haunt you. You could have been straight with them, told them how it is, and if they didn't like it, they could get off at the next stop. That's how you've usually operated. They expect that. They're all too afraid of you to mutiny or even think of crossing you by stealing your bounty. You don't need to worry about the crew. Felgard, now. That's a problem. If you don't manage to cut off the head with one swipe, that particular viper is going to kill you."

"I'll keep your words in mind, Garland."

His second-in-command ran his hand along the table one more time, then walked out. Once again, Viktor found himself wishing for his old friend's counsel. Perhaps one day, if he survived the next week, Ankari would become someone in whom he could confide. But in the meantime, he had better keep his distance, lest the crew have reason to guess at...too much.

———

Ankari stood up, flexing her back and stretching legs that had been sitting for too long. At least she was clean and had experienced three straight nights of sound sleep in an actual bed. So what if the beds were simply set up at one end of their lab? And so what if their "lab" was nothing more than the equipment they had been carrying in their backpacks set up in what was nothing more than an environmental controls room, complete with an engineer wandering in every hour to check the systems? And so what if there was a guard who stood outside day and night and had their meals delivered? It wasn't the brig.

She had access to the net and all the information the system could offer. Oh, she would have preferred to share Viktor's bed at night, but he came by once or twice a day to check on them, and during an unobserved hug and kiss had intimated that he would like shared beds, too, and that he planned to make that a reality as soon as they were done with Felgard and he could officially change their status from prisoners to business partners. A few people seemed to know the truth, but the rest of the crew was still under the impression that she and the others were to be turned in for money. So long as that wasn't the case, she didn't mind going along with the ruse. Lauren was twitchier about the whole situation, and Jamie, despite having a romantic streak, seemed uneasy, too, as they traveled closer to Paradise, the planet where Felgard owned an island. Ankari occasionally wondered if she was being naive in trusting Viktor so fully, so early in their relationship, but he seemed like someone who preferred blunt honesty to chicanery. Even if, as Lauren was quick to point out, he had to be lying to someone: either his crew or her.

But Ankari had come to accept that they had to face Felgard one way or another, and whether someone got paid or not probably wouldn't change much for her team in the end. She had sent messages back and forth to Fumio, and had done more research on Felgard on her own, enough to learn that he had seen a number of doctors in the last couple of years. The tightest security locked down his medical files, but she could guess that he thought Microbacteriotherapy, Inc. might have a solution the other practices hadn't. Ankari still didn't know why he had chosen to kidnap her people rather than simply contacting them to make a deal.

"How's it going?" Jamie asked from a pile of spare parts on a counter. She was trying to build Lauren a bioreactor for cell culturing using a schematic she had scrounged off the net, since she had no piloting or engineering duties at the moment and didn't know much about the research and experimentation side of the company. She didn't seem to have much of a knack for—or perhaps an interest in—helping Ankari with the marketing and customer acquisition aspect, either.

"For me?" Ankari asked. Lauren was working two feet away from her, reviewing blood and stool samples more modern than the twenty-thousand-year-old alien ones acquired in the ruins, but she didn't seem to hear the question. "Good. We've already got a few customers signed up, and several people have given their financial information to prove they're willing to pay. Of course, I can't charge them until we arrange a way to perform the procedures or figure out a way to ship specimens so their own doctors can do the insertions. Being on a ship is tougher than having a static clinic, but it may actually be a boon in the end, since it'll allow us to service more worlds." Ankari had spent the last two days building a virtual clinic, listing services, and marketing their company, something made easier by the publicity Lauren's work had already received.

"That's impressive," Jamie said. "I thought it would be years before we made money."

"It'll be years before the *alien* angle is ready to try, I think." Ankari glanced at Lauren. "But there are plenty of people with health issues that can be improved, if not absolved altogether, by a microbiota transplant. There are already clinics that do that, but those who sign up to perform the service with us will have early access to the alien microbiota when we're sure it's safe for human implementation. There are people signing up now who want children they haven't even conceived yet to be able to take advantage. I find it interesting that those from fundamentalist religions who won't consider the benefits of genetic engineering are willing to consider this. Maybe it's a workaround? I don't know. Oh, and we have some interest in the Grenavine human strains we may be able to introduce shortly. It's widely known that the inhabitants adhered to a natural lifestyle on a world with a rich and varied eco system, and that they were relatively disease-free compared to the galactic standard."

"I can't believe you got Captain Aloof to give you a sample." Jamie grinned, pointing toward the refrigerator that held recently acquired specimens.

"He's not aloof; he's just reserved with who he opens up to."

"Mmhmm. So long as he lets us—"

The door slid open. Instead of the expected environmental-systems engineer, Dr. Zimonjic walked in carrying her medical bag and wearing her sweater with the stuffed pockets.

"Good evening, Doctor," Ankari said with a friendly smile, though the woman's presence made her nervous. She wondered if word had reached her that Ankari and Viktor had spent some time together on Sturm. Even if it wasn't as much time as she would have liked, she had definitely gotten the impression that Sergeants Hazel and Tick had connected the dots. Ankari sat down and propped her arm on the counter, trying to look casual, but she doubted she managed it.

"Good evening." Zimonjic looked around the lab. She had been a skeptic when Lauren had first explained the research in the brig. Had something changed?

"Are we getting another check-up?" Jamie asked. "I feel fine now."

"No, not unless someone needs one. I'm on my way to the station to pick up medical supplies."

A couple of hours earlier, faint clunks and shudders had reverberated through the *Albatross* as it docked at the space station where repairs would be done, the last stop before the ship continued on to Felgard's home world.

"And you came by to ask if we needed anything? How thoughtful." Ankari smiled, though she doubted that had anything to do with the doctor's visit.

"No. I came to…" Zimonjic glanced toward the door, but it had shut behind her, so there was no chance of the guard or anyone else in the hallway overhearing her. "I heard you were collecting fecal samples from Grenavine natives and that there might be payment down the line if they were used."

Ankari sank back in the chair. Oh, that was what Zimonjic wanted? Extra cash? Nothing to do with crushes on Viktor and dark feelings toward the one who was getting all the hugs from him?

Lauren, who had heretofore ignored their visitor—and the rest of the lab in general—spun around in her chair. "That's right. Are you interested in making a deposit? Oh, are you Grenavinian? Not that we wouldn't consider samples from those of other origins, but Ankari said—did you tell her how much interest there's been?"

"I was telling Jamie that, actually, but, ah…" Ankari could tell Zimonjic didn't want the spiel. She was wearing a long-suffering look. She probably just wanted extra spending money and was still a skeptic in regard to the business. "Here, Doctor. The form and more details are on the tablet."

"I'm sure it's all fine. And, yes, I grew up on Grenavine. I was married for a time and never went back to the typical plant-derived surname." Zimonjic made a hasty signature in the air over the tablet, then set her bag down on the cluttered counter and rummaged through it. "I already took the liberty of collecting a specimen."

"Oh? That's very efficient." Ankari took back the tablet with the now-signed form, surprised that a doctor wouldn't have wanted to read more details, but maybe she had already received them from one of the other Grenavinians.

"Yes." Zimonjic placed an opaque tube on the counter by Lauren's microscope and closed her bag. "I'll check back with you later and see if you need anything else."

"Thank you, Doctor."

Lauren made sure the sample was dated and labeled, then stuck it in the refrigerator and returned to her work. Zimonjic walked out the door without another word. Ankari found the encounter a touch strange, but she was relieved not to have been interrogated or denigrated over her relationship with Viktor and decided not to worry further about the doctor.

She returned to her marketing project, but was yawning within a minute or two. Odd, she hadn't been tired before. The guard hadn't brought their dinner yet, so it couldn't be very late. It wasn't until she glanced at Lauren and saw her slumped forward in her chair, her cheek pressed to the counter and her eyes closed that Ankari realized something was wrong. Very wrong.

Zimonjic.

When she had set her bag down…Ankari stood up and almost fell over. Her legs had turned into leaden weights. She caught herself on the edge of the counter. "Lauren? Jamie?" Her voice came out in a croak, as if her vocal chords were falling asleep too.

Neither woman answered. Jamie was slumped in her chair too. They were both closer to that section of the counter where Zimonjic had been than Ankari was.

She stumbled toward it, using the counter for support. A faint gray smoke was wafting from behind a rack of test tubes. Ankari couldn't smell anything, but whatever Zimonjic had left was having an effect. Hers eyelids were heavier than mountains.

She tried to maneuver around Lauren without knocking her out of the chair, but her dead legs and numb feet were useless. She couldn't feel the counter under her hands, either. When she tripped over the leg of Lauren's chair, there was no hope of saving herself. She struck the deck, the side of her head smacking down. It would have hurt more than it did if her nerves were functioning correctly…

Ankari tried to get up, but it was useless. Her muscles had no strength. She looked for a tablet, a comm patch, a way to send a message. Anything. But the floor was empty.

The door whispered open.

"Get the gurney in here," Zimonjic said.

To whom, Ankari had no idea. She couldn't move her head.

"These ladies are going for a ride."

It was the last thing she heard.

CHAPTER THIRTEEN

"Three thousand…fifty-two hundred…eight hundred and ninety…Is that everything? No, wait, forgot to charge you for those…" The merchant cheerfully recited a few more engine parts for his tablet to compute while a robot puttered around the shop, sucking wrappers, screws, and other floor detritus into its built-in trash receptacle. For the third time, it tried to suck up Viktor's boots. He hoped the robots that were jetting around outside the giant view port, welding, scrubbing, and painting the hull of the *Albatross*, had their bolts secured more tightly.

"Sure you don't want to change your mind about that bounty?" Commander Borage asked. "I told you this was going to be costly."

"It'll be fine. If Cosmos Circuits and Cogs doesn't give us a fair price, we'll torture and kill Cosmos, then blast our way out of the space dock." Viktor gave his coolest, hardest look to the pasty-faced pencil pilot totaling the bill.

"Erp?" The man blinked a few times, cleared his throat, and said, "There's not actually a Cosmos. It's just a name. I'm Ralph. And we have fierce security robots to deal with recalcitrant customers." He pointed to two sleek, black human-shaped bots standing guard at the door.

"Oh? What part of me will *they* try to vacuum up?" Viktor waved to the cleaning bot, which was in danger of running over his boot again.

"Your wallet most likely," Borage said.

Viktor's comm chimed. "Sir? This is Striker. Corporal Tungsten's not at his post, and that lab is empty."

Viktor forced himself to take a deep breath and control the urge to run over and treat those security bots like punching bags. "How long?"

"Not long, sir. I've been keeping an eye on the lab, just like you said." Striker sounded worried. He better.

"The tube's guarded, right? All the shuttles still in the bay?" Viktor looked up at the ship, floating in space beyond the window, attached only by an airlock tube on the side opposite from him. He couldn't see it, but he had more guards stationed there than usual and trusted they were at their posts. He couldn't see the shuttle bay from here, either.

"The women haven't gone out the tube. Rubber and Jiang are there. I already checked with them. The shuttles...Sergeant Sethron is leaving the bay right now. Commander Garland cleared him a few minutes ago. He's picking up medical supplies for Dr. Zimonjic."

Or he was kidnapping three women to sell to the highest bidder. Viktor growled deep in his throat. The merchant backed a few steps away.

"Check the cameras and see if anyone except him walked onto that shuttle," Viktor said.

"I, ah, just did, sir. The data is unavailable. It says the camera was taken offline for repairs."

Viktor clenched a fist. "I'll bet. Striker, I want a security team waiting for the sergeant when he lands." Wherever that would be. This station had at least ten shuttle bays. "If those women are on the shuttle, I want them recovered and back in their lab within the hour. I left you in charge of security. This is your responsibility."

"Yes, sir. I got it. Uhm, if Sethron puts up a fight...how much force do you want used?"

Commander Borage, who had been standing silently and listening to the exchange, raised his eyebrows at this and looked Viktor in the eyes.

Viktor couldn't be lenient, not with this. A slap on the wrist would only encourage others to try the same thing. This had to be a lesson to his crew. He didn't want to lose a man, but if Sethron was stealing the women, he would have been lost anyway, kicked out of the company at the least. "*If* the women are there, use whatever force is necessary. Deadly force is authorized. Sethron won't want to live to deal with me, anyway, if he's stolen my prisoners."

"Yes, sir."

"Borage, I'm authorizing you to sign for the repairs. I'm going to find that shuttle."

"Viktor," Borage said softly. "That vein in your forehead is throbbing, and you're holding your gun."

"What's your point?"

"That you may regret actions taken in anger for something so trivial."

"It's not trivial," Viktor growled and stalked away.

———

Ankari had no idea how much time passed before she regained consciousness, but she awoke on a bed, or maybe it was a medical float stretcher. When her gritty eyes opened, she was staring up at a gray ceiling. Were they still on the ship? She hoped so. The stretcher didn't feel like it was moving. When she tried to lift a hand, she found her wrist strapped down. Her legs were too. Not good.

"Awake already?" a familiar voice asked. "You must have been farther away from the gas than the others."

Dr. Zimonjic's face came into view. She peeled back Ankari's eyelids and shined a light into them. Or maybe that was some kind of brainwashing wand. A bulging pocket brushed Ankari's thigh. Picking a pocket would be difficult with her wrists bound, but she could try if Zimonjic stayed this close.

"Afraid I'll die?" she asked. Her mouth was dry, like she'd had a pair of socks stuffed in it for the last hour.

"Your young friend went into cardiac arrest a short while ago. I resuscitated her, but anesthetics of any kind aren't without risk, especially such a potent fast-acting one."

Ankari gulped. "Jamie?" She lifted her head. The doctor blocked much of her view, but she glimpsed two other float stretchers, a row of seats, and a control panel. They were in a shuttle. If they hadn't left the ship's bay yet, maybe there was a chance to escape.

"She's fine now." Zimonjic tugged down Ankari's collar and dropped a monitor onto her skin, the cold device sending a shiver through her as it took its readings.

"It'd be a shame if you couldn't deliver us alive, I suppose." Ankari flexed her hand to the limit of the restraint, dipping her fingers into the top of the big pocket. She brushed the tops of several tools and tried to identify them while being careful not to nudge them. Since Zimonjic had already been pickpocketed once, it wouldn't take much for her to realize it was happening again. Ankari couldn't reach her own pocket, either, so she couldn't hide anything she snatched. Maybe she could grab one item and cover it with her hand. It had to be the one item that could get her out of these straps. Ah, were those scissor handles?

Zimonjic grunted and removed the monitor.

"Why are you doing this?" Ankari rushed to ask, sure the doctor was about to move away. She couldn't quite reach those scissors, damn it.

"To save him from his own stupidity."

"Viktor?"

Zimonjic's eyes closed to slits, and she leaned closer to whisper, "Yes, *Viktor*. Captain Mandrake. He never invited *me* to call him by his first name."

Good job, Ankari. Piss off the person with access to all the deadly drugs...At least Zimonjic was close enough now that Ankari could squeeze the handle of those scissors between her index and middle finger. Just barely. She had to be careful pulling them out.

She licked her lips. "Is this really about saving someone, Doctor? You just want to make money, don't you? Not that I blame you. Two hundred thousand, that'd be enough to retire nicely on if one invested wisely."

"Please, Felgard would have me shot if I showed up at his door, whether I'm an upright GalCon citizen or not. Those finance lords are so high above the law that they're probably not even aware it exists. I certainly don't have the clout to ensure he pays, not without the rest of the company at my side, and Mandrake will probably kill me for this, but...it's for his own good. I don't know what he sees in you, but I'm not going to let his infatuation destroy all he's built. Destroy *him*."

"What are you going to do then?" Ankari slipped the scissors out of the doctor's pocket a heartbeat before the woman straightened up. She palmed them, using her body to hide them from above.

"Knock you out again, tie you up, and dump you in a trash bin somewhere. Or, if Sethron can find an outgoing ship that's not guarded well, we'll throw you in their cargo hold. I don't care where, just so long as you can't get back aboard the *Albatross*. I don't know what you did to talk the captain into helping you, but I can guess." Zimonjic's lips curled into a frigid sneer.

"It's time for you and your friends to deal with your own problems, not drag us into your mess with you."

"I didn't talk him into anything. I told him we'd go our own way if he'd just let us go. He's the one who wanted to help."

Zimonjic didn't deny the statement. From the wry twist of her lips, maybe she believed it was true. "Well, he's not going to help. The company doesn't need to start a war against someone with unlimited money and resources."

"Doctor?" A second face came into view, nobody Ankari recognized. She wondered what had happened to the guard who had been stationed outside of their lab. Bribed to look the other way? Drugged and locked in a cabin? "We're cleared. We can unload."

Unload? Then they weren't back on the ship after all, but already on the station. Ankari held back a groan.

"Thank you, Sethron," Zimonjic said. "Let's get them out of here before anyone on the *Albatross* realizes they're missing."

"It's another hour until shift change. We should be fine." The man—Sethron—walked to the control console, hit a button, and the rear door unlocked with a hiss and lowered.

"Does *he* know you're not planning to collect the bounty?" Ankari asked, speaking normally, so the doctor's helper would be sure to hear. If he hadn't been clued in yet, this might cause some dissent between them. "That there's nothing in this for him except the captain's irritation?"

But Zimonjic calmly said, "He knows."

"Uh, then why would he agree to do this?"

She lowered her voice. "He has feelings for me. Men will do foolish things for love."

After she recovered from her surprise, Ankari said, "So will women."

Zimonjic gave her a hard look but said nothing further.

As soon as the door lowered, Sethron pushed the first stretcher out of the shuttle. Ankari glimpsed another shuttle and various loading and unloading machines on the deck outside. An indifferent robot rolled by, pushing float pallets full of boxes. This looked like a cargo bay rather than a concourse with regular human activity. When Viktor realized Ankari and the others were gone, he would go looking for them—she didn't believe he would, as Zimonjic seemed to think, simply forget about her and continue on to the next mercenary mission. But if they were in some back alley of the space station, he would have trouble finding them. Unless Ankari could get a message to him somehow.

As soon as Zimonjic turned her back to grab Lauren's float stretcher, Ankari flipped the scissors, attempting to get the blades around the restraining cuff. A laser knife would have been much easier. Maybe that had been in the doctor's other pocket.

Zimonjic and her helper disappeared down the ramp. Ankari stopped being subtle and flexed her fingers backward, hacking with the blades as well as she could. She had always had flexible joints, otherwise she doubted she could have cut anything except a chunk out of her leg. Even so, it took dozens of snips before enough of the fabric broke that the cuff loosened. She yanked her wrist out, freed her other arm, and sat up, grabbing at the ankle restraints.

Her captors and the other stretchers were out of view. As Ankari swung her legs to the floor, a man shouted something in the distance. Something about no guns? She couldn't be sure.

She took a step and nearly tumbled to the floor, her legs still heavy and quivering from whatever anesthetic Zimonjic had slammed them with. After catching herself on a seat, she took a moment to look around, rather than charging out. She had better arm herself in case Zimonjic and the guard had weapons. Unfortunately, there weren't any laser rifles mounted on the wall. The doctor's bag was sitting in one of the back chairs. Ankari rifled through it, grabbing the laser knife she had been hoping to find earlier. Not much of a weapon, but she didn't know what most of the other things were.

More shouts came from the cargo bay. Ankari stumbled to the door, beating at her thighs with her fist to try and get the blood flowing. Her feet could have been encased in cement blocks for all that she felt.

Just as she reached the door, the whine of a laser rifle blasted through the bay. Ugh, what was Zimonjic doing? Getting in a fight with station security?

Jamie and Lauren were still strapped to their float stretchers, but they'd been abandoned near a stack of blue crates. Neither the doctor nor Sethron was in sight. No, wait. There was Zimonjic's sweater. She was hiding behind a crate, leaning around the corner.

Ankari sneaked out of the shuttle, beelining for the first stretcher. Lauren lifted her head, her eyes wide. Jamie was starting to wake too. Ankari held a finger to her lips, then grabbed Lauren's restraints, opening them as quietly as she could.

Lasers fired somewhere on the other side of those crates. Zimonjic turned and ran back toward the shuttle. She stumbled when she spotted Ankari. With nothing better for a weapon, Ankari brandished the laser knife.

"Don't!" a man in the distance yelled at the same time as a crimson laser beam streaked between two stacks of crates and blasted Zimonjic in the back. She sprawled forward, hands outstretched, landing spread-eagle on the deck. Smoke wafted from the back of her sweater. She didn't move.

Lauren yanked her legs free of the restraints, and Ankari was lunging to tear off Jamie's before it registered in her brain that the voice that had shouted that *Don't* had been familiar. Viktor. Indeed, the next words were his, as well. "Just...secure the shuttle." He sounded weary, defeated.

A squad of armed and armored young men jogged around the crates, wearing the patches of Mandrake Company. Two ran toward her while the others ran into the shuttle. One planted a hand on Ankari's shoulder, as if she had been planning to flee.

"We've got them, Captain," the man called.

Viktor strode into view. He looked over at Ankari and the stretchers, his face a mask, but his eyes haunted. He went first to Zimonjic and knelt, his fingers touching her throat to check her pulse. This wasn't what he had wanted. She could read it in his expression. He must have expected some other kidnapper, not the doctor. If Zimonjic had been speaking the truth, she had just died trying to *help* the company, however misguidedly it might have been. Ankari hung her head. *Had* it been misguided? She wasn't even sure. From the doctor's eyes, it surely hadn't been. Ankari could all too easily see what had prompted the woman to take this action. She stared at the floor, reminding herself that she hadn't asked for any of this. She hadn't *wanted* to be picked up by Mandrake Company; she'd had no choice in the matter. All she had been trying to do all along was save herself and her partners, her friends.

Even knowing that, she couldn't help but feel guilty as Viktor stood up, shaking his head.

"Load them up and take the shuttle back," he told one of the mercenaries.

"Yes, sir."

He walked away without looking at Ankari or the others again. She didn't know if it was because he was shocked and distressed by Zimonjic's death or…if something had changed. Maybe he realized he had made a mistake.

CHAPTER FOURTEEN

It had been two days since Zimonjic's death. Ankari hadn't seen Viktor since then. She, Lauren, and Jamie had been returned to the lab, again with a guard stationed outside, and they were still receiving meals, but she had no idea if the plan to storm Felgard's island was still in effect, or if Viktor had changed his mind. Maybe he would simply drop them off and leave them to deal with the finance lord on their own. Maybe he wanted to forget about the time they had shared and back out of his contract with her—after all, they had only agreed to it verbally and with a handshake, not by signing anything that would hold up under legal scrutiny.

She missed his company and lamented that he had never made good on his promise of "later," but Ankari didn't know if she was even in his thoughts at the moment. Even if she hadn't had any control over Zimonjic's actions, she felt as if she might have disappointed him. She wasn't sure when his favorable opinion of her had started mattering, but somewhere along the way it had.

A poke in the shoulder roused Ankari from her thoughts. She was supposed to be marketing the business, not dwelling on mercenary captains. "We should be close to Felgard's," Jamie said. "Don't you think you should find out what the plan is? Or if there is a plan?"

"How would you suggest I do that? I'm stuck in here with you two, talking to all the same close-mouthed people." Which consisted of a day guard and a night guard, neither of who knew much about what was going on. Or, if they did know, they weren't answering the women's inquiries.

"Can't you see if the captain will talk to you? At the least, I'd like to know if I should be trying to build weapons or booby traps that we can take in with us, or if we're going to have an escort of well-armed mercenaries."

"Do you know *how* to build weapons and booby traps?" Ankari asked.

"Uhm. Perhaps I should have said I'd like to know if I should be trying to *learn* how to build weapons or booby traps."

Ankari snorted.

"It's too bad that man came in and took our generator," Jamie said. "I felt like we were close with programming it to make an EMF charge that could interrupt a power system."

Ankari must have been sleeping when that had happened. She didn't remember any equipment confiscation. Did that mean Viktor was once again worried about them trying to escape? Maybe he had reviewed the brig video footage and figured out what they had been trying to accomplish that night.

"I'll try to get a meeting with the captain and figure out what's going on."

Ankari knocked on the door, having learned before that it was kept locked. They were taken out if they needed to use a latrine, and escorted to do so. She hadn't asked to be taken anywhere else to test the boundaries, but she couldn't help but feel like a prisoner who had simply been moved to fancier accommodations. Maybe Viktor had changed his mind about everything and was now thinking how much easier it would be to turn her team over to Felgard and about how few men he would lose in such an exchange. Maybe he was thinking about the men…and woman he had already lost…

The door slid open.

"What?" the guard asked, as friendly and chatty as always.

"I'd like to see the captain," Ankari said.

The guard shrugged and shut the door in her face.

"That went well," Jamie said.

"Things have changed, haven't they?" Lauren asked, turning her back on her work to face them.

"I think so." Maybe they should have tried to escape when they had been on that station. But she didn't know when they could have done so. There had been such a brief moment between the time Ankari had freed herself and the time the mercenaries charged into view. "I don't suppose microbiologists know how to build weapons or booby traps?"

"I...don't know," Lauren said. "We do have some toxic and flammable lab components in here."

"Why don't you two see what you can come up with? I'll—"

The door opened again.

"Let's go," the guard said.

"To see the captain?" Ankari asked, since he had said it in the same grim tone one might use if one was taking a prisoner to be pushed out an airlock.

"Yes."

Ankari gave her friends nods and followed the guard into the corridor. It was late evening ship's time, but she didn't know if Viktor would be on the bridge or in his cabin. It occurred to her that she had never seen his cabin. She imagined something with a dearth of chairs.

As the guard led her up a ladder and toward the officers' quarters rather than the bridge, Ankari found herself slowing her pace and wiping her palms on her jumpsuit. She wondered if Zimonjic had left a message, explaining why she had done what she had, that she had believed she was doing the right thing for the company. Even if she hadn't, Viktor might have guessed. He would regret...much, especially if Zimonjic had been a Grenavinian native. His people seemed to mean so much to him. Ankari still believed some of his interest in protecting her was because of her own similar background.

"You coming, woman?" The guard had stopped in front of a door, little different from any of the other gray doors in the gray corridor. Thanks to Ankari's slow pace, he had outdistanced her by several meters.

"Yes." She wiped her palms again, took a deep breath, and joined him.

The guard waved his hand over a sensor. "She's here, sir."

The door opened, and someone walked out, a rangy fellow in a crisp pseudo-military uniform that seemed out of place among the casual civilian garb the mercenaries favored. But a Mandrake Company patch, vines curled around a sword, rode his shoulder. "I'll let the team know, sir," he called over his shoulder and stepped past Ankari, giving her a curt nod.

The guard stepped back and pointed for Ankari to go in, his gesture making it clear he didn't plan to enter himself. She took another deep breath and walked inside.

A pair of three-dimensional maps floated in the air above the friction-mat flooring, one depicting a lush green forest complete with terrain features and roads, and the other showing a large, wooden facility with numerous decks or boardwalks between structures. The holograms were partially translucent, but it took a moment for her eyes to adjust and spot Viktor through the busy maps. He stood on the other side of the cabin, next to a bank of fruit trees potted in a grow system, leaning against a high desk—she had been right; there was no chair. He wore the same black trousers and t-shirt he had donned that night in the temple. She blushed, remembering the way she had tugged those trousers down, her eagerness to do so. Funny how the things that came naturally and without hesitation in the shadows of night could fill one with awkward embarrassment during the light of day, even the artificial light of day of a spaceship. She wondered if Viktor had chosen the clothing intentionally, or if he simply had six black shirts and wore them regularly.

"Good evening," Ankari said, realizing they had been staring at each other through the map for a long time. Or maybe it had only seemed long.

"Ankari," he said. Not exactly a term of endearment. Or even a greeting.

Should she walk through the map and join him at the desk? As she had guessed, there wasn't a sofa, or any other place to sit, either. Except for the bed, which was tucked in an alcove under cupboards. One of the doors was open, revealing his stash of battle armor. The room itself was tidy—how not when there were so few furnishings?—with most of the decor on the walls. One wall held a rack of old-fashioned swords and guns, one a big star map dotted with pieces of paper with snippets of text—quotations?—on it, and the last held framed pictures—landscapes of snow-covered mountains, lush forests, and green meadows along with a family portrait she itched to take a closer look at. But she remained in place, clasping her hands behind her back.

"I'm sorry about Dr. Zimonjic." Ankari wanted to add that it hadn't been her fault, that she'd had no choice but to go along with her, but felt like that had been her excuse for everything from the beginning. Even if it was a legitimate one, Viktor had probably heard it often enough to grow tired of it.

"Yes," he said.

He was full of words tonight. If she knew him better, knew where she stood with him right now, she would tease him for it.

"I'm sorry to disturb you," Ankari said. "I can see you're busy. I just wanted to see if we were still, er, if you were still planning to come down with us and do something to Felgard."

Viktor extended a hand toward the maps. "This is his island and a blueprint of his compound. It's possible they're not accurate—there's misinformation out there—but Lieutenant Thomlin is good at gathering intelligence. We've been making plans for the incursion."

"Oh. Good." Ankari should have realized that was what she was looking at. "I wasn't sure if you might have changed your mind about risking your people to help us."

"No." Viktor tilted his head. "We made a deal."

"I know, but I would understand if you decided it hadn't been wisely made and didn't want to go through with it."

Viktor walked around the holograms, his skin brown and green and yellow for a moment as he brushed through the edge of the terrain map. He stopped in front of her, gazing into her eyes. "Have I…given you reason to want to break off your end of the deal?"

"No, not at all. I mean, I haven't seen you much—at all—these last couple of days, and I just thought you might have been distancing yourself because…I don't know. You were having regrets. Or realizing you'd made a mistake. Or wondering what you'd been thinking. Or all of those things."

"I've been preparing for the mission." Viktor looked thoughtfully at the map. "And, yes, thinking about things. Mostly regretting that I approved the use of deadly force for your…kidnapper without knowing who it was or thinking that something aside from money might have been motivating that person. It was my mistake. Nothing to do with you."

"Except that if I wasn't here, none of it ever would have happened. Your life would still be normal."

"As I recall, you didn't volunteer to be here."

Viktor took her hands, his skin warm, pleasant. He wasn't sweating and nervous the way she was. The callouses on his palms, rough against the backs of her hands, sent a little shiver through her. This first inkling that he wasn't mad or disappointed with her filled her with hope, and maybe something more. Her eyes were level with his collarbone, and when she lowered them, she could admire the swell of muscles beneath his shirt, remember the taste of the skin beneath it.

"No," she whispered, "but I feel like I've been trouble for you ever since we met."

"*That* I won't deny."

She lifted her gaze to his face, not entirely certain she had piqued his humor or if there was some frustration in the admission. Maybe some of both. The corner of his mouth did quirk up, and he rubbed the backs of her hands with his thumbs.

"I wish we could have met in different circumstances," Ankari said. "At some little bar on a space station somewhere. I could have bought you dinner."

"Would you have approached me if you saw me in a bar?"

"It depends. How many guns would you be wearing in a bar?"

"Two. Some daggers. Throwing knives. Bars are breeding spots for trouble."

"You and I must frequent different bars."

"It's possible."

"Would you have approached *me* if you saw me in a bar?" she asked, curious if he had been attracted to her from the beginning or if her heritage or something about this mess had caused her to grow on him.

He gazed thoughtfully at her. "I don't approach women in bars. Since we're always moving around, it's less complicated to rent them by the hour, then leave."

Ankari mouthed, "Rent them by the hour," and he winced, maybe realizing that hadn't been the smoothest thing to say. She decided his rough edges were charming rather than crude and merely smiled, though she couldn't resist teasing. "Not much of a romantic, are you?"

"No."

"Well, since I've been so much trouble for you, let me offer a little advice that may help you save money in the future. You're a handsome man, Viktor. You could get women without paying for them. Just walk up, smile, and talk to them. You wouldn't even have to talk that much. A few grunts would suffice. Oh, but leave the guns with someone else when you do it. You *are* on the intimidating side at first glance. Some women will be drawn by that, but your odds are better if you appear vaguely approachable."

"I'm only interested in one woman," Viktor said. "My new business partner. Will grunting work with her?"

"Grunting and possibly keeping something interesting in your pocket for her to find."

Both corners of his mouth quirked up this time. "That's *always* there."

Ankari blushed. "I meant, uhm, tablets...keys to handcuffs. Things like that."

"You like to be handcuffed? Is this before or after the grunting?"

Er, she was making it worse. Although he looked positively amused by this conversation, so maybe it was worth it. Besides, now she caught herself wondering what he might do to her while she was handcuffed. Their previous encounter had been so abbreviated. She knew very little about his preferences. "Grunting is good at any time, I think. Especially if it's an expression of pleasure."

"Excellent."

Ankari shifted her weight, so that she was gazing through the map toward the bed. It was a tidy bed, neatly made, with a furry blanket folded across the bottom. A soft fuzzy rug on the floor offered a nice alternative to the rubbery matting, and she imagined stepping on it barefoot in the morning. Viktor released one of her hands and slid up behind her, so they were both facing in the same direction.

"Are there any other tactics I should know about for getting this new business partner to sleep with me?" He leaned close, his chest against her shoulder, and lowered his face to the top of her head. He took a deep breath. Smelling her hair? She was glad she had washed it recently.

"You should probably visit her in her lab at least once a day, so she doesn't think you've forgotten her. Or that you're angry with her. Or that you've realized it was a mistake ever to kiss her. Not that she's needy and requires constant reassurance, mind you; it's just that you're a hard man to read. Daily displays of affection would enlighten and delight her, I'm sure. Yes, like that," she added, for he was nuzzling her hair now, and had inched closer, the entire length of his body pressing against her. His free arm curled around her waist, leaving no space between them. Her own body heated in response, and she leaned into his embrace. What had she been talking about? She had already forgotten.

"It was inconsiderate of me not to come," he whispered, his breath warm against her neck.

"Yes, because you promised…things. You promised a *later*." Ankari wasn't truly irked with him—she was so relieved that he wasn't upset with her that all of the tension had flowed from her muscles, and she wanted to melt into him. But she was terribly curious what he'd had in mind that night in the temple when he had said that single word, his eyes scorching as they had memorized her on the way out the door.

"I did," he agreed and kissed her temple, the brush of his lips so gentle that her soul welled with emotion. She had been kissed before—why did it mean so much coming from him? Because he usually rented women by the hour? Because he was known for killing people, not making love to them? "I've thought of you often," he went on. "Most of the crew believes you're still a prisoner. It seemed easier that way. And it seemed I could more easily maintain that facade if I wasn't seen spending large amounts of time with you. But when I was visiting, I never wanted to leave. I always wanted to make your friends leave instead."

"Oh?" Ankari closed her eyes, imagining him ordering everyone out of the lab and pushing her up against a counter…

Viktor bent his head lower, his soft hair brushing against her temple, his lips grazing the tender flesh of her neck. She leaned her head to the side, eager to give him access to her throat, to whatever he wanted to touch. Each scrape, each nibble sent a tingle of electricity through her, charging her to the core. "Actually, I wanted to bring you back to my cabin," he murmured as he explored sensitive flesh, sucking, licking, nipping. "That's what I've wanted since that first night we kissed. It's what I've thought about. In my rack every night." His hand slid up the front of her body, caressing her breast through the fabric of her jumpsuit, then drifting toward the zipper. "Mornings too. Afternoons…"

The idea of him thinking about her excited her almost as much as the deft strokes of his roaming fingers. She released his hand so she could turn and slide hers around his back, anchoring him to her, making sure he wasn't going anywhere. She tilted her face toward him, asking for a kiss.

He smiled, as if he had been waiting all night for the question, then lowered his lips. She opened her mouth, drawing him into her. His tongue stroked long and deep, tasting her, inviting her to taste him. She rocked into him, wanting—needing—more of him.

She could feel his hardness against her and longed to wrap her arms and her legs around him, to press her slick heat against him, to have what she'd yet to experience, to have him in her. But he had pulled her jumpsuit down past her shoulders, tangling her wrists and hands in the fabric, so she couldn't have grabbed anything. Meanwhile, both of his hands were roaming, one thumb teasing her nipple through her thin camisole, the fingers of his other hand drifting lower, stroking her throbbing mound through the fabric of her jumpsuit. She wanted the clothes gone, but the way they rasped against her damp skin was arousing, as well.

"I've never even seen you naked," he murmured. He was deliberately teasing her, keeping it slow when all she wanted was to throw him against the wall and jump on him. She was already panting, already aching for him.

"That could happen," she croaked, finally tugging her hands free, her sleeves falling about her legs.

Viktor released her, and she moaned a protest. She grabbed his shoulders, not willing to let him go. But he wasn't leaving, only pushing her jumpsuit the rest of the way off. She yanked her camisole over her head, wanting his mouth on her flushed body, wanting his lips on her aching breasts. He knelt to tug the legs of the jumpsuit over her shoes. Shoes. Why the hell was she still wearing shoes? She tried to kick them off and stumbled, catching herself on his shoulders. Wrong outfit to wear for easy access for sex. She should have kept the monk robe. But finally, she stood before him in nothing except her panties. She might have yanked those off, too, but she hesitated, a hint of self-consciousness creeping into her mind as he knelt, staring up at her, looking at her from head to toe. What if he was disappointed after his fantasies?

He ran his hands up her bare legs, his fingers curling around the backs, stroking the sensitive skin of her inner thighs. "Even better than I imagined," he said, eyes like lasers as they burned into her flesh.

"Good," she whispered, relief making her bolder. She ran her hands across his shoulders, squeezing the muscles beneath his shirt. She needed to start stripping *him* down, but he wasn't standing back up. Still on his knees, he pulled her against him, breathing deeply, inhaling the scent of her womanhood. She gripped the back of his head, digging her fingers into his hair, and arched against him, wondering, hoping he might...

His hands ran up her thighs to cup her backside, his fingers curling into the band of her panties. Any second he would tear them off. He rubbed against her first, nibbling through the thin fabric, his tongue darting out, tracing the outline of her lips. She gasped, her head lolling back, and groaned his name. "Viktor...please. I want—"

It was as if that was what he had been waiting for. He tugged her panties down, and she kicked them away, supported by his strong hands. She rocked into him, pressing her mound of curls into him. His tongue darted and stroked, and she ground against him, her breaths coming in quick gasps. Her legs quivered, and it was only his hands on her butt, supporting her, spreading her, that kept her upright. His stroking licks turned into nibbles, and she groaned again, bucking with need she couldn't control. With a final nip of his teeth, she cried out, a great wave of release flowing through her.

Her legs gave out and she fell against him, might have fallen to the floor, but he caught her, lifting her and carrying her to the bed with two long strides. She wrapped her arms around his shoulders, still catching her breath. His eyes, blazing like flames, found hers as he lowered her onto the bed, the soft fur of the blanket brushing against her damp back.

He knelt astride her, never looking away from her as he yanked his shirt off. She gazed up at the ridges of muscles gleaming with sweat, his taut nipples, the bulge of him straining against his trousers, and her breath quickened, need building in her anew.

She gripped his thighs and whispered, "I want you. All of you."

"Greedy," he murmured, his gaze roaming across her naked form as he unfastened his trousers.

"Entrepreneurs often are," she whispered, pulling at his waistband, helping him. Or maybe getting in the way. It didn't matter. His trousers soon joined his shirt on the floor, and she could admire his entire body, scars, tattoos, and all. But not for long, for he came down atop her, his mouth taking hers again, demanding and hungry. She spread her legs and stroked his rigid length with her hand, drawing him toward her, welcoming him, wanting him. He groaned, struggling to keep it slow, gentle; she sensed it in the tension in his shoulders, the restraint radiating from him.

"Take me," she whispered against his lips, a command, not a request.

He obeyed. With a growl that brought the panther surging into her mind again, he plunged into her. She cried out, or maybe he did, their heated bodies coming together like comets colliding. She gripped his shoulders, fingernails digging into slick flesh, arching into him, her breaths coming in jagged gasps. Her need grew as they came together, faster, deeper, until he threw back his head and roared. His explosion sent her over the edge, and surges of pleasure coursed through her body. She shuddered, wrapping her arms around his back and her legs around his, claiming him for her own. His contented growl said this suited him fine. He shifted onto his side, pulling her with him, and dragged the fur over them. He kissed her and stroked her waist.

Ankari smiled into his eyes, happy to cuddle with him, though she couldn't resist teasing him. "Do all Grenavinians growl so much?"

He didn't look abashed by her comment—he probably knew he had a sexy growl and that she had panther fantasies about him, so it fit just fine. "I don't know. I haven't slept with many of them." He wriggled his eyebrows and growled. "Do all Speronians bite their men on the shoulder?"

"I didn't do that."

"You did. Twice."

"Well, I was excited."

"Good." He pulled her closer, and they kissed for a while, not talking much after that.

———

Viktor woke to the faint scent of lavender and lilac in the air and the feel of soft tousled hair draped across his arm. He also woke hard, with his shaft pressing against Ankari's thigh, memories of the night igniting his nerves. The map still glowed in the center of the room, giving him enough light to admire her sleeping form. His loins stirred further at the sight of a bare breast rising and falling gently with her inhalations. He tugged the Basaltar mink fur blanket up to her shoulders, lest he be tempted to disturb her sleep with further explorations of her body. Her sumptuous, responsive, agile body....

Down, boy.

The clock on the wall said it was early, and they had been up late. Very late. He would let her rest, simply enjoying the feel of her in his arms, the scent of her beneath his nose. He lowered his face to her hair, rubbing his cheek against it. He resisted the urge to growl, "Mine," though only because she had teased him about growling.

Despite his resolve, his fingers strayed under the blanket, following the sleek line of her waist, the tender skin of her abdomen, drifting up to circle her breast, cupping the soft mound with his hand. She shifted, letting out a soft sigh, and he paused, a small part of him abashed that he might be caught fondling her and a much larger part of him hoping she would wake up and throw her arms around him, and that they would enjoy a couple of hours before he had to be on the bridge.

He rubbed his thumb across her nipple. It hardened beneath his touch, but Ankari's eyes remained closed. He glanced at the clock again, trying to find the resolve to leave her alone, but the blanket shifted, falling away from her and revealing that breast again. He couldn't ignore such an invitation. He leaned over her, exploring that pert nipple with his mouth. He licked and sucked, his own body responding, throbbing against her thigh, begging him to move on top of her, into her...

A hand found the back of his head, fingers curling into his hair, and he looked up. Her eyes were open to sultry slits, watching him through lashes that dusted her cheeks. His arm muscles quivered as he fought the urge to lower himself onto her right then.

"Did I wake you?" he rasped, not quite managing to sound apologetic. It was more of a pleading, *Did you—I hope—want to be woken?*

"Yes."

"Do you mind?" Viktor lowered his lips to her breast again, hoping that if she did, she would forget soon. He slid his other hand down her waist, to the inside of her thigh, and found hot slick moisture there. He breathed in, the smell of her arousing him as much as the feel of her body.

"You can wake me like that any time," she murmured.

Her words were like a starter's gun, and he lowered himself onto her, taking her lips in his, shifting himself between her legs. She smiled against his mouth, wrapping her arms around him, arching into his body, letting him know that she didn't want him anywhere else. He found her warm entrance and crashed into her, a wave surging up the beach. Their movements quickly became fast, frenzied, as if they had been apart for months instead of a couple of hours. They came together, the wave becoming a tsunami, a great blast that stole all of his strength and left him atop her, his face buried in her neck.

"You're very good at that," Ankari whispered in his ear, her nails scraping lightly down his back.

He feared he'd been doing little more than answering his body's desires, but he accepted the compliment, knowing he'd taken his time and pleased her the night before. "I'd like to wake up to you in my arms every morning," he said. It sounded hokey and maudlin, but he couldn't find non-crude words for telling her about how he usually had nothing more than his hand when he woke up hard and that this was much better. He decided she would appreciate it more if he moved so he wasn't crushing her with all of his weight, so he pulled her over with him, holding her against him, stroking her butt, not ready to leave her warmth yet.

"I'd like that too."

The comm chimed, and Viktor sighed. At least someone's timing had been better today, even if it was still two hours before his shift. Ankari kissed him, extricated herself, then pointed toward the door that led to the latrine.

"Mandrake here," he said, watching the sway of her naked hips as she walked through the hologram to reach the door.

"Thomlin, sir. We got word back from Felgard. He refuses to meet you at a neutral location and sent the coordinates for the shuttle port on his private island instead."

"He has his own shuttle port?" Viktor asked dryly.

"Apparently so, sir."

"All right. How long until we reach orbit?"

"Less than three hours."

"Good. Mandrake out."

The comm fell silent at the same time as Ankari padded back across the room, allowing his admiration from a different angle this time.

She paused at the edge of the bed. "Do you need to get up?"

Viktor lifted the blanket. "Not yet."

Smiling, she snuggled in beside him, and he wrapped his arms around her, resting his chin on her shoulder.

"You look like you were planning on going into his base, not meeting in a neutral location." Ankari waved toward the maps hanging in the air.

"Yes, I just made the request so he would believe we meant to deal straight, prisoners for money, that's it. He has all of the advantages in his own lair, so he can't be surprised that I'd want to do the exchange somewhere else. If I *hadn't* made the request, he might have been suspicious."

"He doesn't have *all* of the advantages, either way."

Viktor arched his brows.

Ankari smiled and slid her hand along his forearm, lightly tracing the muscles with her fingers. "You're an advantage."

Her faith pleased him. He hoped he would deserve it in the end.

"He'll have good security too," Viktor said. "I had my men trying to dig up information on any meetings he might be attending or public appearances, times when he'd be away from his base and we could ambush him, but he stays in his sanctuary these days, making others come to him. We'll land and go in with a small team, our prisoners' escort ostensibly. I'll have another combat shuttle waiting over the mainland, ready to come in and help if needed."

"Do we need to do anything?"

Stay out of the way and don't risk getting hurt, he wanted to say, but she wasn't the type to hide behind a man's battle armor. More than once, she'd said she was willing to go in alone. Because she didn't want him to feel obligated to help or to risk his people on her behalf, he knew, but he hoped he had a chance to show her just how valuable his people were. How valuable *he* was. When that had started mattering, he wasn't sure, but it did now, no doubt. He kissed her shoulder.

"Is that a no?" Ankari asked, amused.

"Talk to him if you like, distract him. Figure out what he wants with you in the first place. If he's busy trying to get something from you, he'll be less aware of us and what we're doing. Just don't go off with him and let him dismiss us. I don't want to lose sight of you."

"I'd definitely rather be standing at your side. But if it's possible we can reach an accord with him, make him a legitimate client, I think it'd be wiser to pursue that instead of jumping to violence. As you said, I'm sure he'll have a lot of defenses, a lot of security people around. My guess, the only logical guess I've been able to come up with, is that he wants to force us to work for him illegally, chained in some basement, or to work on some project that we wouldn't otherwise be willing to do on our own. But maybe we can get creative and make a deal."

Viktor's arm had tightened around her at this talk of forced service and basements. He made himself relax. "Will you think me unforgivably bloodthirsty if I admit I'm hoping he drives us to kill him?"

"You don't think we'd ever be safe again if we just walked away with a deal?"

"There's that, but mostly I'm irritated that he betrayed me to all those other bounty hunters. I'm irritated that he's caused you to be hunted and endangered, and I'm also irritated that he's ultimately the reason that I lost my doctor. I want to jam a rifle down his throat and shoot. Many times." His voice had descended into a low hard register as he spoke, and he checked Ankari's eyes, worried he might have alarmed her. This wasn't exactly bedroom talk.

She wore a thoughtful expression rather than an alarmed one. "She surprised me too. Your doctor. I think I understand her now, but when she came to see us...I wasn't expecting her to become one of our would-be kidnappers."

Viktor's first instinct was to brush away this topic, to steer Ankari back to their plans for Felgard, but her words about understanding Zimonjic's motivations made him pause. He so rarely spoke of personal matters and private thoughts to others in the company—even when he'd had Doc Aglianico, their meetings had been infrequent and had usually involved alcohol—but there were times, such as when he lost someone on his team, that he wished he did have someone who could commiserate with him. Punching the bag was an outlet, but when the anger waned, he was still left with an emptiness that grew harder to ignore as the years passed and the number of fallen comrades increased.

"I didn't expect her to betray me," Viktor said. "I wouldn't have included her in that board meeting if I had." Nor would he have authorized the use of deadly force if he'd thought for a second that she would be on that shuttle. "She was one of the inner circle. Even if she hadn't been with us as long as the others from Grenavine, she understood."

Ankari twisted her head to look in his eyes. "Can I speak openly about something?"

He frowned. "Of course." It wasn't as if she was one of his soldiers.

"Since I haven't known you that long, I don't know if it's my place to… advise. Or, uhm, judge…"

"You wouldn't be the first to point out my flaws."

"I don't know if this is a flaw exactly, but from what I've seen, you seem to put the Grenavine natives, the ones who work with you, anyway, onto a pedestal. Well, not a pedestal exactly. But I think you trust them more quickly and more fully than you would someone from another world." He opened his mouth, but she rushed to add, "I don't mean to imply that your people aren't trustworthy or quality comrades—even Zimonjic thought she was acting for the greater good, protecting you from yourself."

He closed his mouth. He had gotten some of the story from Sethron— the sergeant had been injured instead of killed outright in the firefight, and Viktor hadn't had the heart to execute him after seeing Zimonjic on the deck. But he was still struggling to accept what she had been trying to do and how he had let himself become so unapproachable that she hadn't thought they could find a solution that didn't involve mutiny.

"All I'm saying," Ankari said, "is that you seem to believe being from your home world and having shared the loss that you had makes them automatically more dependable and less likely to go against you. Even with me, you were only interested in me after learning about my father and my past, that I'd come from a destroyed world too."

"It was the fact that you knocked Striker on his ass that interested me."
Actually he had found her attractive even when she was slumping against his
chest, nearly unconscious after that first crash.

"All right, but you started to trust me more when you learned I was
Speronian, didn't you?"

"Yes, but also because you had learned mashatui from your father and
that I knew honesty and integrity were always taught alongside with kicks
and punches in that art."

"And then I kissed you so I could steal your key," Ankari said. "I wasn't
being all that honest with you."

Viktor grunted. "You were a prisoner trying to escape. Your actions
didn't mean you couldn't still be a person with integrity."

"I appreciate that you were willing to think well of me, especially if
that's what got me here now." She smiled and stroked the side of his face.
"I just think it's worth remembering that we're all…people, no matter where
we came from and what's befallen us. We have all the failings of humans."

He wanted to point out that he was very aware of the failings of
humans, but he kept his mouth shut, grudgingly admitting that maybe her
observations were worth considering.

"Perhaps this is too heavy a topic for before breakfast," Ankari said,
dropping her hand to his shoulder and rubbing the side of his neck with
her thumb.

He didn't mind heavy topics when they came with rubbing. Unfortunately,
he should get up if they were going to be in orbit soon. There was still planning to do and meetings to call. "I can offer you breakfast if the night's
exercises made you hungry." He shifted her aside so he could swing his legs
over the edge of the bed.

"Certainly, and we can discuss something lighter while we eat. Such
as…who this Willow fellow is."

Viktor grunted softly. "I'd hoped you'd forgotten about that."

"Not in the least."

"It's what my parents named me. You're doubtlessly aware that trees,
bushes, and flowers are—were—an important part of Grenavinian culture
and religion. Plants have inspired a lot of names. I never found Willow to
sound particularly manly, and when I got out into the rest of the system,

I came to find it even less so. I wasn't quite as brawny at eighteen—that's when I left home to join the fleet—as I am now, so I was worried about being bullied. I signed up using the name Viktor, and that's what it's been ever since."

"Why did that monk know it?"

"I've worked for the Buddhists before. Even though druidism was our official religion, there were a lot of Buddhists on Grenavine, too, and many of the temples out there today have Grenavinian roots." He gave Ankari a significant look—she hadn't yet crawled out from beneath the covers. "Speronian too. Anyway, they must have researched my past at some point, because they have me in their databases. I think they just insist on using the name because hiring a Grenavinian named 'Willow' is more in line with their tenets than calling in an ex-Crimson Ops soldier named Viktor." He walked across the cabin to the kitchen wall and fished out a pair of glasses along with a couple of sausage-and-cranberry logs.

"Interesting. So your name changes, depending on the needs of the caller."

"Guess so." He plucked an apple from one of the trees, pulled out a few vegetables, and cut everything up for the blender. He hit the coffee button, too, in case one experience with his green drinks had been enough for Ankari. "What are *you* going to call me?" he asked a little warily as the blender wound down.

"That's a good question. I confess I'm inordinately attracted to your soldier side…" A wry smile—or maybe that was a concerned one—flitted across her face. Right. Because being drawn to a killer wasn't all that socially redeeming. There were times even he found it repelling and thought of heading off to pastures less bloodied. Unfortunately, he wasn't qualified to be much else. He'd been a troublemaker as a kid and an awful gardener—nobody had been surprised when he had left home young to join the military. "I do like the idea of you having a sweet poetic side," Ankari added.

"Hardly that."

"A thoughtful philosophical side?"

"Hm." Viktor took the glasses, mugs, and logs to the desk. "If you find you like being here for breakfast often, I can probably locate a chair."

"The privileges of rank, eh?" Ankari shed the covers and walked over to join him at the desk. He admired the view and dearly hoped she wanted to spend more nights with him. Many more. Distracted by the thought, he almost missed the twist to her face—that was definitely wryness this time—as she picked up one of the sausage bars. "Which do not, it seems, extend to receiving better meals than prisoners get."

He probably shouldn't admit that he actually liked the prepackaged food logs from Dekaron VI. He'd had various kinds of shelf-stable field rations and found these tastier than most, with all the requisite vitamins and minerals. Perhaps the titling lacked flare, but he liked a thing that stated what it was without pretension.

"Prisoners don't receive fresh vegetables." Viktor waved to her glass.

Ankari picked it up. She didn't sneer, but she didn't bounce with enthusiasm, either. "A perk only available to those who sleep with the captain?"

"Actually, there's a hydroponics room and anyone on the crew can pick the vegetables and berries in there. Even Striker could have snatched you some if you'd gone through with your night of *amore* with him."

Ankari had been in the process of taking a sip and managed to snort some of the drink up her nose at his comment. He smiled, pleased to have amused her.

"Did you just say *amore*? Maybe you're a poet after all."

"When you're done, we'll meet with your partners and my team and make our battle plan to maim, kill, or otherwise slay Felgard."

"Or...maybe not a poet."

"No," he agreed.

They chewed and drank in silence for several minutes, made companionable by the way she leaned against him.

Eventually, she asked, "Will we be putting on clothes for this meeting?" and gave him a pat on the butt.

"I do allow for a liberal dress code here."

"So, as long as we have a patch on our shoulders, we'll be acceptable?"

"Yes." Viktor had actually gone to a command meeting naked once. He decided that was a story for another time. They had a lot to do before heading down to Paradise.

CHAPTER FIFTEEN

A sparkling blue ocean stretched beneath the shuttle while a cloudless azure sky filled the air above. They zipped past small islands, but the craft did not slow. Ankari, sitting beside Lauren and Jamie, watched Viktor for cues.

He occupied a seat across from her—apparently his standing-only preference had to give in to the seats-and-harnesses-required rule of shuttle flight. He appeared grim and fierce, clad in his mesh battle armor, with pistols and knives strapped at every imaginable access point. The butt of a laser rifle sat on the deck between his legs. The soldiers at his sides were similarly armed and sat in similar positions, none of them craning their necks to see out the front of the shuttle like Ankari was. Nor were any of them wiping damp hands on their clothes. Jamie and Lauren were the only other people displaying signs of nerves. Lauren had the look of someone who needed a paper bag to breathe into, and Jamie kept fiddling with the straps of a backpack. She and Lauren had supposedly managed to cobble together some booby traps.

"Did you ever find out what happened to our generator?" Jamie whispered.

"It didn't come up," Ankari said.

"You were gone all night."

"Not talking about generators." At Jamie's disapproving frown—more for the lack of a generator update than the fact that Ankari had spent the night with Viktor, she was sure—Ankari asked, "Captain? I suppose it's too late to do anything about now, but we were wondering why one of your people took our portable generator."

"I had it sent to my engineer and worked on," Viktor said.

"Worked on?" Jamie asked.

"It should take down a brig force field now," Viktor said. Ah, yes, he *had* been reviewing that security footage after all. "That may come in useful down here."

"I hope we can avoid being thrown into cells," Ankari said. Maybe that was a delusional hope.

Viktor gave her a quick, tight smile that she didn't know how to read.

Ankari and her friends couldn't carry any weapons of their own in, not when they were supposed to be prisoners. She had objected to that, but Viktor had pointed out that they would likely be funneled through a security screening and that he, too, might be deprived of his weapons. He had growled a little at that notion. Maybe that would keep him from trying to kill Felgard. Ankari didn't know how good of an idea that was. Even if a finance lord could buy all the lawyers in the system and thus get away with committing crimes, that didn't make him a criminal in the eyes of the law. If it were known that Mandrake Company had made the man disappear, there might be…retribution.

"Looks like we're going to have an escort to the coordinates, sir," the shuttle pilot said.

"Not surprising," Viktor said.

"What? Old Felgard thinks we might ignore his landing instructions and drop down on his rooftop instead of in his shuttle port?" Tick asked. The tracker sat beside Viktor, chomping on his gum and stealing occasional peeks through the porthole behind him. He had muttered a few longing words about tropical beaches and rum.

"Maybe we could just drop the girls out in chutes and take us a nice long dip in one of his swimming holes," Striker, who was sitting on the other side of Tick, said.

Joke or not, Ankari wasn't sure she liked that attitude from one of Viktor's elite men, chosen to help protect her team. "I guess he's gotten over his interest in you if he's willing to dump us so easily," Ankari muttered to Jamie.

"I'm fine with that."

The shadow of wings flashed past a porthole behind Viktor's head.

"Mandrake Shuttle," a voice sounded over the comm. "This is Starstrike Alpha. Proceed to the assigned coordinates. We will escort you."

"And my guess is proven correct," the pilot muttered, then raised his voice to respond with a clipped, "Acknowledged."

"Starstrike?" one of the soldiers near the back said.

"Someone has an inflated opinion of the ferocity of his civilian security craft," someone else muttered.

The nose of the shuttle dipped, and a lush green shoreline came into view, lined with a sandy white beach. Trees of impressive stature rose from the verdant inland, some hundreds of feet tall. Ankari thought she saw structures in some of them, but maybe they just had interesting branches and foliage. She had never been to Paradise, but had heard about it, one of the only planets in their trinary star system that had been hospitable—pleasantly so—for human life *and* showed no sign of the past terraforming. Her pre-mission reading had told her Felgard's island had been a global park and wildlife preserve for most of its history, until he had found some loophole, dumped a whole lot of money, and purchased it.

"That's an *island?*" someone asked.

"Looks like a continent to me," Tick said.

"It's just under a million square kilometers," the pilot said.

Tick grunted. "Oh, is that all?"

"Must be nice to have all that money. Think of all the women you could buy." Striker eyed Jamie, having apparently not forgotten about her, after all. "Or maybe women would throw themselves at you, on account of the lavishes you can give them."

"You don't *give* lavishes, you idiot," Tick said, "you lavish someone. With things."

"Whatever. I bet women are jumping on Felgard's dick every hour of the day, hoping for lavishes."

Tick elbowed Striker. "Try harder to be crude, will you? It's not coming through as clearly as it could." He gave Ankari, Lauren, and Jamie apologetic looks.

"What crude? I can't talk about dicks because there are females listening?"

"Quiet," Viktor said, his voice soft, but cutting through the snickers and whispered speculation. "We'll be landing shortly."

A soft beep came from Ankari's pocket. Her tablet. Paradise must have planet-wide net coverage. She almost ignored it, figuring it was something mundane, like her mother wanting to know why she hadn't written lately, but decided to check it in case it was important. Her own research hadn't brought up any more interesting information on Felgard, but she had sent Fumio a note that morning, letting him know that she was going to confront the finance lord and asking if he had found out anything new.

When she pulled up the message program, she did, indeed, find a response from her friend.

No time for a long chat, Sweet Cakes, but I had a fresh thought on the way to work this morning, and took the liberty of investigating. We've been focusing on Felgard, not his companies. Felgard's past has been shrouded and obfuscated, and his present isn't all that clear, either. But in a testament to how much the corporations take preeminence in the system, it's harder to obscure the records of a company than it is to hide a man. I'm not sure if it'll mean anything to you, but his first company, Trak Teck Enterprises, originated on Spero. Standing by, Fumio.

Ankari stared at the words. She hadn't thought to look up the company, either, not beyond the basic information out there on the public exchange, but should have poked deeper. Spero. Just a coincidence? Or did it mean something? That Felgard came from the same planet as she? If that were true, then wouldn't they be all the more likely to be allies rather than enemies? The new information was interesting, but Ankari didn't know how it could help her, especially at this late stage in their plan.

Aware of Viktor's gaze upon her, she handed him the tablet. He read the message in silence, then handed it back to her. If he found anything enlightening, it didn't show on his face, which remained as hard and grim as ever. Even if Felgard did prove to be a victim of a destroyed world, nothing in Viktor's eyes said he was interested in extending the same solicitude to the finance lord that he had to her.

"Landing, sir," the pilot said.

Ankari put her tablet away. She was out of time for speculation.

Tall green grass waved in the ocean breeze as the craft touched down on a brick landing pad next to a hangar. The bricks looked to be gold-plated;

they gleamed beneath the strong equatorial sun. At least twenty armed men waited outside, all wearing crisp white uniforms, and there were ambulatory robots as well, with built-in protrusions that looked like weapons. They floated a couple of feet above the landing pad, idling at the corners.

Ankari took a deep breath. This was it.

Viktor unbuckled his harness and stood behind the pilot for a moment, looking alternately at the view screen and the displays on the console.

"Big welcoming party," the pilot said.

"Big island," Tick said. "You've got to have a big staff, or people will just think you're scrimping."

Ankari eased out of her seat. At least the security men—and robots—didn't look like they were preparing to shoot anyone who stepped out of the shuttle. No, of course not. She was wanted alive. All three of them were. She probably wouldn't be shot until *after* she rejected Felgard's demands.

"We're clear, sir," the pilot said.

"Drop the door. I'll go out first. Striker and Tick after, then Ankari and the others. Sergeant Aster, follow with your squad. Keep them protected."

"Yes, sir."

"You keep the engine running, Sequoia. I'll be in touch if we need one of your special pick-ups."

The pilot glanced back, a hint of a smile stretching a face that was oddly boyish and unscarred for a mercenary. "Yes, sir. I packed the parachutes and thruster bikes, just in case."

"Good."

Viktor was all business, none of the humor from the morning on his face, but he gripped Ankari's hand and met her eyes before passing her and heading out of the shuttle. Ankari was glad he hadn't suggested that she and her friends be handcuffed. She might not have a weapon, but she wanted to be able to act if she had to, even if that just meant running and hiding. With all the hulking soldiers, Viktor must have assumed it would be believable that they wouldn't bother binding their prisoners.

After he went out, the rest of the men herded Ankari, Lauren, and Jamie after him. Ankari tried not to feel useless surrounded by the sea of armed soldiers, but all she could do was clasp her hands behind her back and walk across the brick landing pad—it *was* gold-plated. How superfluous.

The scenery stretching around them was beautiful, though, palm trees, a beach in the distance, and the brilliant blue sea beyond. The thick vegetation inland reminded Ankari uncomfortably of Sturm—she hoped there weren't raptors—but the trees were different. Towering hundreds of feet in the air, they were amazing, some with trunks broader than the shuttlecraft. Long vines snaked down the sides from branches that stretched for what seemed miles to either side, creating a latticework between the trees.

There wasn't much speaking between the two teams of men, Viktor's squad of twelve and Felgard's white-uniformed contingent of over twenty. A hover truck waited, and with a few grunts, Mandrake Company and its prisoners were ushered into the big cargo bed in the back. Viktor sat beside Ankari. He was busy scanning the foliage for danger and keeping an eye on the Felgard men, who had also climbed in the back with them, so he didn't make eye contact with her, but she appreciated his solid presence, the reassuring touch of his shoulder against hers.

The truck wound into the darker interior of the island, following a gravel road, even though the hover feature would have allowed it to go anywhere. The trees grew up all around, the wide bases of their trunks blocking out the horizon and the tall thick shafts stretching up like skyscrapers. An innuendo-tainted joke floated into her mind, and she would have shared it if she were alone with Viktor, but she was well aware of all the eyes watching him, those of his people and those of the white-clad men, as well. Prisoners probably weren't supposed to trade penis jokes with their captors.

When the truck stopped, it didn't seem as if they had arrived anywhere. They were still on the road and in the middle of the forest. A couple more armed men stepped out from behind the closest tree. For a moment, Ankari thought they had been dragged out into the woods to be shot, but the men waved the truck off the road. It stopped beneath a square of green moss that didn't quite fit in with the rest of the forest floor. Before she could lean back and examine it further, the truck started rising. Fast. She grabbed Viktor's arm, realized what she was doing, and tried to find a spot on the bench to grip instead. Of course, Lauren was grabbing *her* arm, so maybe no one would think twice of her alarmed snatch.

With speed that inspired vertigo, the entire craft rose two hundred feet, then halted next to a wooden platform. An entire city of platforms spread out on multiple levels with myriad pathways leading between them, some lined with huge potted plants and others with stark, narrow stretches without so much as a railing to protect one from the fall.

"Felgard lives in a tree fort?" Striker asked as the truck floated onto the closest platform, a large loading and unloading area that included a vehicle garage. "That's not in line with the kind of super villain abode you usually see in literature."

"You've read literature?" Tick asked.

"Yes."

"Was it graphically represented?"

One of the other men snickered, muttering about Striker's extensive comic collection.

"Every panel has sentences on it, you meatheads. It's literature."

"Ooooow-splat isn't a sentence," Tick said.

Ankari tried to decide whether she was reassured that Viktor's men were calm enough for this banter or if she was concerned that they weren't taking Felgard as seriously as they should.

When the truck stopped, Viktor was the first out again, his rifle in his hands. Ankari kept expecting someone to tell them they had to leave their weapons behind. She couldn't imagine the men strolling into Felgard's tree mansion—or inner sanctum, whatever super villains had—fully armed.

A man in a less military version of the white uniform walked out of the vehicle house. "This way, Captain Mandrake." He pointed toward one of the bridges, a wide one, fortunately.

Viktor waited until Ankari and her friends were out, along with the rest of his soldiers, before starting across it. Ankari shouldn't have looked over the edge, but she couldn't help it. A dizzying jumble of trunks stretched downward, vines dangling from their branches and blocking much of the view, but she glimpsed some ferns far, far below. A drop would be deadly, no question.

"Walk precisely where I walk, Captain," the butler said when they came to a platform checkered with light and dark squares of wood, each about two feet wide. He picked his way across in some pattern only he knew.

Ankari thought Viktor might snort at this ridiculousness, but he grabbed a head-sized pine cone and tossed it on a random square. When it first struck, nothing happened, but then it bounced onto another square, which flipped open from invisible hinges. The cone disappeared, falling into the depths below.

Without a word, Viktor strode after their guide, hurrying to catch up so he wouldn't lose the pattern. The other men also rushed to follow, Ankari included.

Three steps in, her heel landed on an edge, and a trapdoor fell open. Even without having her weight on it, the sudden gap and view of the distant ground made her heart jump into her throat. She dropped into a fight stance, more for stability and balance than any thought of fighting, and let out a slow breath, composing herself. She caught Viktor looking in her direction, his eyes intense, as if he would have leaped across the intervening squares, chancing trapdoors, if he'd needed to catch her. The concern touched her, but she was relieved he hadn't acted on her fumble. If *he* were the one to fall…

She gulped. This wasn't the place to contemplate what he had come to mean to her.

A few more heels caught, causing trapdoors to fall open, but the Mandrake soldiers kept their calm and reached the other side without anything more disturbing happening. The guide continued up a ramp to a new platform where he waited for them. Viktor looked back across the checkerboard—trying to memorize the safe route?—for a long moment before joining the man.

Several more men in white butler-style uniforms waited on the new platform, each carrying a bucket in one hand and a long fork in the other. Odd. A bridge stretched ahead of them, lined by huge pots housing strange green plants the size of trees. Their thick stems were more than six inches wide with vines that twisted and writhed in the breeze—or maybe they were doing that independently of the breeze? Trumpet-shaped flowers bigger than a man's head swayed with their movements. Ankari couldn't guess if they were genetically engineered, someone's pet project, or native plants. After all, the trees were enormous too.

At the end of the long bridge, a big building with numerous conical wooden roofs rose up from an elevated platform. Felgard's mansion?

Once all of the soldiers were gathered on the platform, the guide nodded to the men with the buckets. They exchanged long looks with each other, took deep—bracing?—breaths and inched out onto the bridge. Each man stabbed a fork into his bucket, pulling out what appeared to be fresh raw steak. Ankari stared, puzzled, until the trumpet-flowers rotated toward the men, revealing sharp protrusions that she could only think of as teeth. Fangs.

One of the flowers lunged, taking a proffered steak with a strange undulation, not unlike a jaw snapping shut. Others descended on the steak-carrying men. Ankari had heard of plants that ate insects, but this was crazy.

"Hurry," the guide said, waving for them to follow. "They're not sated for long."

As the guide hustled forward, staying in the middle of the bridge, his shoulders hunched inward, his nervousness didn't seem like it was for show. One of the men leading the way, feeding the plants, jumped in surprise as a flower snapped close to his arm. He thrust a steak at it, and the trumpet shifted, swallowing the offering and leaving him to hurry onward.

Lamenting her lack of a weapon more now than before, Ankari trotted after the mercenaries—they were all hustling now, crowding the guide and the men doing the feeding. Those steaks disappeared with alarming rapidity. A big serrated dagger had appeared in Viktor's hand, in addition to the rifle strapped across his chest.

Halfway across the bridge, someone behind them snarled, a mixture of rage and pain. One of the flowers had clamped onto a mercenary's shoulder. He jerked back, shooting at the trumpet point blank. More plants reared and undulated toward him, like sharks roused by the scent of blood. A huge flower from the other side of the bridge darted in, clamping onto the mercenary's ribcage.

"Keep going, keep going," Viktor said, pushing Ankari and the others toward the far side even as he raced back toward the attack. All of the men around the victim were helping, shooting and slashing at the plants.

Ankari felt cowardly for running away, but what could she do to help? A side kick to the stem wouldn't harm the flexible foliage—though it might piss it off. A kick to its pot might do more, but the huge containers must weigh hundreds of pounds each. No, she didn't know how to help. Not from within the mess. Ankari raced through the closing tunnel of greenery, dodging as a trumpet whipped toward *her*. Even though its attack missed, the snap of fangs inches from her ear filled her with fear, and her run turned into a dead sprint.

Lauren and Jamie made it to the platform ahead of her, but she tumbled out on their heels, almost crashing into one of the men with the buckets. Zookeepers, that's what they were.

A couple of raw steaks slumped in the bottom of the closest man's bucket. Ankari grabbed them and hurled them into the swirling mess of plants and men. Not waiting to see if it helped at all, she rushed from zookeeper to zookeeper, grabbing any leftover steaks and flinging them onto the bridge. She didn't pause to watch the effect until she had thrown the last one. It spun through the air, droplets of blood flinging, and splatted against someone's chest. Viktor's. Oops.

The mercenaries had escaped from the fray, leaving severed vines and scorched trumpets on the bridge boards. Many of the plants still writhed, twitching in irritation like cats' tails, but they let the men finish crossing. Something about those twitches made Ankari certain the plants were only saying, "Until next time." The man who had been attacked was dripping a trail of blood as he walked, but his curled lips proclaimed his anger more than they proclaimed his agony. Viktor's people would probably die before admitting to pain.

"Conscientious of you to assist your captors," the guide said mildly, standing next to Ankari's shoulder.

He was watching her through slitted eyes. The zookeepers were, too, and she had the distinct feeling that they would have been pleased if the mercenaries were all devoured on the bridge, since Ankari's team had made its way through.

Ankari mustered all the righteous indignation that she could when she said, "Nobody deserves to die that way." Yes, *that* was the only reason she had helped...

"Felgard somewhere in this maze?" Viktor asked, planting himself in front of the guide. "Or are you just taking us on the grounds tour in the hope that we won't make it to our meeting with him?" He still carried the wicked serrated blade—viscous green plant juices dripped from it—and looked like he was contemplating a throat slitting.

The guide eased back a couple of steps. The zookeepers disappeared down side bridges, none of which were lined with plants.

"He is waiting for you inside." The guide waved to a ramp leading up to the large platform that held the mansion. "This way."

As the man scurried up the ramp, Viktor bumped Ankari's shoulder. With a smirk in his eyes, he murmured, "If you throw raw meat at your friends, I wonder what you do to enemies."

He was gone, striding after the guide, before Ankari could come up with a good answer.

"Be careful, Ankari," Lauren whispered. "These people might figure out beforehand that we're not exactly Mandrake Company prisoners here."

"Was I supposed to let the mercenaries be eaten by plants?" Ankari headed up the ramp.

"Maybe just some of them," Jamie muttered, walking behind her.

"A few more minutes and the ruse will be over. One way or another."

CHAPTER SIXTEEN

Not surprisingly, Viktor and everyone else were funneled through a security screening tunnel before being granted entrance to the big house. Bored-looking guards pointed toward cubbies where guns, knives, and nail files—Keys carried one of those—could be tossed into baskets and "picked up later," or so the promise went. Viktor hated disarming himself, but he had expected it, so he unstrapped everything the security personnel pointed at. He had hoped he might sneak his bone dagger in—sometimes it didn't show up on scans programmed to look for higher tech weaponry, but they found it, as well. It took nearly a half hour for his team to pass the checkpoint, and they left the cubbies overflowing with gear.

The delay grated on Viktor's nerves, but he hoped it was irritating Felgard, as well. Irritated and impatient enemies were more likely to make mistakes, after all.

The guide finally led them to the front door of the mansion. Even though Viktor had seen the blueprints to the Felgard estate, he expected to have to endure another maze inside, perhaps with more ill-disguised booby traps. Those plants had *not* been mentioned on the maps Thomlin had dug up. But the cool, climate-controlled home was open and spacious, with large rooms, high ceilings, and windows in every direction, providing views of the forest on three sides and the ocean in the distance. The guide led the squad past a computer area and a dining room, then up a ramp to a circular chamber that took up the entire top floor. Here, the windows were tinted and doubled as screens with financial news and tickers scrolling down them. One displayed a talking head reporting on an economic upheaval in the southern province of Novus Earth. The sound was muted, but the words scrolled through the air below.

A few white-uniformed guards were stationed around the perimeter of the room, armed and fit. They gave Viktor hard stares. Viktor thought his people could handle them, even starting out unarmed, but the ten Prodigal 700 androids were another matter. The stony-faced humanoids were fleet issue and designed for combat—he'd seen them in action with the robots, cyborgs, and droids units in the army. They could withstand short bursts of laser fire and deflect knives and bullets; they could be knocked down by physical force, but would simply rise up again. The laser pistols holstered at their waists were a threat, but so was the way they could rip human limbs and heads right from their bodies.

Victor gave Sergeant Aster a long look as he came up the ramp. Aster had been carrying the generator that his team had modified. It was supposed to be able to affect anything with a circuit board now, at least momentarily. It was back in the cubby with all of their weapons, but Viktor wanted his sergeant to know he still expected him to try to get to the equipment and use it if a fight broke out.

Aster glanced at the androids and grimaced—probably doubting if the generator would work on them—but nodded once. Viktor doubted it would, too, but they could hope.

At the center of the room, a man sat in a reclining chair, his legs tilted up off the ground, his arms supported by fancy rests with data input devices at his fingers. A holographic display hovered at the perfect angle to be readable by the occupant. Though Viktor had only spoken to the reedy man through the net, he recognized Felgard promptly. He wore the same top hat tugged over his gray hair as before, along with the old-fashioned spectacles with the bleeping light on the frame. A black suit suggested he rarely strolled into the tropical warmth outside of his home.

"How's that chair?" Tick whispered to Striker. "In line with what the comic literature suggests for a super villain's furnishings?"

"If it can shoot lasers out of the armrests, it will be," Striker whispered back. "I might add it to Volume 237."

Viktor took note of a balcony door behind the fancy chair. It and the ramp they had walked up were the only visible exits to the room, but the windows might be openable, as well. He didn't look at Ankari or her friends or the rest of his men as they joined him in the room, fanning out and ready to fight, whether they had their weapons or not, but he was aware of their presence.

"Welcome, Captain." The chair rotated, seemingly of its own accord, so that Felgard faced the group. "I'm glad you weren't overly delayed by your Sisson Hood mission."

"The bounty hunters attacking my ship and trying to raid my brig were more of a delay than Hood." Viktor didn't bother subduing the growl in his voice; Felgard would expect him to be irked about that.

"It seems they inspired you to come promptly though and that you're unharmed. Mostly." Felgard frowned at Rowan, the man who had been maimed by those weird predator plants. "That fellow is bleeding on the floor. Beaumont." Felgard flicked his fingers.

The guide who had led Viktor's team through the maze sighed and jogged down the ramp. He returned shortly with a rag.

"We'll take our two hundred thousand now," Viktor said, "and leave the girls for whatever you want them for. They're trouble. You're welcome to them."

"Trouble?" Felgard regarded Ankari and the others mildly. "Hard to imagine."

"If you didn't think they were trouble, you wouldn't have offered so much to have them delivered." Viktor tried to make that sound like a leading question. He still wondered why Felgard hadn't simply sent his own men out to find Ankari and her friends, not that they had been easy to find on that remote planet. It had been luck and Thomlin's restless net explorations that had led Mandrake Company to them.

"Hm," was all Felgard said.

"The money," Viktor prompted again. He wasn't in a hurry to leave Ankari in here, but Felgard would expect this attitude from him. He wondered if the finance lord would try to get away with a hundred thousand, his original offer. He expected it, in truth. Or he expected the man to give him nothing, except a guide to lead them past even deadlier traps on the way out. He hadn't missed the way the guide had stood by while Viktor's team dealt with the bridge attack.

"Yes, yes, the money, of course," Felgard said. "If you and your hulking men will return to your shuttle, I'll have it delivered on a truck. Solid gold, right? Isn't that what you bounty hunters always want? No flimsy digital money?"

Viktor hesitated—a lot of bounty hunters and mercenaries *did* require physical payment, gold being the only constant in a galaxy where GalCon was always fiddling with the amount of fiat currency out there, causing the value of an aurum to change from day to day. But if Viktor accepted a transfer of funds into the company account, there would be no reason to return to the shuttle to accept delivery of anything. They needn't leave the women's sides until they knew why Felgard wanted them.

"Gold isn't necessary. Transfer the funds directly to the Mandrake Company account, and we'll leave promptly."

"Ah?" Felgard tilted his head, watching Viktor through those quirky spectacles. "I'm afraid the physical gold has already been prepared. It *is* how you'll be paid. As soon as you arrive at your shuttle."

"I have a man at the shuttle. You can deliver it to him while we wait."

"You'd trust a mercenary not to fly off with that much gold? And your shuttle?"

"I trust my men, yes." Viktor met Ankari's eyes. He didn't give her anything so obvious as a wink, but she had been watching him, waiting for his signal, and she stepped forward immediately. It was doubtful whether Felgard intended to deal honestly, so Ankari might as well ask her questions sooner, rather than later, before Felgard tried to *force* Viktor and his men to leave.

"Lord Felgard," Ankari said. Her voice came out steady, even though she must be nervous. She met his eyes, and Viktor allowed himself a moment of pride before returning his focus to watching Felgard and the guards. "You've gone to great lengths to bring us here." Ankari gestured to her friends. "And to say you've inconvenienced us would be an understatement. These gun-happy clods blew up my *ship*." She might have forgiven Viktor for that—though he hadn't actually asked—but she wouldn't ever forget, that was a certainty, and there was nothing feigned about the aggravation in her voice. "If you're done chitchatting with the bounty hunters, I'd sure like to know why."

Felgard sighed at her, as if she were some tedious gnat batting about his ears. "I suppose I must talk to you since you started the company, but I'm far more interested in discussing things with your microbiologist."

The Keys woman looked more like she wanted to step back than to step forward. She glanced at the armed men around the room, swallowed, and didn't say a word.

"I want these thugs out of here first though," Felgard said. "I have no interest in discussing business matters in front of gun-happy clods as you rather politely called them." He smiled at her.

Viktor wanted to punch him, but the chair was a good twenty feet away. He would be shot countless times before he could cross that distance.

Felgard's eyes flickered, issuing some command via the spectacles, and the androids came to life. They strode toward the group of mercenaries.

Viktor hadn't planned to make threats until later, but he lunged to the side and wrapped his hand around Keys's neck. "Stop them, or she dies," he barked.

He hadn't disclosed this contingency to the women, and Keys's eyes widened with believable fear. So long as Ankari didn't think he meant it.

"Please, Captain," Felgard said. "You'll be dead before her body hits the ground. The rest of your men will soon follow." Despite his words, he *had* ordered the androids to halt.

"So long as whatever nefarious plan you're concocting is thwarted too."

"As if you care about my plans. This is about you not believing I intend to pay you, is that it?"

"You *are* being shifty about it," Viktor growled.

"Very well." Felgard's eyes twitched a few times.

The tablet in Viktor's cargo pocket bleeped.

"You'll want to take a look at that," Felgard said blandly.

"Tick," Viktor said. He wasn't going to release Keys's neck; the androids probably had orders to shoot him the instant he did.

Tick unbuttoned the pocket and withdrew the tablet. He unfolded it and held it up so Viktor could see it. An alert informed him that a deposit for the full amount had been dropped into the company account. That was unexpected. And not particularly desirable, because he now had no reason to stay.

"Take it and the men back to the shuttle," Viktor said. "I'll stay to make sure you don't meet with trouble on the way." He glanced back, finding Aster and meeting his eyes again. Only for a heartbeat.

"Really, Captain," Felgard said. "Are you going to stand there with your hand around that woman's neck for the next hour?"

"Only until I'm sure my people have safely left your compound. Someone seems to have installed booby traps."

"If you're referring to the results of my botanical hobbies, I assure you those are merely pleasant decorations."

Rowan, the man who'd been bitten twice by those botanical hobbies, scoffed loudly.

"They do keep the staff on their toes," Felgard added with a smile.

Viktor tilted his head toward his men. They hesitated, but finally trooped out. He was relieved they cared enough not to want to leave him, but he definitely had the feeling Felgard wasn't going to talk about his hopes and ambitions—or problems—in front of so many. With just Viktor there alongside the women, maybe he would. Especially if he had plans to eliminate Viktor, which, given the pest Viktor was making of himself, he might.

"You've been paid, Captain." Felgard's tone was harder now, his eyes cooler.

"Release my new microbiologist."

———

"*Your* microbiologist?" Ankari asked, noting that Viktor's fingers didn't leave Lauren's throat. Lauren looked as nervous at that as she was about Felgard. Ankari didn't dare signal her that she would be fine, at least insofar as Viktor was concerned. "Do you think that you've bought us, Lord Felgard? As if we're exotic pets on sale to the highest bidder?"

"Don't flatter yourself, girl. You're not that exotic."

Viktor's eyes narrowed, as if he wanted to punch the man for the insult. Or kill him.

Ankari jerked her head toward Lauren, willing her to talk. Felgard seemed more interested in speaking with her than with anyone else. If she was the only one he had needed from the beginning, why had he bothered to have all three of them captured?

Lauren took a deep breath and lifted her chin, grimacing at the fingers resting on her throat, then spoke. "What do you want from us, Lord Felgard?"

Felgard gave Viktor an annoyed why-are-you-still-here look, but answered.

"I want what you offer, or what you believe you'll be able to offer soon," Felgard said. "You and your friends will work for me here until you've created a viable treatment plan. You'll do the research, and they'll continue to search the galaxy, retrieving whatever samples you need. With an escort of people and my fastest ship, of course." He smiled at her, as if he were displaying the epitome of generosity. Jamie's face grew speculative, as if she was faintly intrigued by the notion, and Ankari frowned at her. "Your company's time estimate is, however, too far out for my needs," Felgard continued. "You'll have to come up with a viable treatment plan within six months."

"And you intend to keep us as slaves until then?" Ankari asked.

"You'll be kept well, and once you've completed what I've asked, you may leave." He smiled again. He was trying too hard. Out of desperation? Or because he was lying and didn't want them to see through it?

"I don't understand," Ankari said. "Why didn't you just contact us? Aside from your slavery and sleepless nights proposition, we may have been willing to work with you."

Felgard snorted. "That's highly unlikely, given my history. You've researched me by now, I'm certain."

Ankari didn't respond right away. Did he think she had dug up more than she had? Or was there something in what she had that meant more than she realized? "I'm an open-minded woman, Lord Felgard." There, that made it sound like she knew what he was talking about. Probably.

He snorted again. "I'm sure you would say anything at this point to avoid your fate, but come now. You're telling me that you would have worked with me? You a Spero-born woman and me...a Spero-born man?"

Yes, thanks to Fumio, she had known that, but she still didn't see why it should affect her opinion negatively. After all, a common background had drawn Viktor closer to her. Surely it ought to be the same with finance lords. Except she didn't feel closer to him, not at all. His expression told her more was coming, the unpleasant part.

"A Spero-born man who betrayed his people," Felgard added, his gaze shifting from her toward one of the window displays showing market tickers for Novus Earth and Paradise.

Viktor stirred, his eyes closing to slits. He still had Lauren by the neck—she didn't appear pleased by this fact—but there was no bite to the grip.

"People make mistakes," Ankari said. She doubted very much she would be in the mood to absolve him when she found out what his "mistake" had been, but she wanted to keep him talking. What had he done that was so terrible that he had been certain she would never agree to work with him?

"Mistake." Felgard barked a short, harsh laugh. "What a strange word choice for you. When I…" He looked at her curiously. "Do you even know?"

No. But she could guess that this had something to do with the destruction of the planet. He couldn't possibly be responsible or blame himself for that, could he? He was a civilian and always had been—that much was in his public record.

"GalCon was determined," Ankari said. "Our people were stubborn. Proud. They would have been defeated one way or another."

"But how easy it was for the fleet to sneak in once the planetary defense grid was lowered. At precisely the time they requested." His mouth twisted. "Like you, girl, I had a lot of companies in my youth. I started many, seeking that elusive route into the upper crust of society, the financially independent, the untouchable. The lords. Like with you, some of those businesses failed, some succeeded moderately well, and perhaps I would have found what I sought eventually if I'd kept plugging away, but humans are not known for patience. Especially young and ambitious ones. I wanted it all overnight, and that's what they offered me. Felgard, founder and owner of Trak Teck Enterprises, the company that installed the planetary defense grid and serviced and maintained it. And programmed it." He was looking at the screen again, or perhaps the ocean view in the distance. "They offered me a fortune. What I considered a fortune at the time anyway. And the opportunity to meet all the right people, to schmooze and network, to ensure my company became a famous entity on the exchange. To ensure I had everything I could ever want."

Ankari's blood had chilled in her veins, and the climate-controlled air was suddenly far too cold for her tastes. She was staring at the man who had brought about Spero's destruction? Or at least assisted it along? What might have happened if the planetary grid hadn't fallen? The news had always blamed the Crimson Ops for that disaster. No one had ever whispered of betrayal from within. From a civilian contractor who had been hired to defend the planet…not make it more vulnerable.

"And I did have everything I ever wanted after that," Felgard went on, almost as if he were confessing to some priest of old. "For the next twenty years, I had it all. But not even the rich can escape the passage of time, the disease it brings." His eyes sharpened again, and he looked at her.

Ankari composed her face, lest he see how much his words had stunned her.

"Needless to say, I'm intrigued by what those alien microbes might be able to offer. My problem…" He touched his abdomen. "I've always had problems—a psychologist would doubtlessly point out I must have a guilty conscience that troubles me—and the bacteria that plagues me, that keeps coming back…the doctors understand what it is, how it affects the system, how long I likely have, but they don't know how to rid me of it. It's something I picked up in my travels. Apparently those with compromised systems are more vulnerable, but it's problematic for many in the outlying, less civilized, worlds. Aradica Trifilcarius." he said, nodding at Lauren. "I'm sure you've heard of it."

"Yes. It's native to this system, and resists our antibiotics, manual irrigation, and the drugs currently on the market. It even kills nanobots. You're right, Lord Felgard, in that we do believe the alien microbiota would deal with it. Those people were so similar to us, except that they evolved here, or at least lived here long enough to find immunity to many of the native bacteria. It's highly likely that we could help you."

"That was my hope. I'm not a theist, you know. I don't believe there's an afterlife, a heaven or hell. I never did, anyway. I suppose there are naturally doubts when the end nears. Most people hope that a heaven exists, that this isn't the end. I only hope that a hell doesn't exist. I'm sure you can understand."

Ankari was glad he was talking to Lauren instead of her. Lauren wasn't Speronian. She might be appalled, but couldn't be affected so deeply. Ankari needed a moment to recover before she could speak to him without rancor dripping from her voice. If his guilt was stressing his system so that he had been more susceptible to bacterial plagues, then good. He deserved it. He should have died twenty years ago, when millions of others had. *He* should have died, and *they* should have lived.

Felgard had been right. Ankari never would have worked with him if she had known. And now? Did she have a choice? She looked at the guards, the androids, Viktor…wondering if he had come in with a plan greater than walking off the shuttle with men and guns and a vague hope of being able to use them.

For the moment, he appeared to simply be waiting and watching Felgard. Absorbed in the story? Had Grenavine been betrayed in a similar manner? She would have to ask someday.

The displays showing the market tickers blinked out, returning the windows to nothing more than windows. Before Ankari could wonder what had happened, Viktor blasted into motion. He was so fast that she wouldn't have seen him move at all, except that Lauren stumbled forward, flailing for her balance. Flesh smacked against flesh, then a laser rifle fired, the beam streaking wildly into the room.

Ankari grabbed Lauren and Jamie. "Down," she whispered and dropped to the floor. "Stay down."

There weren't any posts or any beams to hide behind, or she would have scrambled toward them. Maybe they would be safer near the wall?

More crimson beams fired. Two of the white-uniformed guards were already down and not moving. Ankari finally spotted Viktor, rolling to dodge fire from the other guards in the room. He came up behind one of the androids—one of the *unmoving* androids—using the broad-shouldered male figure for cover.

Felgard slammed his hand against something on his chair, then threw himself out of it, moving adroitly for a man with less than a year to live. Lauren and Jamie were taking her advice to heart, their eyes wide and their bellies to the floor. Ankari spotted a gun next to a fallen guard. At the rate Viktor was going, he might down the rest without a scratch, if the androids didn't start up again. She didn't know how he had arranged the power failure or how long it would last. Wait, it had to be more than power if the androids were affected...The generator?

Felgard was sprinting out the back door. There was no time to contemplate the hows further. If he got away, neither she nor Mandrake Company would ever be safe, especially not if he figured out a way to extend his life.

She crawled toward the fallen guard. Lasers continued to fire, one beam biting into the floor not five feet to the side of her. Scorched wood flew up, pelting her. She gulped and veered around the new hole in the floor.

Ankari reached the fallen guard and grabbed his rifle. Two of the androids had toppled, and Viktor was hurling himself through the air, dodging more fire. She hesitated, tempted to help him, but he must have been tracking where she was and what she was doing, for he yelled, "Get Felgard," even as he skidded behind another android and fired at two men charging up the ramp.

Ankari crawled toward the door, but realized Felgard would be on another island by the time she caught him if she continued at that pace. She risked leaping to her feet and sprinted for the rear exit.

She charged outside onto a balcony, the warm humid air smacking her in the face like a wet towel. Some of those awful plants lined one side of the balcony and she gave them a wide berth. A long, curving ramp led down to a lower level, but she ran to the railing first, trying to spot Felgard.

There. He was running down the curving ramp. She took a step after him, but Viktor blasted through the door first, charging past her without hesitation. With a dagger between his teeth, a pistol in one hand and a laser rifle in the other, he raced after the finance lord, his face as determined as an avalanche. But Felgard had a big head start. He was running at top speed for the lower level. He must have something down there that could save him. No, not down there...coming in from above. The drone of a small personal shuttlecraft came from the sky. It was heading their way. It had to be coming to pick up Felgard.

Ankari took a step toward the ramp, but skittered back when the door was thrown open again. The androids were awake. *All* of them. She backed up so far she almost ran into the fanged man-killer plants. But the androids didn't look at her, didn't *care* about her. As one, all ten charged down the ramp after Viktor. Some had lost their rifles, but others hadn't. And they were as fast as he was. No, faster. Shit.

When Viktor had almost reached the bottom of the ramp—he must have heard those thunderous boots racing after him en masse—he stopped and turned around. Ankari gaped. He *stopped?* What was he thinking? She lifted her rifle, intending to shoot at least one in the back, though she couldn't imagine what good it would do, but Viktor was already firing on his own. Not at the androids, like she would have expected, but at the bridge itself. The laser ate into the wood like butter, chewing holes and blasting entire boards away. He was relentless, shooting with both weapons, creating a huge gap.

The first android reached the chasm and didn't slow down. It leaped into the air, its legs carrying it farther than a human's would have. Viktor dropped something on the bridge beneath him, turned and ran for the bottom of the ramp. At the same time as the android landed on the far side, the wooden boards beneath its feet exploded. The way it flew back upward made Ankari feel she was reliving the last five seconds, except in reverse.

The other androids stopped at the edge, watching as their comrade flew up…then down. A human would have flailed, hoping to find some branch or vine, but the android must have analyzed all the possibilities, found them lacking, and accepted its fate. It soon plummeted out of sight. Ankari couldn't imagine even such a sturdy construct would survive the fall to the ground. She hoped it didn't anyway.

After the grenade blew—where had Viktor gotten that, anyway?—more of the bridge crumbled on both sides of the chasm. The other androids leaped back, then turned, probably intending to find another way across— or to simply return to the balcony and jump down. That lower level was right under the railing next to Ankari.

Though she was afraid that they would focus on her, she lunged forward and shot at the top of the ramp. Boards blasted away under the barrage, but it wasn't going to be enough damage fast enough, not when those androids could leap twenty meters as if it were nothing. But something else sailed up from below—another grenade? It landed on the platform at the top of the ramp. Worried it would bounce right back off, Ankari shot at it, hoping to detonate it first.

Her shot struck true. The grenade exploded with a boom that shook the platform. Even a dozen meters away, the shockwave threw Ankari onto her back. She landed hard, stunned, barely managing to keep hold of the rifle.

A green vine waved into her vision. Ankari squawked and rolled away before a giant fanged flower head could follow. She scrambled to her feet to check on the androids, hoping that blast had stopped them. She gawked at the charred boards at the edge of the platform, smoke wafting from them. The entire ramp was gone. And so were the androids.

Before she could pump her fist in triumph, the whine of laser fire came from the platform below, rising above the drone of the shuttle's thrusters, which had grown much closer. Ankari lunged to the railing. Maybe Viktor had shot Felgard, and the shuttle would have nothing to do. Except Felgard would have had the opportunity to run even farther in the time Viktor had been busy with the androids. The platform below was much larger and longer than the balcony Ankari was on, with plenty of room for an impromptu landing pad at one end.

She spotted Viktor, not chasing after Felgard, but on the ground, grasping at his shoulder. Ankari's heart sank into her boots. That shot must have come from Felgard. He was running, pistol in hand, to the spot where the shuttle was coming in.

Viktor wasn't dead, not yet, and he staggered to his feet, but that wound was clearly slowing him. Ankari fired at Felgard, but didn't take enough time; the laser blasted into the boards near his feet but missed him. Alerted to her now, he raced under her platform. He would doubtlessly use it for cover, not coming out until he could run straight to the shuttle.

With Ankari trapped on the balcony, twenty feet above him, she couldn't do a thing to stop him. Unless she jumped over the railing. She knew how to take a fall—her father's training ensured that—but the height daunted her, nonetheless. Besides, she had to do something in the next fifteen seconds if she was going to keep Felgard from escaping. The shuttle's landing skids were less than ten feet from the platform, and the wind from its approach was whipping up the air, rustling the leaves of more of those plants lining a nearby platform.

Ankari stared hard at those plants, an idea surging into her mind. She took careful aim and waited. Felgard would have to run out…Where? About there? The pilot touched down and waved.

She dropped to her belly, sticking her head through the railing. There was Felgard, about to run for the shuttle. She fired, not at him but at the edge of the platform holding those pots. She wished she had one of those grenades, but the laser bit into the wood effectively. She blasted several of the pots as she sprayed fire.

Felgard must not have guessed her intent, for he merely sprinted for the shuttle. As he ran out from beneath the platform above him, a laser struck him in the side. It hadn't been her shot, but Viktor's. He was sprinting toward Felgard, despite the injury. The shuttle pilot leaned out of a side hatch, aiming at Viktor, who shifted his attention, firing preemptively. Ankari kept her focus on that railing, those plants. Viktor's shot had taken Felgard to the ground, but he was squirming, trying to get up.

A pot exploded under Ankari's barrage. She growled. Destroying the plants wasn't her intent. But when the dirt and greenery flopped to the platform twenty feet below, the plant was still animate. The funnel head came up, like the snout of a dog as it sniffed the air. Felgard was on the deck a few feet away. He must have seen the danger right away, for he scrambled to his feet, even though he clutched his side with his hand, and smoke was wafting through his fingers. At that same moment, the platform above his head gave away, finally damaged enough from Ankari's barrage of fire to collapse. Wood, pots, and plants tumbled to the level below, crashing all around Felgard.

A piece of the railing slammed onto him, and he crumpled beneath it. The pots broke when they dropped, but that didn't keep the hungry flowers from lunging for Felgard. No less than four fanged trumpets clamped onto his body, ripping into flesh. His screams pierced the air. Ankari looked away, ostensibly to check on Viktor, but also because she couldn't watch a man be torn to bits by carnivorous plants, even if they had been his own "botanical hobby."

The shuttle reared away from the platform, jumping into the air like a frightened cat. Blood spattered the platform where the pilot had been leaning out.

Viktor gave Ankari a silent salute, then lowered his rifle and walked toward Felgard—what remained of the man. Viktor kept an eye on the shuttle, but the pilot must have had enough of him, for the craft veered away, heading straight out to sea. Felgard had stopped screaming, but he was still twitching. Viktor pointed his rifle at the man's chest and fired. By that point, it was a mercy. They had wanted to—*needed* to—stop him, but Ankari shuddered, knowing she had been the one to do it. In the future, she hoped to be able to stick to business ventures and leave the killing to others.

Speaking of others...

She gripped the railing, wanting to run down and check on Viktor—or to fling herself into his arms—but with the ramp destroyed, she didn't see another way down. Unless she jumped. Or...her gaze fell upon a vine dangling over the edge of her level. It belonged to one of those awful plants, the ones still lining the back edge of her own balcony, but the vine itself might not be that dangerous, especially if she didn't touch it for long. Maybe.

"Are you all right?" Viktor called up. His left arm hung limply at his side.

"Me? I'm not the one who was shot. Are *you* all right?" Before she could talk herself out of it, Ankari swung over the railing, grasped the vine, and slid down it as if it were a rope. It had a tacky almost sticky flesh that tore at her hands, so she switched to climbing down, arm under arm. Something snapped above her head, and she let go, dropping the last ten feet and landing in a deep crouch, her butt bumping the planks underfoot. Not the most graceful move, but at least she didn't hurt herself.

She spun, intending to race toward the spot where Viktor had been standing, but he had run to her while she was dropping, and she smacked into his chest. He wrapped one arm around her, pulling her hard against him.

"An unusual method of entering a room," he remarked.

Relief and other feelings she wasn't ready to acknowledge made a lump in her throat, so she didn't try to say anything. She threw her arms around his waist and buried her face against his shoulder, the uninjured one. She might have flung her legs and everything else around him, but didn't want to disturb his injury. The scent of smoke clung to him, his flesh and jacket scorched from the laser fire.

"Shall we see if your friends escaped?" Viktor asked.

Yes, that was important, but she kissed him first, needing him to know she cared that he had been injured, that she cared that he—they—had defeated Felgard, and…just that she cared.

His hand slid up her back to tangle in her hair as he returned the kiss. "Or we could stay here," he murmured against her lips.

"All right."

He snorted softly and pulled back, though he captured the side of her face with his hand. "I wasn't truly suggesting that. There are a lot of people still alive around here who may not take kindly to their employer's death."

As much as Ankari would have liked to continue with the embracing, kissing, and gazing into Viktor's eyes, she had to concede to that logic— there was probably something twisted about smooching while a pile of carnivorous plants were finishing their human lunch nearby too.

"How do we get back up there?" she asked.

Viktor tapped his comm-patch. "Sequoia, you still at the helm of that shuttle?"

"'Course I am, sir. Just sitting here, working on some navigational math problems Commander Thatcher assigned me at *someone's* request." The pilot's cough wasn't subtle.

"We're ready for a pickup. Backside of the biggest building here. Grab the others on the way."

"Yes, sir."

"He sounded a little bitter," Ankari said when the communication ended. "Should we be worried that he'll forget to pick us up?"

"No, pilots need to be mentally challenged. Commander Thatcher would be the first to tell you that. Have you met him?"

"I don't remember." Most of the crew was still a blur to Ankari.

"You'd remember him." Viktor smirked.

"In a good way or a bad way?"

"Can the answer be both?"

"Ah, maybe?"

She must have appeared concerned, because Viktor said, "Perhaps you should have spent more time learning about the eccentricities of my crew before making us partners and agreeing to set up your labs on my ship."

"Oh, but I look forward to learning about those eccentricities." Ankari smiled and gave him another kiss.

EPILOGUE

"I'll admit, this is much better than I'd imagined," Lauren said, stroking some kind of fancy cryo-electron microscope with the fondness one usually reserved for a lover. Or at least a cat or puppy.

Ankari thought the lab felt claustrophobic with all the new equipment packing the counters and shelves and cabinets in the small environmental cabin on the *Albatross*, but Lauren had the space to herself now, so maybe she didn't mind. Ankari had a small desk—with a chair—in Viktor's cabin. Since he was on shift twelve hours a day, she could work there without being disturbed, and by the time he came home at night, they were both ready for more physical activities.

"The equipment?" Jamie asked from the doorway. She had been apprenticed to one of the lower-ranking engineers and was getting on-the-job training when Lauren didn't need anyone to repair or make alterations to her equipment. "Or our new position on the ship in general?"

"Mostly the equipment, but this isn't any worse than the freighter with the shaggy carpeting."

Ankari cleared her throat. "Let's have a little respect for the deceased and departed."

"*De*-parted is right." Jamie snickered.

"Ha ha." Ankari swatted at her. "Shouldn't you be down retrofitting our new shuttle, so the interior won't scare off the clients?" Viktor had agreed to let them fix up the craft that had been damaged on Sturm and install some medical equipment, so they could zip off to meet with clients whenever Mandrake Company had a mission in the same area. "Seeing laser burns on the walls and an array of guns bristling from the front of the craft might not fill someone with the calm serenity we want our customers to feel."

"I just came up to double-check your paint choices." Jamie held up a tablet. "I've got a couple of robots working on it, but it's not too late to change things, if there was a mistake. Did you really want the exterior to be...pink?"

"Yes."

"Oh. I thought that might be...an error." Jamie sighed in obvious disappointment.

"I didn't want Viktor to be tempted to borrow our shuttle if his were maimed, blown up, or otherwise indisposed. With as much expensive equipment as we're putting in there, it should not be used to carry thugly mercenaries down to a battle zone."

"I suppose that makes sense."

Since Jamie wasn't enthused with the color, it probably wasn't surprising that Ankari's comm-patch chimed a few minutes later with someone else's input.

"Markovich," Viktor growled. Though the entire ship was aware of their relationship, he still called her by last name in public—and when he was irked with her. "Why is there a *pink* shuttle in my shuttle bay?"

"Because I'm a girl and I like pink," she responded cheerily.

"This is unacceptable."

Ankari tried to decide if he was truly mad or simply blustering. Maybe he had to look good—suitably surly and authoritative—because one of his men had walked into the shuttle bay with him. "Really, Captain, you never stipulated that the shuttle remain its utterly boring gray color. In fact, you gave it to me without stipulations at all. It's not as if I have my *own* spaceship that I can paint and decorate to suit my needs." She winked at Lauren and Jamie. As guilty as Viktor felt about that incident, she could probably use it as a trump card in arguments for years to come.

He growled again, though no audible words accompanied the noise this time.

"Does he growl that much in bed?" Jamie asked.

"Yes, but it's a different kind of growl. Much more enthused."

"We're not interested in those details," Lauren said, her head once again bent over her new microscope.

"I might be a little interested," Jamie said.

"Ah, Jamie, we might have to see if we can find you a nice young man here so you can have details of your own." Too bad the ship had a lot more bitter, middle-aged men who thought women were something to be rented by the hour.

"Just not that Striker." Jamie's nose wrinkled. "He keeps accidentally bumping into me and trying to invite me to his cabin to look at his comics."

"I'm sure we can do better than that for you. Now, shall we see how that paint job is commencing? I want to make sure it's a very vibrant shade of pink."

THE END

AFTERWORD

Thank you for giving *Mercenary Instinct* a read. I hope you enjoyed the story! Want to get in touch? Send me a note at rubylionsdrake@gmail.com. Want early access to future novels, contests, review copies, etc.? Please sign up for my newsletter at http://www.rubylionsdrake.com/. Thank you!

CPSIA information can be obtained
at www.ICGtesting.com
Printed in the USA
LVOW12s0711140518
577027LV00005B/262/P